George Matheson

The Lady Ecclesia

An autobiography

George Matheson

The Lady Ecclesia
An autobiography

ISBN/EAN: 9783337113421

Printed in Europe, USA, Canada, Australia, Japan

Cover: Foto ©Raphael Reischuk / pixelio.de

More available books at **www.hansebooks.com**

THE

LADY ECCLESIA

AN AUTOBIOGRAPHY

BY

GEORGE MATHESON, M.A., D.D., F.R.S.E.

MINISTER OF THE PARISH OF ST. BERNARD'S, EDINBURGH

NEW YORK

DODD MEAD & CO.

149—151, FIFTH AVENUE

1897

PREFACE

IN this narrative, though I have compressed
nations into miles and centuries into weeks,
I have seldom departed from the stream of history,
nowhere, I hope, from the stream of experience.
I do not think the beauty of an allegory is its
puzzle, but its obviousness. As a key therefore
to these pages, let me state that most of the
characters are representative, even when suggested
by individual names. Ecclesia—the New Testa-
ment word for the Church—represents that inner
life of Christianity itself which was originally the
flower of Judaism. Hellenicus represents that
phase of the Greek mind which came into brief
contact with the flower of Judaism. The Lord
of Palatine represents the Roman Emperor, but
not any particular emperor; Caiaphas, the Jewish
Priesthood, but not any special priest. Phœbe

—the letter-carrier of the Apostles—stands for the ministrant influence of the new faith ; the captain of the guard figures the imperial system ; while the "son of the star" in chapter xxiv., though a real historical character, represents the false Christ everywhere. I have had some difficulty in introducing the person of the true Christ. I have felt that to make Him speak directly in broad daylight, except in the actual words of the Gospels, might seem irreverent; I have therefore taken frequent refuge under the cover of the dream. I have only to add that there has been a designed exclusion of all local colouring, in order to keep the mind from dwelling on the accidents. The framework is historical, but the picture ought to be universal—the same yesterday, and to-day, and for ever.

CONTENTS

vii

CHAPTER I

MY HOME

FROM the shores of our island no man had ever seen land. Far as the eye could reach, and far as the memory could travel, there had never been a hint of anything beyond. From the dawn of historic time men had looked out on the sea and beheld nothing more. Generation after generation had tried to see more. The eye had peered into the distance, and had come back without a message. The ear had listened to the moaning of the waters, and had caught no human murmur. Ships had gone forth to explore: some had returned after vain voyaging; some had sunk beneath the wave; none had brought tidings of land.

The sea was our great problem. Almost the first question of our childhood was, "What is opposite?" and the answer was ever the same, "I don't know." Frequently we made journeys from

1

one end of the island to the other; but it was always to look at the sea. We often thought that our pleasure in these journeys lay in the sights of the island; but in this we deceived ourselves. Our search was really for a voice from the sea. It was the hope that some new angle of the road might waft a fresh breath from the ocean—a breath that should bear upon its wings the murmur of the shells upon another shore.

This is really the answer to a charge which has often been made against the people of our island. We have been accused of frivolity, of inability to rest, of perpetual search for the new. After long experience, I say it is not so. I, Ecclesia, daughter of the island, born of its rulers, bred in its customs, recipient of its pleasures, with a full knowledge of its men and women, and, better still, with an adequate knowledge of myself, declare that I and my countrymen, where we have sought at all, have never sought but one thing—the secret of the sea. All our search for novelty is our search for the opposite land. If we flit from flower to flower, it is because in each flower we fail to find what we sought. It is not that we have found the new thing and grown tired of it; it is that we have never found it. There are those among us who climb height after height unsatisfied; but they are not really changeable. At every height they seek only one thing—a commanding view of the sea. If they found it, they would stop.

I have said that I was descended from the rulers of the island. I have rather expressed a claim than indicated a possession. My father was Moses ben-Israel. He professed to be the head of the oldest clan in the community. He claimed to have received the island by a deed of gift. He did so on very peculiar grounds. One of his ancestors, a namesake of his own, had spent his life in the long search. His eye had rested on a height called Pisgah, far above the mist and the haze. He felt that, if he could get there, he might learn something of a world beyond the sea. One day, in a serene sky, he ascended its summit, and returned no more. He was sought for by crag and stream; but he returned no more. There was no trace of his living; there was no trace of his dying; only, on a cleft of the hill, there was found a tablet of stone, on which in clear letters there was graven this inscription: "Moses, the man of Pisgah; unto thee and to thy seed will I give this land."

My father held this to be a divine bequest—a deed of gift which committed the island to him and to his heirs for ever. He had no doubt about

its supernatural origin. Neither had I ; yet to me
the value of the inscription lay in something very
different. What *was* the land of which this
ancient Moses had received a promise? Was it,
as my father thought, the island on which we
dwelt? Was it not rather the land for which he
had been seeking? Did not the tablet say that—
though the outer eye had failed—the inner sight
had been victorious? Did it not mean to tell
that the vision of faith had seen what the vision
of sense could not, and that beyond the waste
of waters there was a home for the spirit of man ?

I remember making the suggestion to my father.
I shall never forget how he received it. It was the
first occasion on which I ever saw him angry—the
only subject on which I have ever seen him ruffled.
" Ecclesia," he said, " let us have no more of these
fancies. It is bad enough to be denuded of one's
rights without having it sanctioned by a theory. I
have lived here all my life in poverty and struggle.
Families but of yesterday have passed me by.
They have patronised me—me who was in flower
before they were in root. I have caught the dust
from their chariot wheels ; I have seen them smile
in benignant pity. But I have been sustained
through all. What is it that has sustained me ?
It is the knowledge that this island is mine

by right to-day and shall be mine in fact to-morrow. You speak of a land beyond. If it were only a romance, I would let it pass; but it is a romance that spoils the reality. I have been striving all day to hit the mark on a tree, and you tell me that perhaps there is another tree—a tree beyond the ocean. You are diverting the strength of my aim, and I want it all. My promised land is here. My duty has been bequeathed to me by a hundred sires, and I shall bequeath it to you by-and-by."

And so I sought to turn my mind from the great sea—from the mystery of the ocean to the promise of the land. It seemed more loyal, more sacred, more religious, to be prosaic. It was against my nature, and therefore I felt it must be good. I had always been taught that virtue lies in doing what we don't wish to do. I had always been told that the value of a deed was in proportion to its pain. To me the thought of religion was inseparable from the thought of sacrifice. Surely religion was here. My heart was in the murmur of the shell, and my loathing in the murmur of the world. Ought not my heart to yield to my loathing? Should not the secular life by its very repugnance become to me the divine life? Why should I not take up my

father's quarrel—the trampled honour of his family?
He was only a servant in his own house. He
paid rent for his small estate to the lord of the
island—his island. Who was his master? Cæsar
of Palatine Hill—a man, comparatively, of yesterday. Did he not well to be angry? ought not I
to be angry too? Was not this to me the first
and great commandment, "Thou shalt revive the
glories of the house of Israel"?

The greatest events of our lives are the events
that are purely inward. One day something
happened to me—something known only to myself. I was in the sitting-room, and I was alone.
I was thinking what I could do to bring back
the fortunes of my race. What *could* I do? I
was a girl of eighteen, and had seen little of life.
I was an only child. I had never known a
mother's care; she had died at my birth. I had
been brought up in much seclusion; the family
pride and the family poverty had combined to
isolate me. I felt at this moment the burden of
the land to be as heavy as the burden of the sea;
I was impotent from sheer ignorance. Suddenly
there befell a thing which happens periodically
to old furniture; there was a crack in the wood
behind the mirror. I rose mechanically and approached the direction of the sound. I looked

mechanically at the polished surface. I had done so a thousand times before, and seen nothing but the commonplace. All at once I started. If the heavens had opened, I could not have been more surprised. A revelation came to me, unsought, undreamed of. I was beautiful—distinctly, unmistakably beautiful. I stood in the presence of myself with unveiled face, and I admired.

What boundless conceit! you say. You are wrong. It was the most impersonal revelation I ever received in my life. I said, "I am beautiful," as I would have said, "The day is fine," or "The fields are green." If you ask me why I said it to-day rather than yesterday, I cannot tell ; but neither can you tell why you do the same thing. There is a time in the life of every man and woman in which he or she first said, "This is beauty." It is a matter of small consequence whether the object be one's self or another ; the point is that there is a definite time for the revelation. When or how it comes, I know not ; but this I do know, that in the large majority of cases the hour of its coming is not the hour of its first appearing. To-day the child treads ruthlessly over the flowers ; to-morrow he comes back to admire them. A few minutes ago the mirror simply reflected ; it now did more—it revealed. I took the old step over the old stile, and in the act there came to me a new world; I had stepped from despair into hope.

For, standing before that mirror, there flashed into my heart a great design. There came to me an intoxicating moment of self-conscious power. I lost sight of the shore and the waters. For the first time in my life there rose before me a vision of empire. I was not the poor creature I had deemed. I had a gift; I had a talisman. What was wanted to restore the glory of my race? Was it not wealth, and wealth alone? I would bring back the glory; I would recall the ancient splendour. I looked down to the valleys, where my people were struggling. I looked up to the proud crest of Palatine Hill, where dwelt the lord of the island. And I said, "I shall draw them together; I shall unite the mountain and the vale." The image of an earthly kingdom swam before my eyes; the ambition of a human greatness leapt within my heart. Yet I know that even then it was another form of the old, old story; and ever from the lonely beach came up the low surge of the sea.

CHAPTER II

THE LETTER OF HELLENICUS

THE next scene reproduced by memory is after three years. I am sitting in the same room ; I am looking at the same mirror ; I am beholding the same figure ; and I am again alone. I have triumphed—beyond all my dreams I have triumphed. It was no deception, this perilous gift of beauty. It had led me, like the instinct of the bee, to the making of a great house. A letter is before me. It is from Hellenicus, brother of him who rules the island—Cæsar of Palatine Hill. He offers me the alliance of his interests—his heart and his hand. For three years I have been the magnet of the social circle. I have known my power ; I have used it. It has been no surprise to me to receive this letter ; I have seen it coming. And now it is come, and I have conquered : ought I not to be glad ?

Am I glad? You, who read these memoirs,

9

consider the peculiarity of my case. Do you
imagine that at any time my ambition had been
personal? Do you think that for a single moment
my vision of empire had been a girl's forecast of
individual wealth or power? Ambition there was
forecast there was; but for myself, never. It was
for my race, my people, my buried lineage. My
act of worldliness was to me an act of sacrifice.
It was a consecration, a surrender, an altar fire.
Personal joy was out of the question: if I had
wanted personal joy, I would have mused by the
sea. My love was in the mystery of the ocean;
my duty was in the pleasures of the land. To
me the spirit of the world had become the will
of God. It was the will of God because it was
contrary to my own will. It was the cross which
I had to take up, the penance to which I had
to devote myself. It was my asceticism, my
solitude, my self-denial. I had yielded my individual life to the service of my family, and, if
there was any joy for me, it must come in the
glory of my people.

Had I reached this joy? The letter was before
me. What did it say? All that was luscious, all
that was gushing. There was a picture in one
of our rooms of a man in a garden who is allowed
to eat of every tree but one, which was consecrated

to the will of God. This letter seemed to me to
go beyond that picture. It offered the trees
without any prohibition and without consecrating
a single spot. The note from beginning to end
was, " Get rid of trouble." Strange to say, it was
this element in the letter which disturbed me. It
ignored the only thing which had been my motive
—the desire to sink myself in my race. As I ran
my eye down the passages I felt annoyance at the
very places where most would have experienced
delight. " Leave these weeping valleys and come
aloft. Come up into the pure air, into the bright
sunshine. Why drag out your days amongst
things beneath you ? On the uplands where I
dwell the heart is ever light. We forget the cares
of the valley ; we toil not, we spin not. Come to
me, and you shall rest. Your life shall be one long
summer day. It shall move through the path
where the birds sing, where the flowers bloom. It
shall be fanned by gentle breezes ; it shall be
regaled by sweetest melodies. Its morning shall
be the lark, and its eve the nightingale. No sorrow
shall come near you ; no trouble shall dim your
eye ; no work shall soil your hand. All your
burdens shall be borne by others. They shall
bring you the pearl from the sea and the treasure
from the mine. They shall spread for you the

luxurious couch ; they shall furnish your table ;
they shall row your barge ; they shall drive your
chariot. Your sight shall be veiled from all scenes
of misery. Your ear shall be curtained from all
cries of pain. You shall live in the present; you
shall neither anticipate nor remember. You shall
never look at a grave, never listen to the word
' death.' Where the shadows gather, you shall
call on the music and the dance to chase them
away. In the forgetfulness of all that is sad you
will learn what it would be to be divine."

So ran the glowing words. Were they glorious
as well as glowing? Did they express my own
ideal of life, of " what it would be to be divine " ? To
me the divine life had always been the life contrary
to nature—the life which did what it did not wish
to do. Here the divine life was nature itself ; it
was the love of all outward things, and the power
to gratify that love. " Leave these weeping
valleys " ? They were the very things I wanted
to take with me. They belonged to my father's
grounds ; their inhabitants had been the retainers
of his house for centuries. It was for these
weeping valleys I had taught my eyes to look
upon the hills. It was to lift them up that I
wished myself to be lifted up. I heard them ever
saying in the words of one of my old songs.

"Entreat me not to leave thee, nor to return from following after thee." Whoever would take me must take my burden too. Was it fair that this man should be deceived? Was it right he should think me unencumbered? Was it well he should even figure me with an empty heart which he could fill? No; I must speak with him, I must tell him. He must know what I had, what I had not, to give. He must take me with my thorn, knowing it to be a thorn. He must learn that I could not, dared not live for individual joy. He must accept me, not for myself alone, but for the sake of my people.

Hark! what was that? Was the storm rising? Was the surge of the sea becoming more accentuated? My father's house was on the plain between the valley and the hill. From the region beneath there began to ascend a strange murmur. At first I thought it the voice of nature; by-and-by it was like the voice of man. It rose and swelled like a wave, but without its rhythm. There was no uniformity about it. Sometimes it was quick, sometimes slow; now a dirge or wail, and anon a shout of anger. The noise deepened; the valleys seemed to be climbing; I grew cold in every limb. Presently I heard the approach of footsteps. The door was hurriedly opened, and my father came in.

He was deadly pale, though maintaining his habitual calm.

"What is wrong, father?" I said.

"The plague has broken out in the valleys."

"The plague! What plague?"

"The old enemy of this island."

"I never heard of it, father."

"Oh! it is no new thing; but its outbursts are only once or twice in a lifetime. The last was before you were born. We never like to speak of such things."

"But what is the clamour, father? Is it pain? Is it fear?"

"It is the strangest thing that ever entered into the mind of man. This plague comes in the form of a black spot on the heart; but nobody ever feels it in himself. The first intimation a man gets that he is a victim is seeing the black spot in imagination on the face of another. The affected men down yonder believe themselves to be unaffected. They see their own disease on the bodies of those who have given no sign of it. They do not want them to come near lest they catch the pestilence. Some are shrieking in dismay. Some are shouting threats. Some are imploring their brethren to leave them. Some are throwing stones to drive them back into the sea;

and the children are screaming because they hear others scream."

"Oh, it is sad, it is heartrending!" I cried, bursting into tears.

"Sadder than you deem," he said. "How do you think it will affect your prospects? Have you answered Hellenicus?"

I winced. Of all the salt drops I had shed, not one had fallen on account of *him*. "I have not answered him," I said. "I am glad I have not answered; I can release him from any bond on his honour by simply refusing him. A few minutes ago I would have given him the alternative of taking me with my burden or passing me by. But now I cannot; I will bring no tarnished blood into another house."

"Tarnished blood!" he cried. "And who tarnished it? He and such as he. If we had remained as God made us, there is no blood in the island so pure as ours. It is the 'other house' that has infected us. These people in the valleys have done as you were about to do—intermarried. It is from men like Hellenicus that our plague has come. If you went to him, the sacrifice would be all on your side."

"Father," I exclaimed, "if I thought that, I would go. If he had put such a postscript to his letter, he would have had little to fear. It is the want of sacrifice on my part that drives me from him. It seems to me that those of us who are whole are in debt to those that are sick, whoever they may be—Hellenicus or another. Is nothing to be done? Are we to sit here calmly, over-looking the scene of misery, and beholding man's inhumanity to man? Are we to allow men to lacerate one another, exterminate one another, when a soothing word might save? Come, let us go down to them, you and I together. You are their king by right; you shall be their king in truth when you have won their hearts."

"Ecclesia," he said, "I cannot, I dare not. A message has arrived from Palatine Hill, command-ing that all the gates be shut which lead to the valleys. There is to be a public meeting to-morrow, and it will be followed by a more drastic decree forbidding all contact with the infected district."

"Then," said I, "I must appeal to the pity of Hellenicus."

CHAPTER III

THE CONCLAVE OF THE ISLAND

THE next day, within the largest hall in the island, there was gathered the most august assembly I have ever seen. Never before, never since, have I witnessed such a meeting of man with man. It was summoned by a succession of trumpets, each repeating at the farthest audible distance the blast of the other, until the signal became universal. They came from far and near, the representatives of this little sea-girt world. They came to consider the danger in the valleys—the pestilence and the tumult. They came from the leading families, from the leading professions. There were soldiers, lawyers, priests, physicians, landed proprietors. As I sat beside my father, a spectator of the scene, I asked myself if there was any interest unrepresented. Yes, there was one. There was an extraordinary omission. They had come to

17   2

legislate for the valleys ; but from these valleys
themselves there was no representative. No
trumpet had sounded *below*. Not a voice had
been summoned from the contaminated district.
There was every testimony but direct testimony ;
all manner of vociferation round the wounded
comrade, but no contact with the comrade's
wounds. Looking on that great assembly, I felt
then, I feel now, that there was a link wanting to
the brotherhood of man.

In the centre of the building, on a golden throne,
sat the president of the council—Cæsar of Palatine
Hill. I knew him personally ; I had met him
in the sphere of social pleasure. But, apart from
that, I think I should have known him by in-
ference. Command was stamped on every lineament ; his eagle aspect would have revealed him
always and anywhere. His keen eye, his firm
mouth, his haughty bearing, his imperative gesture,
would have marked him out in a crowd. Sitting
immediately below him was one whom I had
also reason to know—his brother Hellenicus.
Many men, and most women, would have said
that his face was more beautiful. Looking at
the two, I formed the opposite opinion. In the
relation in which I stood to him, it seemed
disloyal to say so even to myself. I could

not help it. The two kinds of beauty were radically different. The one was the seriousness of overhanging crags ; the other was the smiling of a bank of violets. It was the bank of violets that offended my eye. At another time it might have pleased me—*had* pleased me ; but, here and now, it was repellent. Cæsar of Palatine was not sunny, but he was serious ; his brother Hellenicus was sunny, but he was not serious. It was his smile that disturbed me. He seemed to regard the meeting as a fine entertainment. He exhibited no sense that there were grave issues at stake. His eye roamed round the building in search of the fashionable and the fair. It was no palliation of the offence that in its restful moments it lighted chiefly on me.

On either side of the throne rose a series of benches, ascending from floor to ceiling in the form of a sloping ladder. These seats were allocated on the principle of seniority. Those on the ground floor were the men and women of the time. In proportion as the benches rose and receded, they were occupied by those who had been great in a former generation and whose immediate day had gone by. It was on these last that my eye was riveted, and increasingly riveted with the measure of the regress. With a strange fascination I fixed my gaze on the occupants of the seat which was highest and remotest. I never saw such a peculiar assemblage as on this topmost bough. They were all old— extremely old. They looked like an anachronism. It was as if, in walking through the fields of this spring, one had seen a leaf of last autumn. Sear and yellow the leaves indeed were ; and yet it seemed to me that in their ruin they were more majestic than anything which I had seen in its strength. I was disposed to realise the saying which an old nurse had taught me concerning the ancient time : " There were giants in those days."

" Father," I said, " who are these men at the farthest distance and the highest height ? "

" These," he answered, " form the section called The Chamber of the Past.' They are a band of physicians. They have been summoned, I suppose, because on account of their earlier day they may be presumed to know more of the origin of this pestilence. But hush ! the president is rising."

" Men of the island," said the Lord of Palatine Hill, " I have called you together because the fulness of the time has come. The fulness of the time is the fulness of our need. A plague, which has been the curse of our valleys, and whose manifestations have been from time to time

suppressed, has broken out again with redoubled
violence. Had it been simply a question of human
suffering, we might have left it to the priests and
the doctors. But it is a suffering which has taken
a peculiar form. Each man believes his brother,
and not himself, to be the afflicted party, and
each wants to expel his brother. It is therefore
an enmity of man against man. Such a thing
cannot exist in this island, of which fate has
made me overseer. For the valleys, indeed, I
care nothing. Let the afflicted parties exterminate
one another. The sooner the better. I desire
that in this island none should survive but the
strong. I would have every element eliminated
which cannot be put to outward use ; I would
have nothing preserved which is incapable of
active service. But the question becomes very
different when there is danger of the valleys
infecting the uplands. My whole policy in the
rule of this island has been based on concentra-
tion. I have sought to bring man and man
together by the force of a common interest. I
have studied to unite the conflicting sides of
human nature by throwing open to all capable
men a common path of ambition. If the contagion of this pestilence should reach the uplands,
my work is undone ; the enmity of man with

man would in the higher circles spoil all. I was not called upon by the laws of this island to ask your advice on this matter. I have an interest and I have a duty which I can depute to no other. There is no dubiety in my own mind as to the course which I ought, which I am bound to take ; nor shall I shrink from the responsibility which fate has imposed on me. Yet it seemed good to me, before taking any action on this grave and solemn case, to ascertain with perfect accuracy the nature of this social malady. I would hear first of all from those who have been nearest to it, and specially from those who have been nearest to its beginning. I seek my information mainly from the Chamber of the Past. I appeal to those eminent physicians in the remotest part of this building, whose life has touched the boundary-line of a more primitive generation, and whose experience is more in contact with the earlier developments of disease. Have they any light to shed upon the nature of this great catastrophe ? "

Then through the hall there ran a buzz of expectation. Presently, like a mist-figure on a mountain, there rose on the topmost round the form of a little old man, bearing all the decrepitude of age, but with an eye which sent forth inter-mittent flashes of an earlier day. He never looked

at the president.   He addressed his words direct
to the assembly; but his voice for a time was
quite inaudible.

"Who is that, father?" I said.

"That is the great physician Amos.   He has
long retired from practice, but he still remains
one of our foremost authorities.   He is a self-made
man, and he is not ashamed of it.   As a boy he
was one of the retainers on our estate in the time
of my grandfather.   But listen; his voice begins
to catch the building."

And, indeed, it was so.   In short, jerky sentences,
like the scintillations of his own eye, the old man's
words flashed forth.   " I come as the spokesman
for the valleys.   I am proud to be their spokesman.
None has a better right to speak for them.   I am
myself a child of the valleys.   I am come of no
high degree; I began life as a herd-boy.   You
will hear to-day many voices from the outside;
mine is from within.   Listen, then, to my testimony.   You have been told that a plague has
risen in the valleys.   There has risen nothing
anywhere.   The plague is not in the valleys, but
in man, and it has been in man since ever he had
a history.   Don't flatter yourselves that the uplands
are clean.   I tell you that the pestilence is all
round.   It is in the house of pleasure.   It is in

the scene of commerce. It is in the home of
kings. It is in the haunts of fashion. It is in the
camp of war. I may say of it what one of our
poets has said of God, 'Whither can I flee from
Thy presence?' Think you that the valleys are
more tainted than other parts? I tell you they
are less so, and less so just by reason of their
unrest. It is the remaining health in them which
makes them sensitive to what is a universal
calamity. If they are more punished, it is because
they are more favoured. Why should they feel
specially what every man endures? Simply because it is more foreign to their nature. Do the
dead feel pain? Do the blind know darkness?
Is not the sense of darkness a proof of day? Why
despise ye the valleys, ye who dwell in the upper
grounds? Behold in them the mirror of yourselves. Their pestilence is your pestilence; their
taint your taint. Every man here is an undetected
leper. Every woman here is an undiscovered
victim. You are walking in the night; but the
day alone will declare it. The men of the valley
are in advance of you; they at least have recognised their shame."

With these startling words the old man sat
down. Strong disapprobation was expressed on
the faces of the audience, and some hisses arose·

"Silence," cried the president; "there must be no sign of either approval or disapproval. This medical gentleman has informed us that we have all the plague latently. We shall not dispute the point. We are here to administer law, and law has nothing to do with latency. Law can only take cognisance of what can be seen, heard, or felt. There is a pestilence in these valleys which has made itself visible, audible. It has taken the form of the enmity of man with man ; that is the danger, and that is the problem. It is no answer to this problem to tell me that others may be as bad to-morrow who are harmless to-day ; to-morrow we shall deal with them. To-day I ask if any physician among you can put his hand upon a cure of the distemper as it exists now and here. I appeal again to the Chamber of the Past."

Four old men started up simultaneously, and began to speak together.

" Who are these ? " I said.

My father proceeded to describe them. " The man at the west corner is the famous Plato. He too is long retired from practice ; but at one time he was principal of the College of Surgeons. The man a little to the east of you is Zoroaster— the proprietor of that strange building called ' The Tower of Silence.' The one farther east still is the founder of our largest medical school—Gautama Buddha; while the shrewd-looking man at the opposite angle from Plato is Confucius, whose success as a physician has raised the fortunes of one of our wealthiest families of tea-planters."

The old men, as I have said, began to speak simultaneously. The president interposed. " I give the preference to Plato because he has been the physician to my brother Hellenicus. Each shall have his turn. But I desire above all things that the judgment of each shall be an independent judgment, neither biassed by the friendship nor dictated by the enmity of his brother. There is an agreement which comes from common interest, and there is a disagreement which flows from mutual jealousy. I want neither. I wish each man to speak in ignorance of the sentiments which have preceded him. Therefore, while Plato gives his voice, let his brother-physicians retire. Let them be kept in separate rooms, awaiting their separate summons. Let there be no collusion, no comparing of notes. So shall the verdict, in any case, be satisfactory. If they be agreed, their unity shall be hailed as the voice of nature ; if they be at variance, their disunion shall be accepted as a proof that the voice of nature is impotent to solve the problem."

CHAPTER IV

THE DECISION OF THE CONCLAVE

IN recording the verdict of these eminent physicians I shall confine myself to the conclusion of their speeches. Each of them spoke for about half an hour, but the opinion of each was summarised in his closing utterances. Plato's address was an elaborate account of the human constitution. He was strongly of opinion that the relative value of man's functions had not been rightly estimated, that one side of his nature had received too much and another too little development. He attributed the plague to this absence of order, this excess on the one hand and neglect on the other; and he thus summed up his indication of the cure:

"Gentlemen, there has been a neglected element in the life of this island. Everything *in* the island has been utilised, but not the thing which surrounds it—the sea. There has not been an

adequate amount of sea-bathing. You may ask
me why, then, the plague has taken hold of those
who are *nearest* to the sea. Just because they *are*
near—too near to see its wonders. The men of
the valleys are in the presence of a great mystery ;
but its very presence makes them blind to it. You
who are farther off from the wonder will better
understand me. The men of the valleys have had
their eyes rooted on the land. They have found
there what they can see and taste and handle—
what satisfies the needs of the hour, and costs
them no trouble in the gathering. Yet it is not
what we can see or taste or handle that gives us
health ; it is what eludes the eye and the hand.
There is a mystic element around you. Sail has
never rounded it ; plummet has never sounded it ;
man has never seen what is beyond it. But its
mystery is its power ; its wonder is its stimulus ;
it refreshes by being inexplicable. If there were
more sea-bathing, there would be less headache,
less heartache. Bathe, I say, in the sea. Seek
more the bosom of the waters. Cultivate the
element which is foreign to you, which escapes
you, and yet surrounds you. Surrender yourselves
to the thought of the boundless, the fathomless.
Lave your weary limbs in that mighty deep whose
circumference is everywhere, whose limit nowhere ;

and the weary limbs shall wax strong, and the heart shall grow calm, and the head shall become clear, and, in all the bounds of the island, plague and pestilence shall for ever flee away."

With these words Plato resumed his seat, and the president next called on Confucius to offer his suggestion. He gave him the second place on the principle of impartiality. He had selected a voice from the extreme west wing of the building; it seemed good to hear one now from the extreme east. Confucius came forward from a side room in utter ignorance of what his predecessor had said. He too entered into a description of the human frame. He too insisted on the necessity of regimen and order. He too maintained the paramount importance of subordinating the lower functions to the higher. But when he came to state what *was* the higher and what the lower, he quite startled the audience by way of contrast.

"Gentlemen," he said, "there is an element in the life of this island which has received too much attention to the disparagement of others; it is the sea. There has been an overplus of sea-bathing among you. You have been attempting to stimulate the mind by a contact with the boundless. There can be no contact with the boundless. If you would stimulate either mind or body, you must study, not the water, but the land. You must fix your eyes upon that which can be seen, felt, measured. You must avoid what is above the senses, what carries you beyond your depth. You must confine yourselves to the things of the day, the objects of the hour. There may be things beyond the day, beyond every day ; that passes my knowledge. Because it passes my knowledge, I refuse to think about it. I turn to what I can comprehend. I consider the markets. I calculate what I can buy or sell. I sow seeds. I plant trees. I build houses. I take my place in society. I do speculate at times, but it is not about land on the other side of the sea; it is about this land wherein we dwell—its crops, its harvests, its trade, its prospects of wind and weather. It is to these homely pursuits that I would point my brethren. In them I see the secret of long life. Live for the present, and you shall have a lengthened future ; enjoy to-day, and you shall possess to-morrow ; no plague shall come nigh your dwelling, if your whole aim shall be to keep your dwelling clean."

As Confucius concluded a murmur of applause ran through the assembly, which, however, was instantly suppressed. Remote as was his generation, there was something in his speech which exhaled the very atmosphere of Palatine Hill, and made one feel that he belonged to modern days. Zoroaster was the next called. Knowing nothing of previous utterances, he devoted himself to a review of contemporary opinion. He said that there were some who believed in the salutary influence of water, and others who were more favourable to an inland life. For his part he did not believe in the benefit of either land or water. He criticised at length the properties of both, and he thus wound up : " Neither on your sea nor on your shore do I find the secret of health. To me the specific for health is sunshine. We are saved by fire. Not from the soil, not from the wave does our safety come ; it is from the light. In the warm glow of the day our flagging strength is renewed. In the divine flame of heaven our weary frame is reconstructed and made strong. Ye who are land-locked, sea-locked, come up into the light. Come and bathe in the beams of the morning. Come and bask in the brightness of the noon. Come and rejoice in the warmth of the midday. Come and be kindled at the glory of the setting. Get out into the free spaces where the day is not cabined nor confined. Go forth into the open where the sun is still untrammelled. Climb up into the high places where the glow strikes first and fullest ;

and in these towers of silence the elements of corruption shall be borne away."

Then came Buddha, the last of the volunteers. He said there were four constituent parts of physical nature—the land, the water, the light, and the air. He proceeded to examine them one by one, and he summed up in these words the result of his analysis : "There is only one possible remedy for the ills of man, and it is the only one which has never received recognition in the past. The soil is not salutary ; the water is not salutary ; the luminous fire is not salutary. But there remains a neglected element of which something might be made ; it is the air. At present the air is as bad as the others ; but that is by reason of the winds. If we could lay the winds, if we could make the air stormless, voiceless, if we could establish in the atmosphere a great calm, man would be calm too. He would cease to desire. Desire is the root of all pain, of all unrest, of all disease. Show me an atmosphere without storm, and I shall make the man to mirror it. I have constructed such an atmosphere. It is as yet only in my mind ; but the plan is half the battle. I have already given it a name. I have called it the Nirvana—the place where the winds never blow. Come and inspect my plan, ye tossers, ye toilers. Come and behold in vision what one day you shall see in fact. Come unto *me*, and *I* will give you rest."

When Buddha had finished, the president rose. "Men of the island," he said, "you have now listened to the representatives from the Chamber of the Past. You have heard four of the oldest and most revered physicians of that chamber. And you have marked how sublimely and how eloquently they have differed from one another. Each has selected as his panacea a separate element of nature. One has taken the land, another the water, a third the air, and a fourth the fire. I need not say that, in such divided counsels, I, as ruler of this island, can have no confidence. When these gentlemen are agreed among themselves, it will be time enough to consider their specific. I have now to ask if there is any man of the audience who has a suggestion to offer different from these."

A buzz of voices followed, but for a long time there was no response. At last a form stood up whose every lineament was familiar to me. It was Caiaphas, my father's head chaplain, popularly known as the high priest. He addressed himself direct to the president, as if it were a private transaction between man and man. "Lord of Palatine Hill," he said, "I have no human remedy to propose. You have truly observed that the world by wisdom

3

has failed to know. You have rightly pointed out how utterly contradictory have been the efforts to solve the problem made by the Chamber of the Past. But, my Lord of Palatine, I am the spiritual servant of a house which has always professed to have a more sure word of prophecy. You have abandoned the claims of fire, air, earth, and water. But there is a fifth power ; we call it God. What He is in Himself I know not, any more than I know what in themselves land, water, air, and fire are. But I do know that we can no more live without Him than the bird can live without the air or the fish without the sea. I say, then, Lord of Palatine, let us not neglect this element of life. It is expedient that a victim die for the people. Let us offer that victim. Let us present to the God of heaven a great sacrifice, a gift of the costliest we can find. Let us raise a mighty altar, and lay on it the choicest of our fold, and let the smoke ascend on high as our intercession for the dwellers in the valley."

The president asked: "Where do you propose to offer the sacrifice ? Will you come into contact with the plague-stricken ? If so, I shall forbid it."

" No, my Lord of Palatine," answered the chaplain Caiaphas ; " I propose to present the oblation on the top of one of the hills, not only beyond the sight, but beyond the reach, of the valleys."

"In that case," said the president, "it is to me a matter of indifference. It is a private and individual question, and does not concern this assembly Are there any more suggestions?"

A wild thought struck me. My blood was boiling at the apathy of man to man. A sacrifice at the top of the hill! A sacrifice which shunned the contact of those for whom it was offered! A sacrifice which brought no danger, involved no humiliation, required no touch of human sympathy! It was indeed an awful thing. Was there to be no voice raised in support of human contact with the valleys? Had it not been tacitly conceded that their plague was only the outward exhibition of a disease which was latently in all men? Why, then, should the mountains hold aloof? Was not the true form of sacrifice a descent into the valleys themselves? Would no one tell this to the assembly? Then I would. Had any one a better right? Was I not by the will of God the heiress of this island—and did not the will of God press on me to speak? In a moment I was on my feet facing that vast audience. "Are you mad?" cried my father, grasping my arm. "Yes," I answered, "mad with the indignation of a wounded heart." Then, turning to the assembly, I said: "Natives of the island you have mistaken, this day, the nature of your mission." But I got no further ; for immediately there arose such a storm of voices that my own voice was annihilated. There was murmuring, jeering, hooting, shouting, yelling, and for a few minutes I felt like a small boat tossed by the great ocean.

Then rose the president, and the loud waves grew still. He said : " We cannot hear the Lady Ecclesia. Much as we respect her family, and greatly as we admire her sex, we are constrained to deny her this boon. We cannot concede to woman the prerogative of a voice in this assembly. Her sphere is at home. Let her kindle the fires of the household, and leave us to put out the fires of the community ; happy is she to have a task so light. And now, men of the island, it is plain that your counsel is exhausted. If you had been able to suggest any remedy for this vile distemper, it would have had my best attention ; but you have none—none on which you are harmonious. In the absence of remedy there remains only restraint. I cannot cure the pestilence, but I can prevent it from spreading. In the right of my lordship over this island, I do prevent it. I make a law for the preservation of the public good. I enact that there be no communication with the valleys on pain of death. I command that all the gates be shut, that all the approaches be closed, which lead from you to them and from them to you. I ordain that between you and the valleys there be a great gulf fixed, so that there be no passage from the one to the other. Whoever shall attempt such a passage, whoever shall open the gates or clear the approaches, will do so with the forfeiture of life. I utter it in no spirit of cruelty or arbitrary despotism. I bind myself by my own law. Should I transgress that law, should I break these boundaries, let no power intervene to save me. Should my brother Hellenicus transgress that law, I would be no respecter of persons; he would suffer like the meanest in the island. Let no man say that I exercise with tyranny the power that fate has given me. I am a subject, not a sovereign. I am master only till the command is uttered; the moment it is uttered I am, like you, its servant, its slave, bound by its observance, answerable for its infringement. Such is the spirit in which I make this law. If it is drastic, it is not drastic against a class; you and I shall stand equal before the bar of an even-handed justice. Does this meet your approval? have I the support and the countenance of this assembly?" And through the deluded audience there ran a great "Amen."

CHAPTER V

THE INTERVIEW

"THEN you refuse to help me?" I spoke to Hellenicus. I had summoned him to an interview in my father's house, and he had come the day after the great meeting.

"Refuse to help you!" he said; "is it not to help you that I am here? Have I not offered to lift you for ever above the sight of these valleys? Have I not asked you, nay, implored you, to spread your wings and be free? Have I not laid at your feet the fulfilment of all possible ambitions? I have offered you wealth, luxury, rest, freedom from care, scenes and sounds of beauty, days of pleasantness, and paths of peace. Is there any greater help to life than these?"

"To some lives there is not; but to me there is a jewel missing from your casket."

"Name it, and were it from the other side of the sea it shall be added to your store."

" It is the love of what I love. I do not believe that a mutual affection is a sufficient reason for marriage. I think a love should be common as well as mutual; or rather, it should be common first and mutual afterwards. If you and I had begun by loving a tree, there would have been the basis for a starting-point, and the agreement in taste might have ripened into a personal attachment. I see you are smiling at such sentiments on the lips of a girl. They are not mine; I have been born in them, bred in them. I have received them from a long line of ancestors. These all died in the faith that marriage should be regulated, not by the mutual admiration of two young persons for each other, but by the admiration of both for something outside of themselves. I received this as a faith; it has now become a conviction."

" Be it so; I accept the terms. Let us agree that there must be something common before there is something mutual. Is there not already such? Take the tree of which you speak. Do not I love it with all my heart and soul in all its root and leaves and branches ? "

" But I do not; that is just the difference. I have never reached that amount of admiration for nature which is entitled to the name of love. Indeed, I doubt if I could admire the tree at all unless I believed that somewhere, somehow, by some one it was planted. I revere above all things the principle of life."

"So do I ; that is the reason that I revere the tree. To me it is living, breathing, inhabited by a conscious spirit. There is nothing to which I am attracted so much as beauty ; but that is because I believe beauty to be the highest manifestation of life."

"My father would agree with you ; but I am bound to confess that I do not. This is one of the things in which my faith has yielded to my conviction. I, like you, was brought up to believe that the highest manifestation of life was physical beauty, and that any defect or deformity was a deviation from the divine favour. But I have lived to change my mind. To me the noblest type of a human soul is a life encumbered with these very infirmities, yet refusing to give in."

"Well, if the infirmity does not prevent them from working, they deserve great credit."

"But I am supposing that it does prevent them from working, that it makes them helpless, handless, from an outward point of view, useless. I say that there is a glory in ladenness as well as in labour. If these people are able to bear without crying, they are in the highest sense heroic. I

think there are men who are not called to act, but
simply to be and to suffer ; if they can do the two
things, they are wondrously strong. And this brings
me back to the old subject. You know that our
house has always had a special interest in the
valleys. They were originally included in the
boundaries of this estate, and, although the right-
of-way has long become common, I have never
heard that the grant has been repealed. But it is
not on this ground that I appeal to you. It is not
because the valleys are mine that I ask your
intercession with your brother ; it is because they
are his. He claims the lordship over this island,
and in point of fact he has it. I never envied him
the possession so much as now. I think I would
give all my remaining life to be mistress of the
island for this single year. I would call it " the
acceptable year of the Lord " ; it would be my day
for salvation. Your brother of Palatine has at
this moment in his hands the fate of the most
destitute and forlorn among the children of sorrow.
Will he be true to his trust ? does he know the
nature of his trust ? He is a great man ; in his
deepest soul I believe he is a noble man. He has
bowed his head to the majesty of justice ; will he
bow to pity too ? The spirits of just men are not
made perfect till they reach generosity."

" You heard his speech yesterday : did it leave you in any doubt as to his mind ? You heard with what iron determination he consigned to death whoever should have contact with the valleys, himself included. Do you think he is a man likely to depart from his own law ? "

" I think you have mistaken the spirit of his own law. It is not contact with the valleys as such that he condemns ; it is contact with the valleys as long as they are in a state of plague which involves enmity to mankind, and therefore treason against the laws of this island. Do not imagine that, if the valleys were pronounced free from this pestilence, your brother would not at once repeal his law. Now, I ask, how can any one know *when* the valleys shall be free from pestilence? What is to be the sign of their cure ? Can there be any sign but the verdict of a physician ? Surely the Lord of Palatine never meant to enact that the banishment of man from man was to be perpetual. Surely he intended it to be only as long as the patients' malady. And how shall the length of that malady be tested if no medical skill is to be admitted into the valleys ? It is for this, and this alone, that I plead. I do not ask that you or your brother should touch these afflicted forms. But I do entreat by all the laws of the heart that they may be touched by those qualified to heal. I ask that one or more of your great physicians be sent into the valleys to succour, and, if possible, to save. I have implored you to carry this petition to the Lord of Palatine, to intercede for me with him. There is none other to whom I can apply but you. The chaplain Caiaphas believes in sacrifice at a distance. My father is good and kind, but he is entirely guided by Caiaphas. I myself cannot go for the reason your brother gave you yesterday; I have the misfortune to be a woman. Will you take my place? Will you be my representative? Will you carry my request and plead my cause?"

"And what if my brother should grant the request, and decree that the man who goes down to the valleys shall be the physician who attends your house and mine?"

"What! Philo? With all my heart."

"But with all my aversion. If he goes, he shall be no doctor of mine. Do you think I want a vehicle of contamination between my house and the valleys? I have lived all my life in beauty. I have pursued the opening flower as persistently as the bee. I have followed the track of the morning as constantly as the lark. I have never been able to brook the sight of deformity. To me the symbol of the divine is, and has always been, the faultlessly fair. Therefore it is that I come to *you*. As the bee flies to its flower, as the lark mounts to its morning, even so come I to you. Ecclesia—let me call you so—why will you waste time over these shadows? Yours is a dream. Mine is perhaps also a dream; but it is a joyous one. Come into my dream, Ecclesia; come and forget the mist and the rain. Come to the singing of birds and the laughing of brooks and the blooming of roses. Come to the nightless days and the endless summers and the careless hours. I shall deck for you a home in the uplands, and I shall call its name Elysium, and on its doorpost shall be written the words, 'There shall be no want here.'"

"And shall the people be there—the people of the valleys? Shall they too have no want? Shall they too have the bird and the bee? Shall they too have the streams and the roses? If so, I shall come."

"Nay, but the bird would cease its song, and the flower would lose its perfume, and the bee would hum no more. Nature cannot dwell in the presence of deformity. Into our Elysium there shall enter nothing that is unbeautiful, not even a memory of such things. Up on the hill yonder we shall forget all about the valleys—their existence, their very name. They shall fade from our remembrance like a phantom of the night, and there shall be only day—day for evermore. Come, my Ecclesia ; come and forget."

"Nay, it cannot be ; you love not what I love. There is a barrier between us which no bond can join. Yet believe me," I continued, taking his hand in mine, " I am not ungrateful to you. I feel that I have gained something from you—brightness. Before I knew you, my life was too grave, too sombre. You have taught me that there is a loveliness in lustre and a beatitude in outward beauty. And although I cannot give up my cause, I feel that you have strengthened me for my cause by importing brightness into it. I feel that sorrow cannot be cured by sadness, but that they who serve by night must themselves have seen the day. Therefore I thank you even while I bid you farewell. We may not meet often in the days to come, for our ways lie apart, and there are no divergences like the divergences of mind ; but may the God of my fathers bless you, and, in every hour of your sorrow, may your valley be illuminated by the sun in heaven ! "

CHAPTER VI

A VISION OF THE NIGHT

I HAD told Hellenicus that I had gained by his acquaintance a brightness which my nature lacked. Yet the night which followed the day of our last interview was perhaps the saddest I had known. It was not the parting with Hellenicus. I had told him that to me a mutual affection was inseparable from a common sympathy, and it was true. I had no sense of a lost love ; but I had the very poignant sense of a lost hope. I felt that an anchor had been lifted to which my ship was moored, and that I was once more at sea. The weight of the valleys pressed upon me as I lay down on my nightly pillow, and my heart was heavy with their load. Far into the night I remained awake, listening in the silence to the sighs that seemed to ascend. Gradually the impressions became more indistinct. The voices of Hellenicus and his brother began to blend with the plaint of the valleys. I found myself wondering why the two men had not been rolled into one. I found myself asking, If Cæsar had the gaiety of Hellenicus, and Hellenicus the power of Cæsar, would it make a perfect man? I found myself answering that it would not, that something must be added to both. I found myself inquiring what that something could be; and then——

Was it morning already? The light was streaming in at the windows. I thought how grand the sea must look in that light; I must get up and gaze on the sea. I rose, made my toilette, and ran into a room whose casement fronted the ocean, expecting to behold the usual sight of water everywhere. Suddenly I stood aghast; there was land in the midst of the ocean. The space that yesterday was a blank had been filled up in the night. Clearly, vividly, in the morning sun, there broke upon my sight the vision of this intermediate shore between the waters and the waters. And hark! was that only the murmur of the waves? No; there were voices from the opposite bank; and as the ear has more longing than the eye, I strained to listen. Nearer and nearer came the voices, until at last they swelled into a chorus, and by-and-by the very words became audible.

" Glory to God in the highest, peace and goodwill
to men," rolled through the liquid air ; and ever
and anon the refrain seemed to be caught up by
increasing voices, till the whole atmosphere became
vocal with benignant song.

And as I looked out upon the sea a new wonder
met me. Between my eye and the land there
was seen the form of something which had
emerged from the shore. What was it ? Was
it a raft, or a boat, or a sail ? Such things had
been often seen before, but not coming from a
new world. Its course was evidently not aimless.
It was crossing from shore to shore. It was
making for a definite point. It seemed to be
coming right in the line of my father's house.
Nearer and nearer it came ; clearer and clearer
it grew. At last a revelation broke on me ; the
form was human. A man was walking on the
sea. He came with fearless step, with rapid step.
His feet seemed to leave a track of radiance
behind them such as one sees in the chain of
moonlight on the waters. I was half fearful and
wholly fascinated. I dreaded to look, but could
not withdraw my gaze. The vast ocean was to
me concentrated into a single point—the course
of that marvellous figure.

Suddenly a mist fell, and the whole scene was

covered. The sea was blotted out, and the opposite land, and the form on the waters, and the
radiance that followed him. I burst into tears
because of the cloud that had robbed me of the
beautiful vision, and I covered my eyes with
my hands that in fancy I might see it still. And
after I had waited thus a long time, I began to
experience a strange sensation. I felt that I was
not alone in the room. There was a presence
beside me, living, breathing, moving. I heard
the beating of my heart for fear. Then slowly
I withdrew my trembling hands from my eyes,
and I saw——

How shall I describe what I saw? We can
only describe that to which we have an analogy.
But this had no analogy to anything I had ever
known. There stood before me an image of
superhuman beauty. The form was that of a
man—I had almost said that of a careworn man ;
it looked as if it were carrying a burden. But
the face—how shall I speak of it? Never in this
island, never in my waking, never in my sleeping,
had I seen anything like it. It was perfectly,
ravishingly, blindingly beautiful. I think the
beauty came all from within. It seemed to me
that the glory of the outer vision had been extinguished just to show that it was not indebted

to anything outside. If I had been asked to define its type, I would have been puzzled. The moment you caught an expression, it seemed to turn into something else. One glance suggested my father; another recalled Hellenicus; a third brought to my mind the Lord of Palatine. It was a countenance which had in it a blending of sunlight and moonlight, of power and gentleness, of all the things which are supposed to be contrary. And, as I gazed, I lost my self-possession. My soul seemed to melt within me; I fell at his feet with a great cry of rapturous pain.

In a moment he had taken me by the hand and lifted me up. Then he spoke, and a thrill went through me. Fancy a blending of all the congruous and harmonious instruments in the world of sound, each taking the appropriate part of the sweetest symphony. The words were human words, island words; but the accent was quite foreign, unlike what I had ever heard before. The strangest thing of all, however, was that he addressed me by my own name.

"Ecclesia," he said, "I have heard the cry of the valleys, and have come over the sea to help them. I have come to form a band of ministering spirits: will you be one of these?" And I answered, "Yes." "Will you go down to the

valleys to-night?" he said; "will you be par-
taker of my cross?" I answered, "I have no
key, and the gates are shut." Then said he with
the sweetest of smiles, "But I have; I have the
keys of death and of the grave, and I have set
before you an open door."

With these words he faded from my sight,
and with a great sob of sorrow I awoke, and lo,
it was all a dream. I am ashamed to confess
that the first thing I did on waking was to cry
actually. Why wasn't it true, O my God, why
wasn't it true! Ye who have seen your dead
in dreams and then waked to find it illusion, I
know you will sympathise with me. Mine was
not a vision of the past, but a vision of the future;
none the less, while it lasted, was it dear, and
my heart was sore for the want of it. I wept
long and bitterly; I watered my couch with
my tears. "Come back to me, come back to
me," I cried; "come over the sea again on the
wings of the morning. Thy imaginary light
has put out all real ones. Thou art to me
above the brightness of the sun. Couldst thou
have such power if thou wert not a reality? O
thou beautiful, come back, come back."

It was the custom in our house, as it was that
of our clan, to begin the day with a service of

prayer. When I presented myself for the morning orison, and when the retainers of the immediate domicile were gathered in the large hall, I was painfully impressed with a strange experience. I felt that from every side I was being looked at. In strangers I might not have wondered; I would have deemed it simply impertinence. But why should those look at me who knew every feature of my face, who saw me daily, to whom I was as familiar as the light or the air? After the service I was confirmed in my impression. My father came up to me and said: "Ecclesia, what is the matter with you? You are looking divine this morning. Have you been using a cosmetic? I thought you despised such things. I never saw you look so well—never."

I was curious to see what I was like. I remembered the mirror which had been the first revealer of me to myself. Perhaps it would now be a second revealer; I would go and try. So I went into the room of my earliest revelation, and drew near the messenger which had told me the first secret about myself. It had made me start before; it made me start more now. Whose face did I see? It was mine, and yet it was not. The old features were there—the old windows of the house; but there seemed to be a new tenant within. It was as if my soul had gone out in the night, and another soul had entered in its room. What was that face I saw blended with my own? I had seen it before: where? One moment, and the truth had broken on me; it was the face of the man of my dream— the man who had come across the sea. And the more I gazed, the more the likeness grew. Every instant I was increasingly riveted, and, ever as I looked, the elements of the old countenance became absorbed in the light behind it. The face of the dream was vanquishing the face of the waking day, and I beheld myself with speechless wonder transformed into the same image from glory to glory.

CHAPTER VII

THE STRUGGLE OF REASON AND FAITH

"WILL you go down to the valleys to-night?"
The refrain sounded in my ears all
through the day. Was it a command? Yes; a
command in a dream. What had I to do with
that? True it had been a powerful dream; it
had affected my very countenance: yet all this
could be done from within. And were not the
waking facts against it, contrary to it? Had not
the Lord of Palatine shut the gates? Where could
I find admission to the valleys? Again there
came the refrain of these other words: "I have the
keys of death and of the grave, and I have set
before you an open door." But was not this also
a bit of the dream, and therefore a bit of the
delusion? I knew the gates had been shut with
that measure of certainty with which I knew the
Lord of Palatine. If a voice should tell me that
one of them had been left open, ought not that to

be a waking voice? Could a sound in the inner ear equal the thundering accents of the Lord of Palatine? Surely I was getting weak; surely I was verifying the president's judgment when he denied my sex a right to speak in the assembly. Let me forget this sentimentalism; let me turn my thoughts to living things.

"Will you go down to the valleys to-night?" still the words kept sounding, sounding. "I have set before you an open door"; still the promise kept ringing, ringing. Day could not drive it out; work could not weary it; the commonplace could not kill it. By-and-by I began to ask myself if I had not misstated my own case. Was not the real question whether God speaks at all? If He does, why should He only speak in the day? Had not one of our poets said, "My reins also instruct me in the night season"? Had not another said, "He giveth to His beloved in their sleep"? Why not? If the will of God could come to me through the impressions of my waking, why should not it come to me through the impressions of my dreaming? Was there any more weakness in the one belief than in the other? If a human messenger had told me in broad daylight that I would find an open door, would I not go and try? The thing would be equally unlikely—

no less and no more ; yet I would assuredly try.
Why should I not try now ? Was not this the real
weakness, the true mark of a feeble mind—to
believe in nothing that I did not see? Then a
great resolve came over me, and I cried : " O
thou beautiful, be my reality for one day. Though
ever after thou shouldst be a delusion, this one day
be thou my guiding star. Be real to me for a few
brief hours. Put out the sun again, and shine on
me with the matchless radiance of yesternight.
This once I shall assume thee to be true, blindly,
unreasoningly, but intensely. Lead on, and I
shall follow thee ; I shall go down to the valleys
to-night."

Many who read these memoirs will be surprised
at the nature of this struggle. It will seem to
them that I had never yet suggested to myself the
main difficulty. The sole question with me had
been whether a gate could have been left open.
Should not the first thought have been, " What if
the gate should be open and you should go
through ? " Was not the punishment death ?
Had not the Lord of Palatine decreed that who-
soever should transgress these barriers should be
guilty of treason and pay the penalty with his
life ? Was not the question of an open door after
all a subordinate one ? No ; to me it was not.

Strange as it may seem, the prohibition of the conclave had never weighed with me. I had not forgotten it, not for a moment; but it had paled before another fire—the fire of enthusiasm. The sight of that ideal countenance had not only put out all actual beauties, but all actual horrors. If I knew that that countenance was real, and that in sober truth it had come from a land beyond the sea, I felt that for me at least there could be no more death. My struggle was not with the weakness of the heart, but with the pride of the intellect; when the pride of the intellect was conquered, my struggle was over.

I do not know how I got through that day. The worst days to get through are not the darkest; they are those whose interest lies at the end of them. I know that during the intervening hours I was very uninteresting to my fellow-beings. We are all uninteresting when we have a secret which we cannot share. It was not the fault of my new faith, but of its unsharedness. None the less it exposed me in the meantime to the reproach of aloofness from common things. My father rallied me that my thoughts were so far away. The chaplain Caiaphas jestingly remarked that "the Lady Ecclesia must be dreaming of the sacrifice to be made for the valleys." The jest jarred upon

me.   I thought it singularly bad taste in a minister
of the altar, and at another time I would have told
him so.   But anger was overborne by a grim satisfaction.   By the irony of fate the man was speaking the truth—a truth dead against himself.   If
my dream was true, the sacrifice had already been
taken out of his hands, out of all human hands.
If my dream was true, God Himself had sent a
victim to the altar.   While man was meditating
how he could avoid contagion, Heaven itself had
plunged into the pestilential stream.   The chaplain
had pronounced his own sentence, and he did not
know it.   He had been deposed from his office.
He had been superseded by a larger ministry—a
higher, holier, purer ministry ; that which was
perfect had come, and that which was in part
was done away.   The words of a condemned man
could not make me angry.

At last the shadows began to gather, and my
heart beat quicker.   The hour was coming ; it
would soon be here.   It had been my custom,
when the working day was done, and no social
pleasure called, to spend a portion of the night in
the library in private reading and still more private
thinking.   Thither I repaired—not now to study
manuscripts, but to observe the sky.   I watched
the last survivals of the February day ; I longed

for them to go, yet feared to see them depart.
By-and-by the latest had faded, and it was night
—moonless night. The moment had arrived.
With a palpitating heart I stole into my room.
I dressed myself in dark attire, yet I did not
labour to make myself uncomely; they who visit
the sick ought not to be outwardly repellent.
Then I fell on my knees, and said, "Be with
me, thou beautiful, be with me"; and I rose
calm. A few moments more and I was out on
the great plain under the sky of night. The
die was cast. The world of girlhood was behind
me, and for the first time in my life I stood
alone.

There were many approaches to the valleys;
but for me, within the short time at my disposal,
there was only one available; it was that which
we called the Sympathy Gate. If this failed me,
the next in nearness was that popularly known as
the Gate of Display, because it ushered into a
slope not steep but prolonged, and affording the
possibility of a carriage drive. But it was five
miles distant, and therefore to me impossible.
Everything depended on the first gate. Was it
open or closed? All the probabilities pointed to
the latter. It was within a mile of my father's
house; it was under his surveillance; it was likely

to be well guarded. And over against this was
what? A voice in a dream.

With trembling footsteps I approached the goal.
It was the crisis moment of my life. It had all
the elements of tragedy in it; yet there was neither
fire, nor wood, nor burnt-offering. It was a theatre
without scenes, an act without persons, a drama
without speeches. I know now what I did not
know then—that the destinies of this island were
quivering on a thread, suspended on the purely
inward conviction of one frail soul. The tragic
hours of God lie below the surface, and have never
been dramatised. Was my ideal living or dead?
—that was the question. If dead, no mother
weeping over the bier of her child was so bereaved
as I.

And now I was at the gate. There are moments
in which suspense is dearer than reality. I wished
there had been still a few steps to go. I covered
my eyes with my hands as I had done in my
dream when the sun went down; faith was low,
and reason was high. Then with a wild, despairing
look I faced my destiny; and with a great cry
I startled the silent air. It was open, it was
open; the gate of brass was burst; my ideal was
alive—alive for evermore.

But this was not all. A new surprise awaited

me. Not only was the valley open; it was lighted
—lighted in the place of its deepest gloom. That
place was the middle. The beginning of the
descent was easy, and the end was easy. But
the centre was steep, precipitous, dark, mantled by
overhanging crags. I would have greatly feared
this spot, had there been room in my heart for any
fear but one. Now the danger was over; it was
revealed only as a ship of sorrow that had passed
in the night, as a thing of horror that *might* have
been. Over the central and steepest part of the
decline a flaring torch was suspended. It seemed
as if some hand had attached it by a string to
the impending cliff and left it blazing there. I
marvelled at the mysteries of God. Five minutes
ago, any spectator would have said, "To what
purpose is this waste?" A torch flaring for nobody, a light in the descent of a prohibited valley,
burning for the sake of nothing—it seemed a
weapon for the unbeliever. And now it was all
explained, vindicated. It had been waiting for
me, for me. It had no mission for its immediate
hour; it was useless for the time of its kindling;
but it was waiting for me. I, Ecclesia, latest scion
of the oldest clan, youngest survival of a race that
was ready to die, had been privileged to explain
the seeming waste of God, had been privileged

to tell why a flower had blushed unseen, why a light had glittered unregarded. " I have set before you an open door " had been the words of my dream ; they were now the words of my experience. God had prepared a table in the wilderness ere yet were found any guests to banquet there ; but He knew that the wilderness would in time break forth into singing, and that the desert would soon be vocal with the myriad claims of man.

CHAPTER VIII

IN THE VALLEY

AS I approached the close of the descent I became aware of the old sounds which had formed such a strange antithesis to the letter of Hellenicus. Not that the murmur was any longer so widespread and diffused. Night brings some relief even to the despairing, and the deepening of the shadows had brought to the valleys partial repose. Yet there were whole masses of men and women, and particularly in the valley nearest to my father's house, who had refused to find such rest. Night could not damp their agony of fear; weariness could not exhaust their passion of enmity. The plague was upon them—upon all of them who were in strife ; but they did not know it. Each had looked into the face of his brother and seen it *there*. The illusion would have been wonderfully helpful had there been love—it would have been a source of ministration ; but when

there was only fear, it became deadly and per-
nicious. Each had beheld in the other the centre
of his danger; each had tried to expel the other
from his life. As I entered the valley, that which
I had only conceived became a sight; and the
seeing surpassed the conceiving. I shall never
forget the scene, never. It will always remain in
the background of my memory as the saddest
picture in all the gallery of life—a picture, lurid,
ghastly, repellent, indelible in its impression of
degradedness, and deeply humbling to the pride
of man.

Shall I try to describe what I saw? The
multitude had divided into groups according to
the centre of their interest—that is to say, of their
enmity. The valley had been brilliantly illuminated in order to detect the blemishes. Naphtha
fires blazed, lamps of oil impended, and the face
of every man was revealed. There was not a
corner of the expanse which did not light up its
own tragedy. On one side was a little band,
united for the moment in a dreadful enterprise.
They were making frantic efforts to stone a young
woman of singularly fair countenance. Undoubtedly she bore on her forehead the mark of the
pestilence, but it was not that mark which they
saw; it was the mark of their own pestilence.

The object which they were trying to strike was inside rather than out, and therefore hitherto they had failed to hit their victim. On another side was a man frightfully marked by the pestilence; they called him a leper. He had been driven within the walls of a graveyard by a party hardly distinguishable from himself in extent of dilapidation. The object was evidently to keep him in quarantine until starvation relieved them of their guard. Here was a little child with the door of its own house shut against it. It had no sign of the pestilence on its person; but its parents were infected, and imputed to it their disease. There were two brothers, fishermen, retainers on my father's estate, who bore on their countenance clear traces of the calamity, deliberately trying to set fire to a collection of hamlets, whose inmates they believed to have caught the contagion. But why prolong the recital? It is sickening even to remember, and I have to record diviner things.

When I entered upon the scene, my presence was quite unnoticed; everybody was too busy to think of *me.* But it was impossible I should remain a mere spectator. It was a matter of life and death, and there was no time for calculation. My eyes turned first to the case of the most immediate personal danger—that of the young woman

who was being stoned. I felt she must be saved
at all hazards. I dashed forward between her and
her assailants, and stood confronting the men
and their missiles. "Do you know me?" I said.
"I am the daughter of Moses ben-Israel—the head
of your clan, some would say the head of your
island. Look at me. I am untouched by the
pestilence, and I shall stand between you and this
woman. You do not need to hurt her as long as
I am here. You have nothing to dread. I shall
be the wall betwixt you ; I shall keep this woman
in the rear ; I shall part you from all contact ;
nothing shall come to you until it has first come
to me. Are you satisfied ? "

I spoke to gain time, and to produce a temporary
calm. For a moment I seemed to have succeeded.
The group fell back a pace and dropped their
implements of destruction, while they kept their
eyes steadfastly on me. By-and-by a voice was
heard, "She has got the plague too : don't you
see the black mark ? " This was not true in point
of fact, but it soon became a reality in belief. The
suggestion was eagerly and instantaneously caught
up, and the faces again grew menacing and lurid.
Once more the missiles were raised, but no longer
for the old object. In the place of the former
woman stood I—the would-be mediator. I had

tried to be the wall of partition between the oppressor and the oppressed. I was now in my turn about to be made the victim. The sensation I felt at that moment is indescribable. I never knew before what it was to meet death face to face. I was meeting it now in its most ghastly dress. Around me were the eyes of a crowd glaring with incipient madness, beholding in me the loathsomeness that existed in themselves, and eager by one stroke to blot me out from their presence. The ground seemed to reel beneath my feet; the lamps appeared to flicker; the naphtha fires grew pale. I saw the stones lifted; I heard the voices raised; I felt, rather than beheld, the arms outstretched to throw. I breathed a prayer to the God of my fathers; I heaved a sigh for the vanishing of my dream; I stood awaiting the end.

Suddenly they fell back; the missiles dropped from their hands; the glare faded from their eyes; and their glances turned aside from me. I followed the direction of their gaze. The next instant I uttered a cry—the first that had escaped me during that scene of terror. Over against the adjoining naphtha fire stood the form of a man not numbered among the sons of the valley, and his figure and face were that identical face and figure which I had seen in the vision of yesternight.

When he came, how he came I know not; I was under the shadow of my cloud, and did not see it. But there he stood in all the radiant beauty of my dream. I would have known him amid ten thousand; I could have identified him in a multitude which no man could number. I had never seen him before with the waking eye; yet my first sight was not so much knowledge as recognition. It was quite old to me, familiar, almost commonplace. It was not the surprise of entering a palace; it was the joy of reaching home. I felt that I could have gone up to him and said, " You have come at last; I have been waiting for you a long time."

Then he spoke; and again the voice was old; it was the voice of my dream. He raised it no higher than he had done in my dream, but it penetrated in a moment every corner of the field. And instantly it seemed as if a cord had been thrown round the multitude to draw them into one. The isolated groups broke up and began to move towards the voice. The parties surrounding the graveyard abandoned their post and left the leper free. The incendiary fishermen gave up their efforts to set fire to the hamlets. The house door which had been barred against the little child was thrown open, and the parents came out and the child went in. By-and-by this whole section of the valley, representing the wants of all the valleys, and therefore the radical wants of man, was gathered around one common centre—the object of my dream, the goal of my waking hours.

Hitherto it had been the music of his voice that had attracted, rather than the sense of his words. It was a voice so unlike the valleys, for that matter so unlike the uplands, that its power preceded its meaning. But now its meaning began to appear. If I attempted a direct repetition of what he said, I would fail; but I would fail, not for the reason you would imagine. I would fall short, not in magniloquence, but in simplicity. If *I* had spoken, my words would have been too fine; they would have passed, not *into*, but *over* the valley, and would have been heard in the halls of Hellenicus. But this man's voice touched the ground; it kindled the lily of the field. Shall I try to reproduce the spirit of what he said? It was very original as well as very simple—should I not say because very simple? I would have expected him to have begun by strains of commiseration. He struck just the opposite keynote. He told them that they had special advantages in belonging to the *valleys*—advantages which the men of the uplands did not possess. He told them they were nearer to the vision of the sky than those who lived on the hills. He said there were colours that could only be seen by the cloudy day, treasures that could only be reached by the lowly heart, banquets that could only be enjoyed by the hungering spirit. It was not more satisfaction they required; it was more want. He had come to cure the pestilence by creating more want. From the land beyond the sea he had brought a draught which increased thirst. If they would partake of it, they would see a strange thing; all the marks would leave the faces of their comrades and appear on his. And then there would happen something more wonderful still, which he would not tell them yet, for he wanted them to find it out for themselves. It was the constant draught in the country from which he came; without it angels themselves would grow weary. Would the men of the valley try?

Then from the vast assembly there rose a great and simultaneous "Yes"; and the majestic voice resumed. He asked if there were any men in that crowd who would volunteer to bear round the draught to their brethren. It would be very easy for him to do it alone; but he wanted them to have a part in their brothers' cure. Within this golden chalice there was a liquid, any single drop of which would transform life and banish every personal pain. Though the cup was small, it was amply sufficient to supply the whole multitude; for, unlike other cups, its contents did not decrease as they were expended. If there were any among them who were willing to be the first partakers and the first distributers, let them come to the front.

For a moment there was a silence. Then a buzz of excitement arose. Twelve men stood forward from the crowd. Our sensational moments are the seasons when others for the first time act differently from ourselves. This was a sensation in the life of the valleys. Twelve men by a voluntary act of independence had marked themselves out from the mass. I knew them, every man. They were nearly all of the fisher class, and had for years supplied, not only this valley, but my father's house with the fruits of the sea; and what I was chiefly struck with was the fact that amongst them were these very two incendiaries who, a few moments before, had been making such deadly efforts to destroy the dwellings of the plague-stricken.

Then came an imposing ceremony. The crowd was again parted—this time into twelve groups; and they were served in turn by each of the volunteers. Each carried the chalice through his allotted sphere, and then passed it to the nearest in rotation. I confess that my own eyes were riveted on the central figure; I rather felt than saw the ceremony. It was impossible for me to withdraw my gaze from that face so divinely beautiful; as the ceremony progressed, it became increasingly impossible. Ever as the chalice moved on from lip to lip, it seemed to me that the fashion of that countenance became altered; it began to take upon itself the likeness of the pestilence. Every moment it grew more marred, and I wondered. And I wondered most of all at the fact that with all the marring there was no change in his beauty. I have seen men and women whose loveliness was undimmed by the meanest apparel. This was a stage beyond. Here was a man whose loveliness was undimmed even by a marred visage. I think at that moment he reached to me his climax of beauty. Whether the contrast helped it I know not. Does the charm of moonlight on the waters lie in the fact that there is brightness in a sphere which ought to be troubled? I cannot tell; let us leave it to the artists and pass on.

For, indeed, my own heart was getting troubled. A great fear began to creep over me. What would the multitude say when they saw the marred visage? As yet they were too tremulous to see anything; the crisis of the experiment pressed on their hearts and blinded their eyes. But what would it be when the experiment was over? Had not that maddened crowd seen their infirmities in the face of each other even when they were not there? The divine beauty of this man had precluded such a deception. But now, without tarnishing his beauty, the marks of the valley were really there. What would that crowd say if their eyes lighted on the marred visage? Would they not cry for his blood as they had cried for the blood of the leper, as they had cried for the blood of the spotted woman, as they had cried for the blood of the suspected village? Oh, if I could only get the marks to come on me! If by any act of will, if by any form of sympathy, I could draw them from that dear face to mine, how gladly, how proudly would I die! These few minutes were to me an eternity as I strove to steal his cross and hide it in my own bosom. Never before, never since have I passed through such an agony. I seemed to be pulling at the bars of fate—frantically, hopelessly, but still increasingly. No human soul ever prayed for deliverance as I prayed for the gift of death. "Father of mercies, clothe me in his likeness, that I may die in his room "; it was the voice of my heart, it was the cry of my soul. And still the chalice moved on, and the visage grew marred. One strange thing was passed ; the stranger thing was about to come.

CHAPTER IX

THE PRIESTHOOD OF HUMANITY

THE cup had come to the last man; the first without the last was not to be perfected. It was a solemn moment, a tragic, tremendous moment. On that final draught the fate of the valley depended. Every eye was turned on the terminus; even my own wandered from their central gaze. There was the stillness or death around, or rather that stillness with which one contemplates the crisis between life and death. What would that crisis bring? Would it be night or day? Would it lift the valleys into splendour, or would it leave them in deeper shadow—deeper from that very promise of the morning which had flattered and failed?

The last man had tasted; the chalice was withdrawn. There was an instant of great silence —silence that might be felt. My heart died within me. I think, in the moment of suspense, we instinctively give the balance to fear. I knew this stillness could not last; it must be broken either by jubilee or by execration. If the latter, what then? The passions of an infuriated crowd, maddened by unfulfilled prophecy, reckless from deluded hope. Nay, what was I myself to feel in such a case? Were there not passions which I, a daughter of the uplands, might well share with the men of the valleys? It was not death from their hands I feared; it was life with my own. To have my ideal shattered, my prop broken, my dream a delusion; to find that, after all, there was nothing higher than myself in this island, nothing to rest on, nothing to lean on, nothing to hope on; to find that the land beyond the sea was but a phantom of the brain, the messenger self-deceived, the help imaginary; to go back once more, however unselfishly, to the search for a merely island home,—my God, sooner would I die.

Suddenly I was interrupted in my meditation. A great shout rent the air. It came from the back row; the last were the first. It was caught up by those immediately in front. It was reverberated by the group still nearer. At length the valley was ringing with one common cheer— loud, long, heart-moving. It shook the silent

night with the breath of a new spirit. The
fires appeared to blaze more brightly; the lamps
seemed to vibrate to the swell of an unwonted
breeze. By-and-by the voices became articulate.
From different sides of the valley came a medley
of utterances, not successive, but simultaneous,
and expressing in varied forms one common joy.
"We are free, we are free." "The burden is
lifted." "The pestilence is over." "The marked
faces have been washed white as snow." "See
that man whom we drove into the graveyard;
he looks now as fresh as you." "Look at that
woman whom we tried to stone; I don't see a
spot on her beyond what nature gives to us all."
"There are the two fishermen shaking hands
with the people they wanted to set fire to; they
have found out their mistake and are sorry." "I
don't see a black mark in all the valley."

"Yes," cried a voice amid the multitude, and
I trembled, "there is one among you who re-
tains the marks of the pestilence; it is the man
who has healed you: did he not tell you that
only by his stripes you would be cured?" In
an instant every glance was turned on the marred
face of the stranger. The event which I feared
seemed to be coming. I saw the streams draw
together; I saw the wave roll forward. For

the second time that night I interposed my frail
person between the martyr and the storm, as if
an atom could break the force of a torrent.   I
stretched forth my hands in piteous supplication ;
I raised my voice to cry, " Save him, save him."
The words would not come—not from *me*.   But
they were to come from a most unlikely quarter.
For now there happened that second strange
thing which the night had foretold.   The words
which my lips could not utter were taken up by
the very crowd to which I prayed.   In a moment
it all burst upon me ; I had mistaken the last
movement.   The second advance of the wave
was no longer from the motive of the first ; that
was hostility, this was compassion.   " Save him,"
cried a hundred voices, " for he has been our
saviour.   Is this man to die by our contagion ?
Is he to die by the neglect of those whom he
has succoured?   Shall we allow him to linger
in the open sky when we have homes and fires
and shelters ?   The night is late, and his own
night is upon him ; let him abide with us until
the breaking of the day."

" Look at him whom you have pierced," cried
Peter bar-Jona, one of the twelve who had helped
to bear the chalice.   " Is not this the very picture
of the man of whom one of your poets has sung

'He was wounded for our transgressions'? Are not these marks ours, our very own? Are not the scars of my own house there? Do you see that woman in the front? That is my wife's mother. She may well press toward her deliverer. Half an hour ago she was covered with the pestilence. Look at her now—as pure as the virgin snow. Why? He has taken her wounds. This man without spot or blemish has been marred for you and by you. Will you let him die?"

Then there was great sobbing in the crowd, for the people of the valleys do not restrain themselves as the inhabitants of the uplands. Strong men were choked with emotion. Frail women pierced their way through the throng to administer help to the solitary sufferer. Some ran to their houses to find restoratives. One brought a cup of cold water; another bore aromatic spices; a third carried a box of soothing ointment, and actually began to apply it to the spots on the face of the sufferer. At this stage there occurred a strange episode. One of the twelve men who had borne the chalice —Judas Iscariot by name—uttered a voice of dissent. "This is going too far," he cried. "Here is a woman actually touching the very marks from which she has been delivered. It is appalling to

see such recklessness. Is it not enough for you to
be healed without seeking to incur your plague
a second time? These valleys have borne sufficient pain ; let them taste their new-found freedom.
We are all, I am sure, much indebted to this
stranger ; thank him, and let him go."

A yell of execration greeted the hapless speaker.
The fury of the crowd was again uppermost—no
longer in the interest of self, but of sacrifice. I was
glad to see that the cure of the pestilence had only
transplanted, and not uprooted, their energy, for
there is nothing so hurtful to the valleys as the
spirit of apathy. It was a fine sight to see these
men and women lighted by the anger of love. It
was too fine for the object of their obloquy. The
fire in these faces blazed above the naphtha flames.
There were muttered curses ; there were ominous
threats ; there were even indications of coming
violence. The culprit saw it and cowered. He
turned his back upon the crowd and moved into
the night alone. Yet I marked then, and I
remembered afterwards, the dark expression on
that brow—an expression which cast a gloom over
the hour of deliverance, and has ever since formed
a background to each moment of joy.

And now there occurred a new wonder. Beneath
the touch of the woman who applied the ointment

the marks faded from the face of the solitary
sufferer. The expression of pain left his countenance, and in its room there came a gleam of
the most exultant gladness I have ever seen or
imagined. It was to me a new phase of his
strangely diversified beauty. I had seen that
beauty already in varied forms. I had seen it
in majesty; I had beheld it in tenderness; I had
witnessed it in calm; I had viewed it in storm;
I had looked on it in sorrow. But to see it in joy
was a fresh thing. It was not merely that the
face had lost all traces of the pestilence. There
was something on it which was not there before
the traces came. The mystery lay, not in what
the ointment had taken away, but in what it had
left behind. "She has wrought a good work in
him," cried the crowd. But I asked myself if the
ointment could have done this. Was it not indeed
a work wrought *in* him rather than on him? I
felt there was something I could not see. I gazed
into his face and marvelled.

Then he spoke once more, and once more my
heart bounded. No music ever equalled that voice.
Shall I try to reproduce it? I might as well try
to reproduce the notes of the nightingale. The
words were like a blaze of diamonds strung on
a plain cord; they were at once too high and too

6

lowly for me to imitate. I shall not try to imitate
them. I shall not even put my own words in his
mouth as the dramatists do; I would not like to
impute my words to him. I shall merely en-
deavour to state baldly and in the most indirect
form what seems to me to have been the burden
of the most wonderfully original discourse I have
ever listened to.

He began by stating that he was sure they all
wanted to know the meaning of that great mystery
which had met them twice that night—the appearance on his person, and the disappearance from
his person, of the marks of their pestilence. The
explanation was very simple. Between his heart and
their heart there was a connecting cord. Although
they seemed to be separate, they were not really so.
It was impossible that *their* bodies should receive
any wound without *his* being wounded ; it was impossible that their lives should receive any healing
without his being vivified. It was true—the union
was not perfect—they could not yet feel *his* pains
and joys, though he could theirs. But while the
completion still lingered, there was enough already
to make them solemn. They often prayed to God
to give them gladness: did it ever strike them
that God prayed to *them* for gladness—stood at
the door of their hearts and knocked? A pestilence

in the island was a pestilence in the universe. He had come from a land beyond the sea. Was it a happy land? That depended on them. He had come to them with clouds because their own clouds had affected his atmosphere. They often cried for help to the unseen land: were they aware that the unseen land cried for help to them? There was joy in that land over the sunshine of a single soul. The lightness or the darkness of its day depended on the lightness or the darkness of their island. Would they help the unseen land to its joy? Would they spread abroad the happiness of man? Would they take away the pain from the heart of God by removing it from the souls and bodies of their fellow-creatures? Let them remember that to lift the burden of humanity was to lift the burden of God. Were there any in that assembly who would continue the bearing of the cup, who would bear it into other valleys and into other sorrows? Let each bring his vial and fill it with the sacred draught. Were there any in that assembly who were willing to be enrolled to lift that cross of man which was the cross of God? Were they willing to be ordained to the ministry of love—the life of the Eternal? Were they willing to impart their healing touch to the least, knowing that thereby they did it to the Highest?

Let all who would submit to such an ordeal come forward and sign their names.

So saying, he unrolled an enormous parchment, which he called the Book of Life. He bade each who should come to the front fill his vial with the liquid, write his name on the scroll, and depart to his home. A great resolve came over me. I had been only a spectator ; I would be so no more. I too would sign with the valleys ; but, because I belonged to the uplands, I would mark my humility by signing last. A multitude of little vials were brought from the houses. Then a long procession filed forward ; first, eleven of the chalice-bearers, then an additional seventy. I thought the ceremony would never end. My heart beat wildly. Through all that night he had never once seemed to recognise me. I was hungry for recognition. Oh, just to hear his voice say again as it said in my dream, "Ecclesia"! As I sat on one of the benches in the valley and watched the procession move on, I figured in fancy the coming of my turn. Would he know me? Would he greet me? Would he commend me? I observed that to each who came he said a word which nobody else could hear. I thrilled with expectation. I too would have a word all to myself—a little secret treasure which nobody knew but me, and which I would

keep locked up in my heart for evermore. Oh
the joy of that moment, the maddening, melting,
morning joy—the picture of the day that was
yet to be !

At last the moment was come. I had waited
to the end. Was there no trace of pride in my
humility, no wish to be marked out from the
common crowd ? Perhaps ; but it was at least the
pride of devotion. I was the last remaining on
the ground ; as I moved forward I said, " I shall
be alone with *him*." I hurried towards the spot
where the open scroll was spread. As I went, I
did not look at the scroll ; I kept my eyes on the
ground, through the tremor of meeting him. Only
when I had reached the spot did I lift my gaze.
With a glad expectancy I looked up to the little
eminence from which he had addressed the multitude. He was gone ; the chalice was gone ; the
scroll was gone : I was alone with the night.

Do you know what it is to get a heart grief at
the end of a great joy ? It is not merely that it
counterbalances the joy ; it annihilates it. Will it
be believed my spirit at this moment went down
altogether ? I say it with shame ; it showed how
far I was from the life I had professed. Had not
the valleys been healed ? Sad to say, that was an
aggravation of my pain. Why should he have

spoken to these men and not to me? Was not I more ripe for him than they? Had not I seen him in a dream? In what dream had *they* seen him? Had they not been wasting the substance of their life in riotous living until the pestilence fell upon them? Yet for them he had brought out his jewelled ring and his best robe, and for me there was not a word. Oh, it was hard, hard! My heart was breaking.

With weary steps I took my journey home. I was tired and sick and lonely, and all things were changed. The way was longer; the ascent was steeper; the torchlight was dimmer. My feet were impeded by the chill of disappointment; my eyes were blinded with tears. I had been sad before, but it was with a holy sadness; this was a grief which needed more of Heaven's help, for it was the pride of a wounded spirit.

CHAPTER X

THE LAST MADE FIRST

ECCLESIA, are you ill?" It was my father who spoke. I had returned in time for the hour of evening prayer, and the household retainers were assembling. I assured him I was not. "Where have you been all night?" he said. "I have long felt that you spend too much time in consecutive study. The beauty you had in the morning has gone out of you. You are no more like what you were than a lamp is like a star." And when the chaplain Caiaphas came in, he said, "You look tired, Lady Ecclesia; I am afraid the sacrificial victim for the redemption of the valleys has not been found to-day." And when the servants appeared I again saw that they all remarked me, but it was no longer with the same kind of observation; there was a touch of pity in their glance.

And now I began to question myself. Why

was it that this beauty of the morning had declined? Was it grief that had caused it to fade? Was there anything in joy that was more favourable to beauty than sorrow? Had I not looked that very night upon the countenance of a man crushed with all the sorrows of the valley, and yet supremely beautiful? It could not be grief that had changed me; it must be that I was grieving for something wrong. And then it all burst upon me like a scorching flame. Was I one whit better than Caiaphas? Was I not exactly doing what Caiaphas was doing—seeking a priesthood of my own? Was I not as selfish as Hellenicus, more selfish than the Lord of Palatine? Was I not trying to have an ideal all for myself and for no other person? Was there one in the room so utterly vile, contemptible, mean, low, despicable, as I?

It was the custom in our house to attach more importance to united than to individual prayer. For the first time in my life I thought otherwise. When I retired to my room that night, there came to me a new experience. I felt that this formal worship was no preparation for sleep to such a one as I. I felt that the voice of the chaplain Caiaphas could not be the closing impression of *my* day. I felt that my prayer must be solitary, private, without intermediaries—not read from a book, however sacred, but uttered in the silence of the soul.

I went down on my knees and prayed. The chaplain Caiaphas would not have called it a prayer. I did not feel the least solemn ; I just felt my heart throbbing with pain and crying to be relieved. I did not even address the great God in the heavens. My cry went down to the man in the valleys, or whom I had last seen there. I did not ask myself whether he could hear me ; I prayed not from reason, but from instinct—not because I ought, but because I must. I just cried : " O thou beautiful one, I have done wrong ; and, what is worse, I have *been* wrong. I have been a poor, miserable, selfish creature, unworthy of even a glance from thee. I should have rejoiced instead of weeping ; I should have thanked thee instead of bemoaning. I thank thee now. I thank thee for lifting the pestilence from the valley and pausing not to look at me. I thank thee that last night the men with most disease had all thy sympathy, and that I who was comparatively whole was passed by. Forgive my meanness, and help me to love like thee."

That was all I said. I had never breathed a prayer like it before. It seemed to contradict all my past training as to the nature of devotion. It surely could not be devotion. Had I not been taught that in prayer we should feel how far heaven is distant from the sea-girt island where we dwell? But this prayer of mine was dreadfully rreverent. It forgot the great God in the far heavens. It forgot to remind Him of His majesty, His omnipotence, His undyingness. It forgot about things above altogether. It just came out as if it were spoken to one on a level with myself; nay, a little farther down than I could reach. It was terribly simple, profanely short, coming far too quickly to the point. I was glad Caiaphas did not hear it; but I did hope it was heard by the man in the valleys.

And somehow, I cannot tell how, there began to steal over me the sweetest peace I had ever known. It was not like the rapture I had felt either in the vision or in the valley. It was something which could not come till rapture was past. There is a great difference between joy and rest. Joy may come before the storm, but rest alone can follow it. This was not sunlight, but moonlight— not rapture, but repose. Yet there is a charm in moonlight that is not in sunlight; I think for one thing it is more revealing. I have no doubt at all that peace is more revealing than joy: " He giveth to His beloved in their sleep."

I was very weary when I laid my head upon
the pillow. The day had been long—the longest
in my life. It had been crowded with incidents.
It had been a series of rapid alternations from light
to shade, from shade to light again. It had exercised every power of my nature—body, soul, and
spirit; no wonder I was fatigued. There came
over me that delightful sense of abandonment
with which in our least disturbed moments we
yield ourselves every night into the hands of
another and are content that for us time should
be no more.

"Ecclesia!" Clearly through the night air I
heard the name; clearly through the stillness I
discerned the voice. There was no other voice
like that in all the island. It did not seem, however, to come from the valleys. It was nearer;
it was within my father's grounds. "Ecclesia!"
The call was repeated, more intensely, more
earnestly, and the direction from which it came
was more pronounced. I felt that I was called,
not merely to listen, but to come. The moment
this conviction broke on me, I lingered not. I
rose from bed and attired myself in the dress I
had worn for the valleys; it was the garb of my
own humiliation, and I wanted *him* to meet me
just in the costume in which my fall had come.

My toilette completed, I hurried along the
corridor. It was unlighted, but somehow that did
not impede me. I passed on without obstruction,
without pausing, till I found myself in the open
air, and in the grounds of my father's house.
Somehow their appearance was changed. They
had caught a likeness to the valleys. The naphtha
fires of the valleys were blazing ; the lamps of the
valleys were impending. I would have thought
it a continuation of the old scene but for the
solitude. Stay ! Was I alone ? No ; there he
stood—the man of the valleys—in the very grounds
of my own dwelling. There he stood in all his
peerless beauty. Before him was a table with
writing materials, and in front of him was that
identical scroll which had been in the valley the
object of my glory and of my grief.

I ran across the lawn as I had rushed forward
in the valley. I was determined I would not
be disappointed this time. I did not look to the
ground as before. I sped towards the spot with
my eyes fixed on the goal, resolved to keep him,
never to let him go. I indulged in no fancies ;
I drew no pictures of anticipation ; I just ran.
Panting, I reached his side. I uttered no word ; I
made no request ; I only gazed into his beautiful face. I was struck with something which

reminded me a little of the marks of pain I had seen in the valleys. I said nothing; but, in the old voice that made my heart leap, he answered my thought.

"Are you surprised, Ecclesia, that some of the marks have returned? Do you know what brought them back? It was your pain. Do you remember what I told you—that all the sorrow and all the joy of this island is reproduced in me? I caught the gladness of the valleys, and my face mirrored it; then came your cloud into my day. And did you think I had really passed you by? Do you not know it was the very nearness of your presence to my heart that made me outwardly ignore you? Do we not speak loudest to those who are farthest away? It was meet to make merry and be glad over the valleys, for they had been dead and were alive again; but I had been with you even in your dreams. Nay, whence these tears? Let there be no self-reproaches. It is all forgiven, it is all forgotten. See, I have brought you back the scroll which has been the cause of so much weeping. I need no such pledge as your signature, for your name is written in my heart; but your testimony may help others; come and sign."

Then I took the pen, and was about to put my

name to the end of the scroll; but with the gentlest of all touches he lifted my hand to the top of the parchment. And there I saw that at the very beginning of the roll a place had been left vacant. The first name signed was that of Peter bar-Jona, and between the first and the last there were no intermediate spaces; but above the name of Peter there was an unappropriated line; I wrote there, " Ecclesia, daughter of Moses ben-Israel."

As I raised my head I caught sight of what I had missed before; at the other end of the table stood the chalice, and beside it a little vial. I made a movement forward. " It is like the scroll," he said—" quite unrequired between you and me. There are many who are called; but there are a few who are chosen. These chosen ones need no chalice, for a fountain runs invisibly from my heart into their heart. They always appear to be served the last, because nobody sees them with the cup; yet they are the first of all. But though you need not the chalice for my sake, fill the vial for your sisters and your brothers; they will not understand your invisible fountain, but they will all appreciate what the eye can see. Unto them which are without, life must be revealed in parables."

When I had filled the vial and tasted it, a strange boldness came over me. I felt as if all fear had been cast out of me. A great thirst took possession of me. Here was a man who could rend the veil and show me what my ancestor Moses had died in trying to see. "Tell me," I cried—"tell me something of the land beyond the wave. I have sought it since I was a child. I have stood down by the edge of the sea and listened to its murmurs as if they could bring me a message. You say you have come from there; give me but a shell from the other shore, and I shall treasure it for ever."

A curious smile flitted across his face. He drew from his bosom a golden cross. "These," he said, "are the shells that murmur on our shore. Take it; wear it; keep it next your heart, and you will always hear the music of the land you long to see." "And is it far away?" I cried. But I spoke to the empty air. He was gone; he had vanished into the night, and on the grounds of my father's house I stood alone. It seemed as if he had taken away the home-feeling with him. All my boldness deserted me. My limbs trembled; I shivered with fear. I stretched out my hands to the appalling shadows and cried, "Light, light, light." Immediately the prayer was answered; morning struck my eyelids; I awoke; it was a dream.

Yes, it was a dream; but of a very peculiar

order. That things were not what they seemed to me I do not doubt. That the thoughts which passed through me were clothed in very inadequate shapes I firmly believe. But I have proof that the process was not wholly inward—shall I not rather say, not wholly confined to myself? I brought something out of my dream which I did not take into it; I was richer this morning than I was last night. I speak the truth of God; I lie not. I declare in the presence of the All-seeing—let philosophers explain it as they will—that in my hand was the very vial which I had filled with the sacred draught, and on my breast was the very cross through which I was to hear the music of the other shore.

CHAPTER XI

NOT PEACE, BUT A SWORD

WE were just completing the morning meal, of which we always partook together—my father, the chaplain Caiaphas, and I. My father was congratulating me on the return of my good looks, and was endorsing his views on the inexpediency of much study. Caiaphas was insinuating that the studies would do less harm if they were less secular. I was listening to both with an averted interest, which sprang rather from a sense of duty than from any spirit of undutifulness. For the first time in my life I had the uncomfortable feeling of seeming to be what I was not. I was not troubled in my conscience, but I was greatly troubled in my consciousness. I was deeply persuaded that I was right; I had chosen my part, and I had no regret. None the less, I felt that I was keeping a secret from my father —a father to whom in the olden times my heart had always been open. It was the first barrier to my household peace, the earliest cloud in my domestic sky.

Suddenly words and musings were alike cut short. Through the morning air there ran the blast of a peculiar horn, only heard in the island at times of great crisis, and always conveying the same signal—alarm. It was never blown for individual troubles, only for cases of common danger. It had not sounded when the pestilence had been proclaimed in the valleys, for the valleys were not held to have any necessary connection with the uplands. This must have been deemed something more serious. Like the blast which had summoned the great assembly, the signal was propagated from one horn to another, each taking up the message where the compass of its predecessor seemed to be exhausted. It appeared to descend from Palatine Hill, and to increase in volume as it came. Presently a horse's hoofs were heard in the grounds. There was evidently something which specially concerned our family. My father and Caiaphas started from the table and hurried into the courtyard. A messenger rode forward to the front of the house. He handed a letter to my father. "From the Lord of Palatine," he said. "Were you to wait for an answer?"

said my father. "No," he replied; "the answer was to be given in deeds, not words."

When the messenger was gone, my father broke the seal. As he read I watched his expression; it was grave. When he had finished, he turned to me. "Summon the household," he said; "this is a matter of vast and vital importance." While I called together the domestic retainers, he consulted with Caiaphas long and earnestly. At last, in the hall where we were wont to assemble for family prayer, there was gathered a company of eager, anxious, expectant faces. Caiaphas took his seat at the head of the table as if he were about to resume the morning service; but the aspect of his countenance was not devotional. For a few moments he faced the household with a menacing look, as if to prolong our torture of suspense; then slowly and coldly he thus delivered himself:

"Three days ago the Lord of Palatine made a law. He declared the valleys to be afflicted with a pestilence which rendered them dangerous to the peace of this island, and he enacted that during the continuance of this pestilence any communication with the valleys should be punished with death. He commanded all the gates to be closed that lead to such communication, and he solemnly asseverated that any breach of this order would

forfeit the life of the offender, were it himself or
his brother. That order has been broken. Last
night the valley in front of this house was
entered ; this morning the Sympathy Gate was
found open. On the threshold there are clearly
discernible footsteps ; that which was done in
darkness has been brought to light. I hold in
my hand a letter from the Lord of Palatine. It
breathes deep surprise and strong indignation.
It is not the indignation of a man who has received
a personal injury, but of a legislator who has seen
his law broken. He has heard in this act the cry
of treason against the government of this island,
and he has demanded an expiation. The sacrifice
for the valleys is likely soon to be made."

He paused, and the faces of the household grew
ghastly. Then in gentler words my father took
up the strain. " I would fain hope," he said, " that
things are not so bad as the Lord of Palatine
deems. The keys of the Sympathy Gate are not
in my hands, nor in yours ; the Lord of Palatine
himself holds them. I do not believe that any
one of you has the ability, if he had the will, to
make a key. My own opinion is that by some
oversight this gate at the first was not properly
locked. It is deeply to be deplored that such
a thing should have occurred on our side of the

valley, but I feel convinced that it does not originate here. Is there any man among you who can testify that any hour, either yesterday or the day previous, he saw the Sympathy Gate open?"

But all the testimonies were on the other side, and they were affirmed with great positiveness. One man declared that he had passed the gate yesterday morning, and found it fast locked. Another said he had seen it at mid-day, and marked how completely it was closed. A third affirmed that he had passed it at five in the afternoon, when the shadows were rapidly deepening and the night was falling fast. He was aware of the existing law, and he had deemed it his duty as well as his interest to see that his side of the valley was guarded. He was prepared to take solemn oath that any interference with the valley must have been subsequent to that hour.

My father looked disappointed. He had no love for the Lord of Palatine, and would have been well pleased to have found him tripping on his own ground. But the eye of Caiaphas lighted with a malign joy. He had always been a subservient tool of the house of Palatine. He had uniformly discouraged those family aspirations in which my father indulged; indeed he was an

enemy to aspiration of every kind, and greatly
feared the leaping of fences. Accordingly I detected in him an ill-disguised satisfaction in the
failure of my father's attempt to shift the blame.
"You have given," he said, "a most candid testimony, and one which greatly narrows our field of
investigation. You have proved that this was a
deed of the night. Being a deed of the night, it is
a deed of evil. It has been wrought in the hour
when men sleep, in the hour when men are blind.
What is worse, it has been wrought in the heart of
this estate, in the very centre of this family tree.
As the chaplain of this house I am concerned with
its honour. I feel that you are under a cloud,
that we are all under a cloud. A responsibility
is laid upon me, and I will not shrink from giving
my advice. Listen then to what I propose. I
suggest that this house offer a reward for any
information which shall lead to the arrest of the
man who has trespassed in the valleys. I advise
that the Lord of Palatine should be requested to
have a placard set up in these valleys, giving notice
of the reward. I propose that the Lord of Palatine
should suspend the law against communication for
one hour only—from twelve to one to-morrow at
noon. I suggest that any man of the valleys who
has information to give shall take his stand at that

hour on the other side of yon fence where he can be seen and not touched. I advise that on this side of the fence the inmates of this house should gather at the appointed time, fearlessly courting investigation of themselves and their surroundings. So shall we be washed white in the eyes of the Lord of Palatine."

"And how do you propose," I said, "that the placard is to be carried into the valleys? Do you think the Lord of Palatine will consent to admit into his own dwelling the contagion which he deprecates for the island?"

"If the Lady Ecclesia had waited till I had finished," he answered with some haughtiness, "she would have found that I had amply provided for the emergency. There is a deformed beggar in the neighbourhood, named Simon, known to all of you and supported by your alms. Him shall we send down into the valley to post the placard, with instructions not to return till to-morrow afternoon. By the hour of one to morrow the communication shall be closed again, and we shall take care that he returns no more."

"And so," I said, "you shall compel a man to bear that cross which you are persecuting another man for bearing voluntarily."

A gleam of lightning shot from the eyes of

Caiaphas. He turned to my father. "For nearly twenty years," he said, "I have been the chaplain of this house and of this clan, and, as law and religion here are one, I have been in these years the legal adviser of your family. Before I came into your service you were my master; when I took your service I became yours, for he that ministers in holy things is the lord of all. By the irony of fate it has been reserved for your daughter to be my first traducer. Never before have I been addressed in such insolent terms. I am accused of persecuting a hero when I am prosecuting a criminal. I call upon you to exercise your paternal authority."

"Ecclesia," said my father, "you forget yourself." But his voice was not thunder; I think he was more troubled than angry.

"Bethink you, father," I said, not deigning to address the chaplain, "the man who has gone down to these valleys has gone with a motive. What motive but benevolence could induce any man to go? It is some one who has heard the cry of the weary, and, to bring them aid, has braved prohibition, law, death. It is some one who feels for your people what you and I ought to feel. It is some one who, in defiance of popular opinion and in spite of legal enactment, has been constrained

by the sheer love of man to seek him at his lowest
ebb and in his most fallen fortunes. Who knows
but God Himself has interposed to stretch an
arm of deliverance across the great sea. Let us
beware, father, lest haply we be found to fight
against God."

"Dreams, dreams, dreams," cried Caiaphas, still
addressing my father, "the dreams which this
young lady used to foster on the sea-shore, and
which cling to her as a penalty. I say, this is not
the arm of the Almighty, but the arm of treason.
It is the arm of one who has lifted his hand against
the laws of this island, and has sought to rouse the
valleys into enmity with the uplands. If any man
might legitimately desire a change of government,
it is you, sir. You have claims to be the head of
a clan which was the original source of all the
families in the island; if so, you are ideally the
island's king. But I ask if such an event as
happened last night is in favour of your interest
any more than that of the Lord of Palatine. The
rousing of the valleys may be adverse to *him*, but
is it advantageous to you? If a nameless adven-
turer has gone down to the valleys in a moment
of popular frenzy, if he has gone down in defiance
of law in order to impress the populace with the
superiority of need to law, if, as the result of that

impression, he has gathered around himself the
sympathy of the multitude, and if that sympathy
should take final shape in rising and revolt, will
not that be more adverse to your claims than any
domination of the Lord of Palatine?   It will break
your influence in the one sphere in which you have
been paramount—the attachment of the lower
orders."

He had struck my father on his weak point, and
I saw he had made an impression.   I hastened to
counteract it, or rather to turn it into a new
channel.   "Yes, father," I said, "he is right; he
has spoken truly.   Your influence has always been
paramount among the labouring and the laden,
among those who toil and spin.   It is this which
makes you different from Hellenicus, different
from the Lord of Palatine—I would say greater
than they.   I ask, will you sacrifice this influence?
Will you stand before this island, before all ages
as the champion of those who would oppress the
valleys?   Will you allow it to be said by con-
temporaries, by posterity, that Moses ben-Israel
offered a reward for the apprehension of the man
who had tried to help the helpless?   It is not the
bribe that I deprecate.   I have no fear that any
man in the valleys would be so mean as to take it
I accept to the full the chaplain's test; I shall

meet him at noon to-morrow; we shall all meet him. But, as your child, nay, as a part of yourself, I protest against that which would dishonour you. I protest against this reward being offered by the head of the clan in the *capacity* of head of the clan. If it were a matter of private enterprise, I would have nothing to say; if it were the public act of the Lord of Palatine, I would have nothing to say; but the official deed of Moses ben-Israel it will never be."

Everybody was startled. My father was startled; Caiaphas was startled; I myself was the most startled of all. I could not understand the boldness of my own words; it seemed as if some one were dictating to me. "Ecclesia," said my father, "where have you got your gift of tongues? I am convinced; you have prevailed—prevailed or once even over Caiaphas. I accept the arrangement of Caiaphas in all respects but one; the reward must not be offered by the head of this house."

"Then," said Caiaphas, "I offer it myself as a private individual, in the interest of that which I believe to be religion. The arm which has intervened to promote dispeace in a household hitherto full of harmony cannot be the arm of the Almighty."

CHAPTER XII

IN FRONT OF THE ACCUSER

IT was the next day at noon, and all my father's house had gathered in the grounds. The Lord of Palatine had accepted the proposal of the chaplain ; the reward had been placarded in the valleys. My father was there, and Caiaphas, and I ; all the domestic retainers were there ; there was a full representation of our family tree. It will surprise the reader of these memoirs to learn that of all the party I was the only unconcerned spectator. The reverse might have been expected. I alone knew the secret. I alone knew certainly that these valleys had something to disclose. I alone had evidence that the scene of the pestilence had been actually invaded. Nay, I was myself one of the very parties for whom the law was in search ; if any one was guilty, I was. Yet there was not in my mind a tremor of anxiety as to the futility of the result. I had

no fear that the valleys would betray the man
who had been their benefactor ; and if they did,
I had no fear that one so great *could* be betrayed.
To associate *him* with the danger of death was
impossible. I could think of him as suffering ;
it was there I had seen his highest beauty. But
suffering was a form of life ; the very greatness
of his pain might be measured by the greatness of his vitality. Death was a negative thing,
a powerless thing, a thing remote from either
pain or joy. My hero could not die ; he could
feel, he could weep, he could groan in spirit ;
but he could not die. I laughed in my heart
at the attempt to track him.

And here, while we are waiting at the fence,
and my narrative is for a space suspended, let
me answer a question which, I am sure, must
be pressing on the mind of all who shall read
these pages. Doubtless it will seem to many
that my conduct throughout this episode has
been pre-eminently unsatisfactory. They will
say : " Knowing yourself to be one of the agents
in this revolt from existing law, and professing,
as you do, to be an admirer of the deed, why did
you not confess it ? " I answer, " Because I *was*
an admirer of the deed." Looking back on every
hour of that and the previous day, I protest

solemnly that there was not a moment in which
I was not prepared to lay down my life for my
convictions. I declare before God that in the
white glow of my emotion I would, like one of
my ancestors, have forgotten the pain even of a
fiery furnace. But what then of the valleys? what
of the work of that man who had to me taken
the place of the divine? Was his benevolence
to be interrupted by a premature disclosure, that
I might enjoy the luxury of self-sacrifice? Was
I to be allowed the selfish pleasure of expressing
my devotion, when by its expression the gates
of charity would have been shut for evermore?
My confession would have exploded the mine
of latent love. Ye who talk of the dread of
martyrdom, I would have you to remember that
love's greatest martyrdom is the prohibition to
sacrifice. I would have you to know that the
most drastic moment the heart has to bear is
the moment of its own restraint, and that its
tears are never so bitter as when it is compelled to swallow them. My time of deepest
sacrifice was precisely the moment when I
made no sign.

A quarter of an hour had passed. The eyes of
Caiaphas were straining towards the gate of the
valley. My thoughts were far away. I was so

sure that nothing was to be expected that I had
forgotten where I was.   Suddenly Caiaphas cried
out, "he comes! he comes!"   I started.   I felt
like one who had been walking in a fit of ab-
stractedness and struck against something.   I
thought it must be a delusion: who could have
come on such an errand?   I followed the direction of the eyes of Caiaphas.   And truly, emerging
from the Sympathy Gate of the valley, I saw the
shadow of a human form.   It came nearer, and
the shadow took substance; it was a man.   It
came nearer still; it was a face I knew.   It
approached the boundary-line; and then in a
flash I recognised him; it was Judas Iscariot.
Strange as it may seem, I had never thought
of such a contingency.   I wondered now that I
had not thought of it.   I remembered the scene
in the valley.   I remembered his effort to check
the rising enthusiasm.   I remembered his adverse
reception by the heated crowd.   I remembered
the malign expression of his countenance as he
slunk into the night; I said to myself, "This
man *could* tell."   And then for the first time
there flashed upon me another thought; I too
had been seen in the valley—seen by this man
of meanness.   I experienced more tremor in the
anticipation of my own betrayal than in the

threatened betrayal of him whom I idolised. I had no fear that *he* could be taken even should he be disclosed. What I did fear was that *my* discovery, my arrest, should strike terror into the valleys, and paralyse on the very threshold the influence of that beautiful life whose contact had promised them the dawning of a new day.

" You have answered the placard," said Caiaphas, addressing the slouching figure, not without an accent of contempt.

" Yes," he replied, " I have obeyed the summons of your most holy office."

" You have information to give as to the valleys ? "

" I have."

" Were you, the night before last, in the presence of any man who was a stranger to you ? "

" A man ?   I doubt if it was a man."

" No quibbling.   For your own safety you have already confessed too much without confessing all.   What stranger did you see in the valley the night before last ? "

" I have no wish to conceal: but how can I tell ?   I know nothing like him by which I can describe him."

" What name did he give ? "

"He gave no name, but the valleys have given him a name ; they have called him their deliverer, their saviour ; they have called him Jesus ; there are some who say 'King Jesus.'"

"Ha ! We begin to see light at last. At last the Lord of Palatine will know his friends and reward them. And what has this man done that they should call him king ? "

"As I said, I doubt if he be a man ; he has cured the pestilence."

"Cured the pestilence ? How ? "

"By the power of his own presence. I have never seen such a presence. The Lord of Palatine is like a child beside it ; his brother Hellenicus is like an ape beside it."

"Silence, miscreant, or you are a dead man. You are come here not as his herald, but as his accuser. Having told so much, you must tell more. When this rebel had persuaded the men of the valley that he had healed them, what did he ask by way of recompense ? "

"The signature of a bond."

"Ha ! A bond of allegiance ; the light is broadening, deepening. And what did you sign in this bond ? "

"I refused to sign."

"Very good ; you were afraid of the punishment

of treason. And what was the compact which you were asked to sign, which others did sign ? "

" It was a promise to band together for the ministration to the wants of the valley."

" A treasonable guild, in other words. Had you any weapons with you ? "

" None."

" Were you furnished with any ? "

" None."

" Did you take anything away from the secret meeting which you did not bring into it ? "

" *I* did not ; some did."

" What ? "

" Each who signed the bond received a little vial with a mysterious liquid."

" I see ; a quicker remedy than the sword ; some deadly poison. Now comes my crucial question. Look round the retainers of this house ; scan their features carefully, and tell me if you recognise any face to-day as one which was present there."

I drew a free breath. Some people overshoot the mark ; Caiaphas had aimed too low. It had never occurred to him to look higher than a retainer. Would Judas keep strictly within the compass of the question ? Could I trust him to answer just so much, and no more ? No ; God had

given me the chance of escape, and I would accept
His deliverance.   I addressed Caiaphas.   " You
are exceeding your commission," I said.   " A
reward has been offered with the consent of the
Lord of Palatine, and without further consent you
dare not go beyond it.   You have proposed to
reach the *source* of the stream ; you are not at
liberty to search for its accessories.   If you want
to do that, you must ask an additional warrant.
How do you know but that in the opinion of the
Lord of Palatine your search might spoil the search
of more skilled detectives ? "

Caiaphas bit his lip, and looked dark.   I had
hit him on his strongest side—his claim to legal
knowledge.   " Surely," he said, "the Lady Ecclesia
has too much respect for the honour of her house
to allow it to be interfered with by a technical
point of law.   Can it be that she and I have
changed places on this question ? "

" I have so much respect," I cried, "for the
honour of my house that I make here and now a
deliberate promise.   If ever the time shall come
when you shall lay your hands on him who has
braved for love the thunders of law, I swear by the
great God, and by all which I deem holy in man,
that I shall offer to you, to the Lord of Palatine, to
all men, a conclusive proof of the innocence of

these retainers. I have reason to know that every one of those servants was elsewhere in that eventful hour, and had no participation either in its joy or in its pain. That is my pledge. Have you ever known me to be untrue? Will you not trust me till the time comes?"

"Be it so," said Caiaphas; "and the sooner it comes the better." Turning to Judas, he said, "Can you give me any indication when and where this man is to be found?"

"There is a thanksgiving service to-night for the cure of the valleys, and at the close he has asked Peter bar-Jona and the two sons of Zebedee to meet him in the Oilpress Garden."

"And could you undertake to identify him?"

"In a crowd of millions."

"Then the pestilential valleys must be braved for once. Be at the garden gate at the close of the hour of evening song. I shall myself hasten to bear the tidings to the Lord of Palatine."

The result of the meeting had been to me more favourable than I had reason to expect. I had passed through the fire, and had come out unhurt. I had escaped without shame, without meanness, without denial of my convictions. I had not only averted the blow from myself, which meant the cause

I professed ; I had succeeded in vindicating even
against Caiaphas the protective power of law over
the meanest subject. True the man of the valleys
had been betrayed, tracked, pursued ; but I had
no fear for *him*. My hero could not die ; it was
not possible that death should hold him ; I told
myself again and again that it was impossible.
Above all, I had done something to express my
devotion. In words which none but myself could
understand, I had pledged myself to make the
hour of this man's arrest the signal of my own
surrender. I had promised to my heart that I
would make the disclosure of my part in this
transaction contingent on the success or failure of
the movement of Judas. And, all the time, God
was preparing a totally different solution, and was
leading me by a way which I knew not to the
advent of the crisis hour. I was saying proudly
to myself, " I shall die for *him*, for *him*, for *him*."
And God was saying : " Your love for him,
Ecclesia, would be more devoted if it were less
romantic. Your offer of surrender is beautiful :
but is it perfect? You will come if the sun goes
down ; very good. But what if only the *candle*
shall go out? what if merely the taper shall be
extinguished ? Have you realised that surrender
is not complete when it is given only to the

highest ? Inasmuch as you shall do it unto the least, you shall do it unto him. You have a chapter of the Book of Life yet to learn, Ecclesia ; I shall lead you into the palace by another door."

CHAPTER XIII

PHŒBE

ABOUT half an hour after my return to the house I was summoned by one of the domestics. I was told that my maid Phœbe was in violent hysterics. She had been brooding over the possible consequences of the indoor and the outdoor meeting, until the terror had got possession of her brain. Twenty-four hours of mental tension had done their work. The dim suggestion of being suspected had grown into a certainty of impending judgment. I felt a pang of remorse in my heart. I felt that I had been just a little selfish. I had measured the effect of these scenes purely by their influence on myself. I had altogether forgotten that there is a difference between a storm to one within the house and a storm to one outside. I had been protected from the cold by a warm lining at the breast—the power of a great emotion. I ought to have remembered those

who had no such emotion, no such lining against
the storm.   I ought to have remembered how
much more toilsome the march is when there is
no music.   I ought to have thrown myself down
into the position of those below me, to have seen
with their eyes and felt with their hearts.   I might
try to do it still.

Phœbe was not of our clan.   I had received
her into my service from the house of Hellenicus,
on whose estate her ancestors had for centuries
been retainers.   She had herself caught much of
the atmosphere of that house—its habitual search
for sunshine, and its constant recoil from pain.
I have often been struck in houses with the
resemblance between servants and their masters.
I was struck with it in Phœbe.   She was like
Hellenicus on a lower plane.   But sixteen years
of age, she was younger in mind than in body.
Her characteristic feature was youthfulness.   She
accepted the sunshine as a right, and received the
cloud as a breach of faith.   She took fine weather
for granted, and looked upon the overcast sky as
a personal injury.   The result was that when the
rain did fall it fell heavily.

It fell heavily now.   I found her on the floor
in paroxysms of terror, wringing her hands de-
spairingly, and sobbing wildly.   I turned out all

her fellow-servants who had gathered as spectators;
I knew that at such times the voice of one is better
than the murmur of a multitude. I found she was
oblivious of everything that had happened during
the meeting. Perhaps it would be more correct
to say that she had never observed anything.
There was only one image in her mind—the figure
of Caiaphas as he asked the betrayer to scrutinise
the faces of the household. She had come in a
state of tremor; she had remained in a state of
vacancy; she had left in a state of nightmare.

I made her sit down on the couch, and talked
to her soothingly. I had little success. She
seemed incapable of being calmed. "They will
think I have been there! They will burn me, they
will burn me!" was her constant cry. It was
in vain I told her that she had nothing to fear.
It was in vain I assured her that I had myself
the power to avert all suspicion from her, that I
had evidence to prove she was not there. There
are deeps of suffering that lie beneath all natural
comfort, and they are by no means confined to
those sorrows for which there is an adequate
cause. If you let the nerves go too low, a trifle
will have the same effect as a tragedy.

All at once a thought struck me; it was the
memory of that little vial which had come to me

in my dream.   Had *he* not said it would help
my sisters and brothers ? had I not felt in myself
its power to make bold ?   If Phœbe's mind had
not been a blank to what had happened, it would
have been a dangerous suggestion ; but it *was* a
blank.   I would try.   I pressed it to her lips and
made her swallow a few drops.   In an instant
she was calm.   The frightened expression left her
face ; the intelligence returned.   By-and-by she
sat up, and a gleam of interest shone in her eyes.

"What did the man go down to the valleys
for ? " she said.

" I believe he went down to help people who
were like you—in great distress."

" And why are they so angry with him ? "

" Because there was a law made that no man
should go, and he has braved the law."

" But why was such a law made ?   Was it kind
to leave the people of the valleys without
comfort ? "

" I think not, Phœbe."

" And wasn't it good of him to go down when
everybody else stood back ? "

" I think it was supremely good."

" And will they punish him for having so much
love ? "

" If they find him, they will put him to death."

Surely they would not do it if they knew he had been so kind. I could tell my old master Hellenicus, and he would speak to his brother, the Lord of Palatine."

"Do you know what would happen if you did that?" I said this by way of experiment. "You would be suspected of favouring his disobedience, and would be punished along with him."

"What should I care for that?" she cried, with a fine flash in her eye. "I think I should like to be along with him anywhere."

I was startled to see how close she had come up to myself in a few minutes. "If," I said, "he came and asked you to go down with him to the valleys to-night, would you go?"

"Yes," she said; and there was a ring of conviction in her voice; "this night or any night I would go."

"And if you knew," I said, "that by going you would suffer, would you do it all the same?"

"All the same," she cried; "would it not be grand to suffer with such a man?"

Did a pang of jealousy go through me? Did I feel the slightest possible annoyance that a poor creature like this should have been transformed in a moment into equality with myself? The heart is naturally so mean, and love is

habitually so monopolising, that I cannot be quite
sure I was altogether free from such a twinge.
But if it was there, it was at once expelled.
' Phœbe," I said, "I see this liquid has done
you good. Keep it by you during the day.
Use it all if you will ; I shall only ask back
the little vial, as it is a gift from a very dear
friend. I do hope it will complete your cure."

It was a trivial act, but, since I had seen the
man of the valleys, it was the most solemn I
had yet performed. Hitherto I had only *received*
his influence ; now for the first time I had *imparted*
it. Something of his had passed from my hand
into the hand of another. Little did I know
how awful this moment really was. Little did
I dream that I was standing on the brink of
a tremendous destiny, touching the crisis hour
of all my life. Little did I guess that the tiny
vial which I meant to reclaim in the evening
would never come back to my hand any more,
and that, when next I should see it, it would
be—— But let me not anticipate.

The day wore on with its rounds and duties.
My father and I dined alone. Caiaphas had
gone to carry his report to the Lord of Palatine.
To me the removal of his presence was always
the lifting of a cloud ; to my father it was the

changing of a view. I invariably remarked that when Caiaphas was absent he became more large in his sympathies and more tender in his judgments. To me the memory of this day, whose afternoon he and I passed together, will always be one of the sunbeams in my life. My secret did not press upon me with the same intensity as it did yesterday; I felt that already it was half out of my hands. And then the new life into which I had entered, so far from dimming the old, had lent to the old a golden hue. I think I never loved my father so much as that afternoon, never came so near to him in the sympathy of my heart. Oh, I am glad that on this day, of all days, my sight of him was fair, for it was the last that he and I were thus to pass together.

The day wore on and began to wear away. At nightfall I went out to the village adjoining my father's house. I wanted to call on some of the cottagers on their return from daily toil. In the old days this would have been my hour for study; but now my heart needed more. My father wished me to take Phœbe with me for company in the night; but I resolutely refused. I pointed to her nervous excitement. I pointed to the clearness of the heavens—to the stars shining in their strength, to the silvery moon in the sky and on the waters. I pointed, above all, to the love which would come to the people from seeing they were trusted by their superiors. And the last argument prevailed ; my father let me go. I cannot but remark here on what small threads our destiny is suspended. If I had taken Phœbe with me, the sequel would never have been written as it is written. I would have entered by my own door—the door I had planned for myself. God meant me to enter by His door, and He wrought out His purpose by a trivial circumstance. Our threads are God's chains.

I made my rounds in the village and bent my steps homeward. It was a gorgeous night, very unlike that in which I had made my descent into the valleys. There seemed to be a promise in the air. We speak almost proverbially of the calm before the storm. I suppose the phrase is generally uttered in cynicism, to suggest the deceitfulness of hope. To my view there is nothing in which God is more kind. I do not believe that rest is merely or even mainly valuable when it comes at the end of the journey. To me it is most welcome when it precedes the labour of the day. Looking back through the glass of memory, I thank God for this night. It was a draught of pure water given to one who was about to enter an arid desert. I am told of one of my ancestors that he was fed by an angel previous to making a journey of forty days. Even so feel I to-day. As I survey that dark past, and reflect that I have actually got through, I thank the All-Father for that evening of strength and calm. It seems to me now as if He had fed me before starting—fed me with invisible food and by an unseen hand. I know that without this nourishment I never could have borne my coming cross.

Through the clear air there came a sound of singing. It ascended from the valleys, and I knew what it meant. It was the closing hymn of the thanksgiving service. "Be at the garden gate at the close of the hour of evening song"; these words of Caiaphas rang in my ears. Was I afraid? No, a thousand times no. My heart caught up the old refrain. He could never be taken. He was beyond capture, bonds, death. He was unfettered by the conditions of this mortal clay. He would vanish from the sight of his pursuers and resume his path of gold. Oh, what a dream they were in, what a delusive dream!

I came to the gate of my father's grounds. I had left it shut; I found it open. Caiaphas must have returned. He must have come back to tell that he had been baffled. How I should like to hear him tell it. I ran through the avenue with the step of my last night's dream ; I reached the house door. Suddenly my heart stood still. It was no longer the home which I had left. There were torches blazing on the lawn. The hall was full of soldiers, and between two of them stood a prisoner ; it was my little maid Phœbe.

CHAPTER XIV

THE CONFESSION BEFORE MEN

WHEN I recovered from my first start, my immediate feeling was one of indignation. I turned to the captain of the guard. "How dare you," I said, "invade the house of a peaceable citizen—a house whose family tree is older than any in the island!"

"Whom have I the honour of addressing?" said the captain.

"I am the Lady Ecclesia, daughter of Moses ben-Israel; this is my father," and I pointed to him as he stood fronting the group with countenance pale but calm.

"I am sorry that I have been compelled to show to your father an act of seeming disrespect, but it is my office to obey commands."

"You are under commands to leave this house immediately."

"These are brave words, my Lady; but there is a power in the island higher than yours."

"Yes, a wonderful power, a military power of the first order, a power that can enter the defenceless home of one of its own subjects, a power that can surround a girl of sixteen with a band of soldiers, and with resistless might carry her away to prison. I always knew that the Lord of Palatine was great, but I never thought him so strong as this."

The captain of the guard turned to my father. "I make allowance," he said, "for the impulse of youth; but I am bound to tell you that the language of your daughter exceeds either propriety or prudence, and might be used against you by one desiring your hurt."

"Ecclesia," said my father, "I am afraid the time has gone by for anger. We are in a very critical position. Caiaphas, who has not yet returned, made his report to-day. What impressed the Lord of Palatine beyond everything else was the distribution of the vials. He fears they may contain either a secret poison or a secret influence, and he has given orders to search for them in every house of the island, and to arrest all with whom they may be found. They have searched my house and have found one."

" Here it is," cried the captain, holding up my own little vial. " This young woman," pointing to Phœbe, " has been caught red-handed, caught with this in her possession."

" And how do you know," I said, " that this was one of the vials distributed by the man in the valleys ? "

" The bottle," he answered, " might come from anywhere ; it is the liquid that is peculiar. I would not, however, have pressed the point if this girl had offered any defence, any explanation. Instead of that, she refuses to say where she got the vial. She will not even plead a lapse of memory. She declines to give any assurance that she was not one of the spectators of that infamous scene."

" But I saw her in this house at seven of that evening," cried one of the servants.

" Ah, yes," said the prisoner ; " but I had plenty of time to be in the valley after that."

I looked at the girl in startled surprise. Was this the same being who, a few hours ago, had been screaming over an imaginary terror. I never dreamed that the effect of the draught would be more than temporary. Here she stood, not only calm, but almost defiant, rejecting a circumstance that would have been in her favour, and simulating a guilt which certainly was not hers. What could

be her motive ? In a moment it broke upon me ;
it was to shield *me*. The instinct of the heart often
makes us cleverer than the power of the brain.
Phœbe's brain was not strong, but her heart had
seen it all. With the piercing accuracy of devotion
she had put together the scattered threads and
recognised my danger. I had become to her what
the man of the valleys had been to me : shall I not
rather say that he had shone to her *through* me.
Her first call to sacrifice had come to her in the
need of a fellow-mortal.

And so had mine. It was at this awful moment
that I first learned the divergence between Heaven's
way and my way. I had decided in my heart that,
if ever I should surrender, it would be for *him*
—for him personally, individually, distinctively.
Heaven had decided that he should be represented
to me by another, and that other amongst the
lowliest. I was called to give my life, not for the
man of the valleys, but for this humble maiden,
this serving-girl, this most commonplace and un-
romantic of all personages. Nor even for her was
it a sacrifice that was asked from me. It was
an act of common honesty, without which I would
have been the vilest, meanest, basest of mankind.
Truly the gates of God are not all gates of gold.

All this passed through the mind quicker than

words can tell, and made no appreciable pause in the stirring scene. On my part there was not a moment's hesitation, not a breath of dubiety. There was only one course to be taken ; it had all the pain, but not the merit, of a sacrifice. I stepped forward to do the only thing which honour could do. Every one looked surprised as I approached the captain of the guard.

" I have something to tell you," I said, "of great importance. But before I do so, I have an act of reparation to perform. I spoke to you just now with much rudeness and with marked discourtesy. I had no idea you had so good a case. I blamed you for discharging your duty. You were right, and I was wrong. Accept my apology and forgive me."

" Do not speak of it, my Lady," he replied ; " it was all most natural on your part. I deeply regret that you have been put so much about. I can assure you that no one suspects you or your esteemed father of knowing anything of this disgraceful business, nor shall any expressions used in the heat of excitement ever be retailed by me."

Did I wince as he uttered these words ? If I did, it was not from shame, but from the sense of being an unconscious deceiver. It is very painful to be received under a false ideal. How absolutely

this man had mistaken my position was known
only to myself, and the fact pressed upon me with
the weight of a solitary burden. I believe nothing
hurts a man or a woman like the impression of
having been deceived.

"And now," I said, "I must ask you to release
this poor little girl. Perhaps you think the calmness and coolness of the demand more aggravating
than the angry heat. Nay, but never fear; I shall
not send you back empty-handed to the Lord of
Palatine. If I ask you to release this girl, it is not
because I would rob the law of its penalty. It
is because I have the proof of her innocence; it is
because I have discovered the guilty party."

A thrill of sensation ran through the hall;
my father looked startled; every servant looked
ghastly. "She knows nothing about it!" cried the
prisoner: "what should she know? Have you not
proof enough that it was I? Have you not found
the vial in my hands? Have I not refused to tell
where I got it? Who else in this house could
have been with the man of the valleys?"

"Dear Phœbe," I said, "those who have been
with the man of the valleys dare not sacrifice truth
even for love."

"Lady Ecclesia," said the captain, "I am aware
what a painful thing it must be for you to implicate

one of your own domestics; but, as you have
yourself said, love must yield to truth.   It is your
duty to your family and to the traditions of your
house to wipe out any stain that may have occurred
within its walls."

"May the stain last for ever!" I cried.   "May it
spread and grow and deepen until it covers every
inch of the floor, till there is not a spot within this
dwelling that is not dyed with the red blood of
sacrifice!   I am come to make my confession
to-night.   This poor girl is innocent as *you* count
innocence.   She had not the privilege, she had not
the glory of touching the hand that filled this
vial; she only received it from common hands like
mine.   But I—I obtained it from himself; he filled
it for me, he brought it to me.   He met me under
the shadow of the night—this man of the valleys
whom you persecute.   He met me in a dream, and
bade me go down into the vale.   He told me he
had the key to all gates, and that I would find
before me an open door.   I came to the Sympathy
Gate, and I found it indeed unbarred, and in the
heart of the dark defile there blazed a torch of
golden light.   I went down, and saw what I shall
never forget.   I saw a man, of beauty absolutely
peerless, of power seemingly omnipotent.   I saw
him stand in the group of sufferers and literally

lift their burdens. I saw the weeping made to laugh and the sighing made to sing. I heard words that man never spoke to man—so simple were they, so human. I beheld the foremost of the healed write their names in his roll-book and bind themselves to the service of the sad. I saw them fill the vials with that mysterious draught of which, unconsciously, you are the bearer. He would not let me sign, he would not let me taste within the valleys, for I was a child of the uplands, and the burden of the vale was all its own. But when I lay within these walls, he came to me again in a second dream. He brought me the scroll ; he brought me the elixir ; and I gave him my name, and he gave me his cup, and I was bound to him for evermore."

The sensation produced by these words was appalling, but it was very different in nature from what I had expected. I had expected cries of astonishment, voices of reproach, perhaps even expressions of personal alarm. In any case I expected that the interest would centre in my *narrative*. To my utter bewilderment, I alone was the object of solicitude. There was only one impression, and it found voice in my father. He put his arm round me, and addressed the captain of the guard. " Don't you see," he cried, " my poor

child is mad.   Her nerves have got above her body.
Ever since the day of the conclave she has had the
valleys on the brain.   She has thought of nothing
else, dreamed of nothing else.   She was always
imaginative, this child of mine.   When a very
little girl she used to look out upon the sea and
figure a land beyond it ; I have heard her say that
voices came to her from an opposite shore.   I have
had great trouble in getting her to see the advantages of this island home ; but for her love to
myself she never would have seen it.   And now
this story of the valleys has set her altogether on
fire and made every fancy real.   Whoever heard of
an actual vial being given in a dream ? "

"Yes," said Phœbe, "she must be mad.   The
vial was got from my hands.   She says she gave
it to me.   Where then did she get it ?   It could
never have come as *she* says."

"The prisoner has hit the point," said the
captain.   " If a vial containing a suspected liquid
were found in the possession of the Lady Ecclesia,
and if she asserted that she obtained that liquid
from the suspected source, I would be bound to
arrest her on the charge, however incongruous her
own narrative might be.   But in the present
instance the vial is not found in the possession of
the Lady Ecclesia.   It is found in the hands of a

serving-maid. The Lady Ecclesia professes to
have given it to her, but she has failed to show
that it ever could have been hers. I have no
alternative therefore but to consider a preliminary
case established against the serving-maid and to
take her into my custody."

The smile on Phœbe's face was positively
radiant. My own nerves were in a violent state
of tension. Those who called me mad had nearly
made me so. In the meantime the excitement
rather sharpened than blunted me. I saw that my
line of self-prosecution had, from a worldly point
of view, been weak, and I sought another. I was
determined at all hazards to save this girl.

" Listen," I said, addressing the captain of the
guard ; " I shall produce the evidence of a sane
woman. I shall give you a proof beyond all
controversy that I speak the words of truth and
soberness. There is one who both can and will
tell you that I was in the valley that night. There
are hundreds who could, but would not ; this man
can, and will. None of your band will dispute his
testimony ; you have taken him for your ally, your
detective guide. He has gone to-night to help
Caiaphas in his fruitless search. He shall never
find the man he seeks ; but he can find *me*. Ask
Judas Iscariot whether he did or did not see me

in the valley on that night of redemption.   I shall
abide fearlessly by his decision.   If he says 'Yes,'
you will believe in my sanity ; the evidence of a
man who lives for material gold will be above the
testimony of a spiritual dream."

At last I had succeeded in deeply impressing
the captain of the guard with the gravity of my
charge against myself.   He turned to my father.
" Your daughter is not mad," he said.   " Excited
she may be, and well may be ; insane she is not.
It is quite possible she has mixed up the ideal
and the real, and is unable to assign their due
proportion to each ; but that does not constitute
insanity.   She has offered evidence which may
or may not be established, but which, whether
established or not, is perfectly legal.   The Lord
of Palatine is a born lawyer, and it is evidence
like this which he solicits.   I dare not ignore it.
I shall therefore release this girl, pending further
inquiry into the testimony of Judas.   Until this
inquiry is completed I shall make no other arrest ;
but in the meantime I put a guard round this
house night and day."

A deadly pallor overspread the face of my
father.   This was the greatest blow he had yet
received to his fortunes, not excepting any
pecuniary losses.   He had such a burning sense of

the honour of his family, and such a conviction
of the link between honour and liberty, that to
interfere with the independence of his house was
to him the calamity of calamities.   I think he was
about to speak.   From his point of view there
was indeed something to say ; if there was not
evidence to arrest, there was surely as little to
restrain.   But all future discussion was cut short
by the sound of hurriedly approaching footsteps.
I knew them ; they were those of Caiaphas.   He
had come home at last ; come home to tell that he
was baffled, beaten, ousted ; come home to say
that the object of his search had escaped him as
the chariot of one of my ancestors is said to have
escaped the pursuit of death.   So I told myself, so
I had always told myself.   There was not in my
mind, there was not in my heart, one shadow of
doubt.   There are some minds even in common
life whom we cannot for a moment associate with
the thought of death.   We can think of them as
labouring, as heavy-laden, as doing any amount of
work, or bearing any amount of pain ; but not as
losing power, not as passing into negation.   So, in
an intensely exaggerated form, was it with my
thought of *him*.   I could believe in anything about
him that involved life, however painful, however
tearful it might be.   But to think of him as ceasing

to be, to associate him with something which was neither pleasure nor pain, neither work nor weariness, to imagine him as simply passive, inert, pulseless, a harp with strings unswept by any hand —it was a thing impossible.

The steps drew nearer. They were not so slow and languid as I would have expected from a disappointed man ; but I remembered that rage often gives one the power of cheerfulness. He entered with flushed face and gleaming eyes. "Well," said the captain of the guard, "what success have you had ?" Caiaphas waved his hand. "The sacrifice for the valleys," he cried, "has at last been found ; he is taken, he is taken." It was the last weight on an already overburdened brain. The ground shook beneath me ; my limbs trembled ; the faces grew dim ; the lamps went out one by one ; there was a sound in my ears like the rending of rocks ; I uttered one long, loud, despairing shriek, and I knew no more.

CHAPTER XV

INWARD WANDERINGS

WHERE am I? Where is anybody? I am all alone, lying on the hall floor; the very lights are out. Oh, I remember! my God, I remember! Caiaphas brought the news, and I fainted. I hear the words still: "He is taken, he is taken." I did not think he *could* be taken ; but is he less beautiful to me for that? Oh no. It was not for being supernatural I loved him, but for being more natural than other people. Who should be with him now if not I? He told me that my trouble made a mark on him : why should not his trouble make a mark on me? And it does. I hear him calling through the night. "Ecclesia, could you not watch with me one hour?" The words come clearly, vividly. I must go. I know the guard-house ; I know where they have taken him. I must leave at once. If my father comes back, he will not let me go ; he will say I am not well enough. But I am. I have stood up now; I am strong; I am fit for any journey.

Ah! it is the same clear night; every star is leading me to *him*. But it is a long, long way I have to go. What if I do not arrive in time? "Ecclesia, could you not watch with me?" I hear the words again quite distinctly. Yes, I am coming, I am coming. Oh that I had the wings of a dove that I might fly to thee and be at rest!

"Who goes there?" It is the voice of the captain of the guard. He is standing at the gate. I forgot the gate. I forgot that I am a prisoner pending the answer of Judas. "Listen to me, sir; I am the Lady Ecclesia; let me pass but this once, and I shall come back. I promise it by the house of my fathers. I have great faults, but I have never broken my word to living man. You know I have not tried to escape the danger of this hour."

What does he say? Do I hear aright, or is it a phantom sound? I am free? Judas can testify no more? Judas dead? Judas dead by his own hand? Judas dead by remorse? The beautiful face too much for him, too haunting for him? Can it be true? I know not; but a living fact is before me. The gate is unbarred; the captain stands aside; I am through; and there rings in memory the refrain of words familiar : " I have the keys of death and the grave, and I have set before you an open door."

I am speeding now through the night with rapid step. I am impatient, but not weary. It is not the length of the way that disturbs me ; it is the shortness of the time. I have read that the sun once stood still in the midst of a battle ; I wish he would arrest his journey in this battle of my heart. If I cannot arrive before the dawn, I may be too late. If I could only learn how long I have ! See ! who is this coming ? Is it possible ? Yes ; it is Peter bar-Jona. He must have escaped from the valley when the detective party came out ; I remember he was to meet *him* after the hour of evening song. He will tell me all about it. But why does he run so fast ? " Stop, Peter, stop but for a moment ; where have you left the man of the valleys ? " What does he say ? He has not been with him ? Not with him ? Not with him at the evening song ? Not with him in the Oilpress Garden ? And now he is gone ; he seems afraid to be questioned. He is hurrying back over the road by which I have come. I wish I could get forward as quick as he gets back.

Whole hours must have gone by ; but there is no hint of dawn. A man opened a window a few

minutes ago and cried, "Watchman, what of the
night?" and I heard the answer clearly, "The
night is far spent; the day is at hand." Yet I
see no sign of it. Rather it seems to me as if
the dark were deepening. The stars are going out
one by one, just as the lamps went out in my
father's hall when Caiaphas brought tidings of the
capture. I can no longer go so fast; my steps are
less clear to me. It is not weariness makes me
go slow; but the slowness makes me grow weary.
My heart is dragging my whole body after it, and
the weight is terrible. I must take out my little
vial. Oh, I forgot; I have it no more; it is with
the captain of the guard.

The last star is gone; it is dark—deeply dark.
I can go no farther. Let me lie down on this
little bit of grass on which I tread. It is no rest,
for my heart is travelling all the time. O Father,
my Father, help me! I am broken, beaten,
wounded; I have none but Thee. Aid me, not
to quietness, but to movement. Thou hast myriad
lights in Thy dwelling; spare me but one. Send
me but a flicker, but a gleam, but a flash of Thine
eye across the night. My spirit cannot rest just
now in green pastures; it can have no repose but
in the wings of a dove.

But God has *made* me to lie down. I have

slept on the green grass, and, spite of myself, I feel
stronger. Yet there is no change in the night;
it is still starless. What shall I do? Shall I try
to grope my way until I meet the dawn? Hark!
I hear footsteps approaching—firm, clear, resolute
footsteps. Who can it be that walks the night so
quickly, that treads the dark with so little fear?
He seems to be coming from the direction where
I am going. Will it be another like Peter bar-
Jona, who has escaped from the garden instead
of following to death? He does not appear to
see me; he is passing me by. No wonder, in
such darkness. I shall call to him.

He has heard me; he is coming. I say *he*
because I am sure it must be a man; his step
reveals it. "Pardon me, sir, for detaining you;
but did you hear anything of a prisoner who was
taken to the guard-house to-night?"

Why does he not answer? I listen in vain for
his voice; I cannot see his face. But what is this
warmth that is stealing over me. I feel a garment
thrown around me, and in the comparative heat
I learn for the first time that I have been cold.
I wonder what right he has to treat me as a
pauper. Am I not the Lady Ecclesia? Am I
to be indebted to a stranger for common charity?
And is it not presumption in this stranger to give

me a covering when I ask for an answer? I shall speak again.

"You seem, sir, to be kind; but it is not this sort of help I desire. I am in search of one who was taken a prisoner to-night from the Oilpress Garden. Stay, was it to-night? It seems as if many days had passed while I slept; I am not even quite sure when I started. But if you have come by the main road, you must have heard of him. He is one that could not be hid; he is like no one else in the island; I am sure he does not belong to the island. If you have any tidings, please tell me; only say he is untouched by death."

Still he answers not. And now I am trembling. What means this silence? Does he wish to break some news to me by degrees? Does he want to prepare me for grief by an inward fear? See, he has taken me by the hand now; he is leading me over the sward. What is this strange thrill that runs through me? Is it memory, or is it hope? Where and when have I felt it before? It does not seem to be quite new. What is this wild joy that is coming over me? Is it only *grief* that needs to be broken gradually? My blood is tingling; my heart is leaping; my brain is burning; they will say my mind is wandering. Save me from delusion, O my Father!

"Ecclesia!" He speaks, and doubt is gone. If he had spoken two minutes sooner, I would have died—died of ecstasy. But the bread of joy has been broken to me by degrees. I have had the sleep, and the footsteps, and the garment, and the hand; and now I can bear the voice. "Speak to me again; say it once more, that I may know I am not dreaming. Oh, I have been seeking you so long, so wearily! Can the moment of my despair be the moment of our meeting? I was coming to watch with you, and you have come to watch with me. I might have known you could not be taken. I might have known my first thought was the only true one. I always said you would pass death by like my ancestor, Elijah: why was I so foolish as to listen to Caiaphas?"

He speaks, and with the sound of his voice breaks the long-expected dawn. "Not like your ancestor, Ecclesia, this night have I come to you. He passed death by; I have passed through it. You start, you tremble: why? Are you afraid to think of me as having had a moment of impotence? Ecclesia, I had not perfect power in your island without that moment. Listen; I will tell you a secret. Until this night there was one thing which I had not learned—what it was to be absolutely helpless. Do you know how I have

struggled for this experience, how I have been
straitened until it has been accomplished? No
one ever strove to rise as I have striven to descend.
Men fix their eyes on the height and try to scale
it ; my aspiration has been to get down. Men are
in search of perfect knowledge ; I have sought to
learn what it is to know imperfectly. I have seen
a great gulf between your island and the land
beyond. You would not be a step nearer to us
if you could dry up the sea, if you could touch our
hands with your hands. What was it to your
valleys that I stood in the midst of their sorrows?
What was it to them that I bore the marks of their
pestilence? It proved my power ; that was the
very thing which to the valleys made me weak.
They said, 'What is the pestilence to *him*? Has
he the dimness of our eye, and the dulness of
our ear, and the faintness of our heart? Can
the same marks make the same soul?' And
truly they were right. I took their cross, but
not their cup ; their burden, but not their weakness : my thorn was the thorn of the rose. I felt
that the rose must die if I would reign over human
hearts. I felt that except a corn of wheat fall into
the ground, it must abide alone. Ecclesia, I have
touched the ground to-night—the common ground,
the ground where the valleys and the uplands

meet. I have reached the limit of human help-
lessness, the base of human impotence. I have
descended the last height that made me more than
man. I have learned the mystery of mortal
weakness; I have all sympathy, and therefore I
have all power."

And now I am clasping his hands in the ecstasy
of possession; I feel them pierced with wounds.
" Oh, do not leave me, do not leave me! Take me
with you; I cannot live without you. My soul
pants for you; my heart longs for you; more than
for the morning I have watched for you. I care
not where you lead me. I will go with you into
the meanest hovel, I will follow you into the most
pestilential valley. To be with you is to be in
paradise; to be without you is to be in my heart's
everlasting fire—unsatisfied love. At however far
a distance, only say that I may follow you."

Has he refused? So sweetly that I hardly
know it is a refusal. " Not yet, Ecclesia; not yet.
The place is not ready for you yet. I have still
to bind the girdle of sympathy which I have put
round the dust of your island—to bind it to the
other side of the sea. In my father's house are
many mansions, and I would not have one of them
foreign to you, Ecclesia. I would not have your
eye to rest upon a scene unfamiliar, upon a light

unsympathetic. I would not have you look at a
picture which shall have nothing of the island
home about it. I go to prepare a place for you.
I shall have the house furnished in the old style,
painted in the colours of memory. Its galleries
shall have portraits of the past. Its libraries shall
contain the record of island deeds as they are seen
from the land beyond. Its music shall repeat on
perfect strings the strains of long ago. Hold me
not so fast, Ecclesia ; it is expedient for you that
I go away. I go to put living waters into human
fountains, to make a home for you across the
wave. But think not I shall leave you comfortless.
In times and places where the island sees me not
you shall see me. Where the common eye reads
only land and sea, I shall reveal myself to you.
In every hour of weakness, in every moment of
agony, in every season of the sinking heart, look
up, and I am there. Measure not the distance of
the waters ; in my land the wish is the wing. We
go in the *spirit*—quicker than the wind, swifter
than the light. In the mansions of my Father's
house all thought is movement, for love is the
chariot of the soul, and to say, ' I long to be there,'
is to be there already."

" But tell me, oh, tell me, what if, when you are
gone, I awake and find it a dream ? See, the

dawn is spreading its gold ; the garish day is coming, and the island forms may rouse me into lesser life." As I speak there breaks over his countenance a beam before which even the morning fades, and on my ear there fall words of infinite music, " Call that the dream, and this the waking."

" She will live," said a voice by my side. " In all my professional career it is the most marvellous recovery I have ever known. I would have said a few minutes ago that the boundary of hope was past. A week of delirium, preying on a physically exhausted frame, gave little promise. But something too subtle for my analysis has brought back the life from the grave. It has been a passion week of storm. The waves have been beating against a bank of sand, and the bank of sand has conquered."

I saw it was the physician. " Have I been ill ? " I said—faintly, for I felt extremely weak. " Ah ! " said the doctor, " her mind has ceased to wander." Exhausted as I was, I began to ask myself why those who wander in mind are so much less esteemed than those who wander in body. We value the testimony of travelled people if only the travelling be outside. The man who has explored every corner of the island, the man who has

gone farther than his neighbours over the sea, is
held in great estimation. But if the wandering
is within, if the mind has left the body asleep and
has gone to journey on its own account, if we have
been put to death in the flesh and only quickened
in the spirit, we deem that our experience has
reaped no gain. Why? Surely in either case the
only question is, Where have we been? I at all
events had been on a road which had brought
me back to life; nay, which had given me life to
carry back. I had experienced a peace that had
passed medical knowledge; my mind had been
stayed by its own wanderings. There had come
to me on my way something which had turned
back the shadow on the dial, which had quickened
the pulse of life and renewed my term of years.
It was all from within. But was it therefore untrue,
unreal? Might it not well be that this so-called
week of wandering was indeed the deeper reality,
and that the island life to which it had summoned
me to return was but a distorted shadow of the
night?

CHAPTER XVI

HOURS OF CONVALESCENCE

YE who shall read these pages, whether ye be natives of the island or citizens of the land beyond the sea—for I feel that my record shall one day be read there—I would have you to know the nature of that abnormal experience which, during this week of suffering, had befallen me. The events of outer life had been presented to me backwards; that is to say, the later had been revealed before the earlier. While I lay on that couch, prostrate in body and wandering in spirit, the actual life of the island had been startled by two great surprises. The first was a stroke of terror. The man of the valleys had been taken, and, with hardly even the formality of a trial, had expiated with his life the infringement of a law of sin. He had suffered a mode of death which had been reserved for criminals of the valleys— the cross. To me the idea of a cross had come

to suggest majesty. You remember where he
had presented me with a golden cross—not in
the valleys, but in the very grounds of my father's
house. His own manner of bearing it had been
so majestic that they who condemned him were
unable to lay him in the valleys; they made
for him a grave in the upper soil.

The act was so sanguinary, so arbitrary, so
instantaneous, that for a day and a half it took
the heart out of every man. The island seemed to
get a simultaneous shock of paralysis, and dawning
aspiration died. At the end of thirty-six hours
there occurred a second surprise. Suddenly, to all
appearance unaccountably, there broke out a blaze
of enthusiasm. Three men, you will remember,
had been summoned by the man of the valleys
to meet him that fatal night in the Oilpress Garden.
Peter bar-Jona was one. The others were James
and John, the sons of Zebedee—the same two
young men whom I had seen in the valley, trying
to set fire to some cottages believed to be infected with the plague. When their deliverer
was arrested they had fled. They had made their
escape, not only from those who pursued the man
of the valleys, but from the valleys themselves.
They were the first who had reached the upper
ground since the alarm had been given of a

pestilence in the vale. All at once, these three men were surrounded by crowds—not of enemies, but of auditors. They proclaimed that the man of the valleys was alive, that they had seen him, heard his voice, received his message to become the ministers to the wants of man. They asserted that, where two or three met together, and partook of the sacred vial in love and loyalty to his name, they had reason to believe that he would be in the midst of them. In a short time there met, not two or three, but five hundred; and it was proclaimed in the very heart of the uplands that this large assembly had obtained simultaneously and indubitably an apparition of him who had been dead.

These were the incidents of the outside life. Now in my so-called wanderings the same incidents had appeared, but in the opposite order. I was in search of one whom I believed to be alive; I found him alive. When I met him in the shadows of the night, it never occurred to me that it was anything more than the fulfilment of my natural desire. I took it for granted that he had proved himself incapable of being slain. Then came his own startling revelation—that he had not passed *by* death, but passed through it. How did that revelation affect me? With wonder certainly, with awe, perhaps even with a mystic dread—but not with depression. I had no doubt whatever of either of the facts. I believed him to be alive on the evidence of my consciousness ; I believed him to have suffered on the testimony of his own word. But the life was the present fact, the immediate fact. How could I be depressed? If you were to awake some morning from a deep sleep, and were to be told that during the night you had been subjected to a severe physical operation, from which you had emerged free from pain and full of vigour, how would you regard that operation ? Certainly not as a subject for tears. The calamity, whatever it was, would be a thing of the past. So was it with me. The power of this man resurrection had to me preceded the fellowship of his sufferings. I had been presented with a leaf of summer before I was asked to tread the winter snow. The result was that the winter itself was disarmed of its sting. It was full of singing birds, redolent of the breath of flowers. The event, to which a week ago I had looked forward with dismay, had ceased to be a prospect of any kind. It had become a retrospect, seen from the top of the hill and invested with the glory of the sunlight.

To you, therefore, who shall read these pages

the thing which surprised my nursing attendants
will be no surprise at all—the calmness with
which I received the tidings. They were no
tidings to me. I only received them in answer
to my own questions, or rather in corroboration
of my own assertions. The doctor had forbidden
any volunteered communication. I was still extremely weak. I was unable to keep my attention
long on the stretch. I had lengthened periods
of sleep, interrupted only by short interludes of
waking. It would be weeks before I was myself
again. Sometimes my mind lay passive, and left
the senses to work alone. I saw familiar forms
flit to and fro, but I beheld them with a mechanical
listlessness. My father was in and out of the
room ; Phœbe was my constant attendant ; many
of the women I had visited in the cottages gave
from time to time a helping hand; but I was
rarely roused to interest. Caiaphas was not admitted ; it was feared to provoke a recurrence
of the old association. Medically I think this
was a mistake. What I wanted was opposition.
Everything had gone too smooth. There was
an over-amount of harmony between the fact
and the dream. There was needed something
to gainsay, to interrupt, to impede, something
to stimulate progress by shutting the door, and

rouse me into energy by arresting the sweep of the hand.

In point of fact, my first complete wakening into outward interest did begin in this way. One day I heard the tramp of many footsteps in the grounds below. I asked what it was. Phœbe said, " You remember the guard of soldiers that was put round the house ? " " Yes," I answered ; " but they have no right to be there any longer. They were put there to wait for the testimony of Judas. But Judas will testify no more. Judas is dead—dead by his own hand." You will see how completely I had blended the horizon of my wanderings with the horizon of the outer life—the blue of the sky with the blue of the sea. The words of the captain in the dream were as real to me as the tread of the soldiers in the courtyard.

" This is shameful," said the doctor. " Any reference to the fact of the suicide ought to have been carefully concealed from the patient. In such cases all morbid topics should be excluded."

" But, sir," said Phœbe, " no one has spoken to her of the matter."

" She has uttered," said the doctor, " the very words which I heard used a few days ago by the captain of the guard. How can these words have

been repeated by her unless they were first reported
to her ?"

How indeed? Yet I am not sure that it was
wholly supernatural. Who can tell the limits of
the ear? Who can say whether, in certain
abnormal states of mind, sounds uttered at a great
distance may not be carried to the sense. The
medical art believes strongly in the laws of nature:
but have we measured the reach of any law of
nature? May it not be that all which we now call
supernatural may yet be included in the domain
of law?

But to return from this digression. I persisted
in my question why the removal of the only witness
had not been followed by the removal of the
guard. I was answered that the reason was
unknown; it could only be accounted for on the
supposition that some other evidence had tran-
spired. To me this came like a refreshing gale.
There is a strength in the sense that our love shall
be called to prove itself. In my night wanderings
I had been merely a recipient; I had gone to
minister, and I had ended by being ministered
unto. I had lost thereby something of life's
stimulus. Premature summer is not good for the
soul. I had reaped a premature summer. I had
come to the top of the hill by a road that involved

less than the normal amount of climbing. I had
seen the power of this man's *resurrection* ; I had
been no real participant in the fellowship of his
sufferings. Hitherto I had suffered *for* him, but
hardly *with* him. I had seen the beauty of his
face even when it was marred ; I had lamented the
sorrow that marred it ; but I had never felt that the
same thing should mar me. I had taken his cross
in compassion ; till the night of my wanderings
I had not perceived its glory. I awoke from my
trance with the feeling of its glory. I came back
to life with an unemployed energy in my nature—
an energy that waited for resistance to quicken it
and to quicken me. The sense that the cloud was
not past was the very thing I needed. It gave me
what I was losing—an interest in island life.

Not so thought my father. The thing which I
counted gain was viewed by him as a very serious
loss. Day by day as he entered my sick-room I
saw the cloud deepening on his brow ; and I
began my new stage of promotion by entering into
his soul. To this man of long lineage there had
come the sorest of possible calamities—a blot upon
his name. It was not the suspicion of complicity
with the valleys that to him constituted a blot ; he
could have borne that with more than equanimity.
It was the guard round his house. His pretensions

had always been high—the highest. He regarded himself as by divine right the heir of all the island. Who was the Lord of Palatine that he should circumscribe his liberty? Was it not enough for him to have lost his birthright, his fortune, his strength? Was he to lose his personal freedom also? Was he to become a slave, a captive, a household retainer, whose every movement was dictated, and whose every exit was watched? Surely the cup of his humiliations must now be full.

And, then, the disaffection in the valleys—that too had an irritating influence on my father. It was not that he disapproved of their attitude; it was his regret that their attitude was not occasioned by *him*. The affection of the valleys had centred round a stranger. They had been attracted by a man whom they believed to be no native of the island at all. Why was *he* not in the place of that stranger? They were willing enough to take the island from the Lord of Palatine—but not that they might give it to Moses ben-Israel; they wanted it for the stranger. And for Moses ben-Israel it was a hard thing. Ought not the outcry to have been for *him*? Why should a stranger have taken the place which he had always felt himself born to fill? Was it not of this place that he had dreamed night and day? Was it not for this place he had thirsted as the hart for the water-brooks? Was it not his by right—by a grant older than any in the island? Why had this flood of enthusiasm risen for another and not for him? Was not the answer clear? Was it not because he had neglected his birthright, sold it for a mess of pottage? He had been living in supineness, in idleness, in lethargy. He had been dreaming but not acting, regretting but not repairing. When the pestilence had come to the valleys, why had he waited for a meeting of the conclave? Why had he not cast himself down into the afflicted region? Why had not he of all men been the first to pro-claim an interest in the welfare of the people—his people? The valleys would have risen in a mass and fulfilled the vision of his ancestor Moses. Another had stepped down before him; a stranger had secured the prize.

And then in my father's mind there rose a tragic question; I record his thoughts as the sequel re-vealed them. Was it yet too late? The man of the valleys was dead. They said he was alive; that was a dream, and would pass. But the dis-content would not pass; it would be fostered by the disappointment. Might he not catch the valleys in the rebound? He had proved himself unworthy of their love; but did baffled love never pass from the worthy to the unworthy? When the dream had faded, when even at the call of fancy the man of the valleys came no more, when expectation had knocked at the gates and knocked in vain, then at last would come his appointed time. Would it not be possible even now to utilise this reaction, to accustom the valleys to the thought that the head of their clan was by right the head of the island? Might they not be brought to believe that the man of the valleys had appeared just for the purpose of awakening their loyalty to the old tree, and that they could not better express their devotion than by resisting the rule of the Lord of Palatine?

So my father brooded; and, as he was musing, the fire burned. Naturally a calm man, the one spark in his nature had been ignited by the traditions of his race. Till now it had smouldered and made no sign. But now it broke forth with such a gleam as the day often casts at its setting. In those hours of loneliness in which he beheld me hovering between life and death, there rose within him a red resolve. He would raise the standard of revolt against things as they were, as they ought not to be. He would turn the passion of the valleys into a new channel; nay, he would make the waters of the old channel minister to the new. Where were those men that had emerged into the uplands—Peter, James, and John? He must meet them at all hazards. He must tell them that the man of the valleys had come to lift them from the valleys—not to seek their personal allegiance, but to waken their allegiance to their family and their home. He must ask them if a guard round the dwelling of him who was the head of their clan was a spectacle which they would tolerate. He must appeal to them by the past—the old, but not the dead past—the past which had inspired their ancestors, and would be vindicated by their descendants. It might be that the dry bones of the valley would live, and that from the region of the shadow of death the resurrection of his house would come.

CHAPTER XVII

A SECRET MEETING

IT was night, and I sat by the fire of my sick-room with a bright lamp in front of me. I was no longer confined to bed, but was still forbidden to leave the apartment. During the fortnight that had elapsed since my re-awakening to island life I had made strides toward recovery. My bodily strength remained weak, but my mind had regained its balance, and my heart had resumed its interest in common things.

All at once the door opened, and my father entered accompanied by three men. " Ecclesia," he said, " I have brought these physicians to visit you—at least, it is only on that pretext that they have obtained admittance. Perhaps they may indeed prove physicians to you. They have been men of these valleys with which you so strongly sympathise. You have heard their names much of late. This is Peter bar-Jona, and these are the brothers James and John, the sons of Zebedee."

The three figures before me were each stamped with a separate individuality. I have got into the habit of describing men by the impression their appearance has produced. I never fix my mind nor even my memory on that which is accidental to them—that which can change. Why expatiate on the colour of the hair when it can alter in a night? If I were asked at this distance to enumerate in detail the features of the three, I would certainly make mistakes; but their different impressions are most vivid. The word that of all others would best describe the face of Peter is mobile. It was its mobileness that made it remarkable. Measured by any single moment, it would have been commonplace. What made it not commonplace was the fact that nearly every moment saw it change. It was now grave, now gay; now exulting, now despondent. You could not depend on it for a minute; it made prediction impossible. Its variety of expression was altogether unlike that of the man of the valleys. His was simultaneous; it revealed many phases in one. But Peter's was successive. It came in a series of flashes. It was not the

countenance of a universal man, but of one who
was a different man each moment. The man
of the valleys made you feel that he had a
place for all ; Peter made you feel that he had
a place for *you* to-day, but would probably reserve
it for *me* to-morrow.

The two brothers had an expression more fixed
and definite. It was here and now that I first
recognised their identity to the two incendiaries of
the valley. There was indeed in the countenance
of each much that suggested fire. But it was
in each a different kind of fire. James was the
fire flaring up ; John was the fire kept down.
The face of James expressed the determination
that was eager to act ; that of John indicated
the determination that was willing to wait. James
was passion outward—passion that must relieve
itself by a blow ; John was passion inward—
passion that did not need to be relieved, but
was able to feed upon its own intensity. John's
was the nobler countenance. It gave the impression of concealed treasures, of having more
in it than was seen. It was full of promise.
One felt in looking at him that, though he
might begin by kindling fire, he would end by
suppressing it.

" I have sent for you," said my father, " to

propose the terms of an alliance. This is the fitting place for such overtures. You are in the presence of two extremes—myself and my daughter. *I* represent the uplands; the Lady Ecclesia has an affection for the valleys. This room therefore embraces both sides of the question. For myself, I have already made the first advances. I have invited you under my roof at a time when the valleys are suspected of contagion. I have assumed therefore that under the influence of the man you reverence you have really experienced healing power. I have chosen also a fitting opportunity. My chaplain Caiaphas, who would never have acceded to this interview, is absent on business. You may speak freely; we are alone."

"Father," I said, "since we are alone, and with a view to promote a perfect understanding, will you allow me to begin the interview by asking your visitors whether they recognise me as one who was in the valleys that night?"

"Lady Ecclesia," said Peter bar-Jona, "we are here to make no such statement. That which passed in the valleys is sacred to us. The eyes of our memory rest but on one form—the man who was dead and is alive. Would that mine had never rested on another! Your challenge

puts me to shame this night. You remind me
that I have forgotten his form in the forms of
his enemies. I have been the vilest of cowards ;
I have suffered like a thief, and not like a martyr.
I fled from the Oilpress Garden—I was going
to say like a woman ; but pardon me—unlike
you." And the strong man burst into a torrent
of weeping.

"Yes," said John, "we left it to that son
of perdition, Judas, to accuse his friends. We
have no wish to be concealed ; but we never
betray."

"This brings me," said my father, "to the
crucial point. Why is it that, when the only
man that could betray is dead, and dead without making a sign, I am still a prisoner in my
own house? Why is it that there is a band of
soldiers round my dwelling when the ground of the
charge against me is removed? *My* dwelling, did
I say? Is it not your dwelling? Have not your
ancestors sheltered themselves under the branches
of this broad tree? Is not my house even now
the nearest to the valleys? Is not the Sympathy
Gate almost adjoining my grounds? Why should
your quarrel not be mine? I have not looked
with equanimity on the closing of the vales :
shall you look with indifference on the closing

of my gates? The Lord of Palatine plumes himself upon his justice : think you this is just? Is it fair in law, is it right in equity, that I, a scion of the oldest house in the island, should have that house guarded with soldiers when the man who was to accuse me is dead ? "

" Have you then not heard," said John, " the ground of this continued watch ? Know you not that, when the man of the valleys was taken in the Oilpress Garden, there was found on his person a parchment roll ? Know you not that in this roll there was inscribed a vast list of names attesting their love and loyalty to the man and to the cause ? Know you not, above all, that the title of the roll was the ' Book of Life,' and that on the margin appeared the motto, ' All things inscribed here shall inherit the kingdom ' ? The words to the Lord of Palatine sound like treason, and he has given orders to examine the roll. Peter's name is the second from the top ; my brother and I follow ; if dis- covered here, our lives would not be worth a moment's purchase."

" So," said my father, " that is the reason of my incarceration. Listen ; let us make the reason true. You want in this island to establish a reign

of righteousness; be it so. You want to fashion
it after the pattern of him whom you call the
man of the valleys; be it so. Let him by all
means be your ideal king. But do you not
need one to *represent* your ideal? must not your
kingdom have a visible as well as an invisible
head? The man of the valleys has passed away.
You could not have an absent king; the man
of the valleys would not have wished you to
have an absent king. He did not ask you to
follow his person, but to follow his teaching.
If you would please him, if you would reverence
his memory, you must set up in this island a
kingdom sacred to the God of your fathers, and
a king who has descended from your fathers.
I offer myself as such. I bring you no supernatural lineage; I have no claim to belong to
a land beyond the sea. But if it be an advantage
to be bone of your bone and flesh of your flesh,
if there be a bond in blood and a sympathy in
family union, if the traditions of the past be
dearer than the fancies of the future, it is in
me that your allegiance should centre this night.
You have heard in the valleys the voice of a
man who has called you back—back to the fields
of your childhood, back to the resurrection of
your home. Obey that voice, and you will do

homage to his cause. Throw in your lot with mine, and you will honour the man you serve. Instil into the growing crowd which follows you that the resurrection you proclaim is a type of the replanting of your family tree, and you will make this night the dawn of liberty."

"But," said Peter, "we who seek a place in the kingdom of our Father do not seek more liberty. What we are in search of is less liberty. We would be clothed in more humility; we would take the yoke upon us; we would tend the sheep; we would feed the lambs. The pre-eminence we seek is pre-eminence in serving; the greatest shall be ministers to all."

"Yes," cried John, "ours is not a kingdom of mere order, not even of mere righteousness; it is a kingdom of love. They who would sit at the right hand of the man of the valleys must drink of his cup and be baptized with his baptism. Their regal robes must be washed in blood, dyed in the tint of sacrifice. The men in front of our throne are the sons of tribulation. They have made their red stains white in the glory of love. They lead the van because they follow the sacrifice; they are arrayed in spotless garments because they serve day and night."

"But," said James, and his eyes flashed in

eagerness, " are we not sons of tribulation in our
fight for freedom ?   Is not our first service to King
Jesus the liberation of his people?   What is the
object of our sacrifice ?   Is it not to be the eman-
cipation of this island ?   Is not this sea-girt home
the sphere of the kingdom ?   Can we shed our
blood more royally than in the place of our fathers,
for the haunts and hearths of our fathers?   Why
dream of sacrifice when the act is before us, ready,
waiting to be done ?   I sympathise much with
Moses ben-Israel."

" Brother," said John, "your own view is too
sea-girt. How know you that this island is the
kingdom for which we are to shed our blood ?
Listen ; I had a dream last night, so vivid that I
doubt if it were a dream.   I thought I stood on
the shore, and there was no more sea—only the
place where the waters used to be.   That place
had become itself a valley, steep to descend and
arduous to tread, yet making a continent withal.
There was no longer a separation between our
world and the other world.   Men no longer spoke
of this as an island ; it was a bit of the mainland.
They no more thought of God as dwelling in a
place beyond the wave.   There was no wave—
nothing to divide ; it was all one region.   The land
at the opposite side of the valley was clearly

visible, and on all points it glittered in the sun. But people never thought of it nor spoke of it as a land beyond anything ; it was a piece of our own country, a room in our own house, which was now the same as the house of God."

"I do not know that I indulge in dreams," said Peter ; " but for me there is sufficient answer within the island itself. What reason have we to think that the centre of God's care is the house of Moses ben-Israel ? If He has set the sun to rule the day, it is not because the sun is the centre of His interest, but because it is not ; it is only the means to something else. Have you heard of this new man that has arisen in the midst of us ? I have never seen him, but he is drawing crowds. His name is Paul. He is not a son of the valleys, but of the uplands. He has made a singular profession. He claims to have a message apart from us altogether. He says that the man of the valleys has appeared to him on his own account—appeared after death with a quite unique command. He has told him that there has been a too exclusive attention to that branch of the tree which we call our clan. He has asked him to remember that the fields of the Lord of Palatine are also white already for harvest. He has bidden him cast his eyes over the sorrows of those whom we have been accus-

tomed to call our oppressors. He has made to
him the startling announcement that he has a love
for the house of Hellenicus as well as for that of
Moses ben-Israel. He has commanded him to
leave to *us* the mission of the valleys, and to keep
his eye upon the cares and griefs of that uppermost
region which we despise. Does this look as if he
recognised our claim to a universal dominion of
the island?"

"And does this look like patriotism?" cried my
father. "Are *their* claims equal even in point of
sorrow to ours? Are they trodden down like us?
Are they circumscribed by limits like us? Are
they under prohibition like us? Look at me, the
head of your clan. I dare not go out of my
grounds without a pass. My servants dare not
leave my grounds without a pass. My visitors
dare not enter my grounds without a pass. You
are yourselves within my house by the permission
of the Lord of Palatine, obtained through false
pretences. And what shall I say of the valleys—
the men to whom your leader first appeared?
Their position is still worse than mine. I at least
can get out on permission; they are told that they
will get no permission. Waive the question of the
kingdom; let it be a question of common sympathy,
helpfulness, humanity. Is there the possibility for

a redeeming power any more than a reigning power when the gates of communication are shut that connect man with man? How shall you yourselves find an entrance back into the valleys? Have you not by your very escape to the uplands put a barrier between you and your past, and cut away the moorings that bound you to the ancient shore?"

A curious expression passed over the face of Peter. For a moment he did not speak; then he drew a step nearer to my father and said in low accents: "Hark! I will tell you a secret. You are the father of the Lady Ecclesia, and may be allowed to know what is not known to those outside our community. The valleys are not so forsaken as you suppose. That night in the Oilpress Garden the man whom we worship took me aside and made me a bequest. He gave me a whole set of keys to the Sympathy Gate. He gave me not one, but many, that I might have power, not only to go in and out myself, but to give that liberty to those whom I thought worthy. It is mine to bind these gates or to loose them according as I shall deem one ready or unready to enter in. He who would enter by the Sympathy Gate must himself have sympathy. Not every one that says, 'Lord, Lord,' is fit to go down into the valleys, nor he that makes lordship the goal of his possession.   He that descends thither must go with a drooping mind—with a heart hungering with their hunger, thirsting with their thirst.   Not every man is fit to bear the keys."

A gleam shot through the eyes of my father. "Will you give me," he said, "an opportunity of speaking to the valleys—just one half-hour to tell them of the relation between them and me?"

"I cannot, I dare not," said Peter, "for the relation between them and you is not one of sympathy.   You seek not them, but theirs—their suffrage, their support.   Your compassion would be a cloak, your pity a pretence, your interest an insult.   Your search for their cross would be the search for your own crown; no, Moses ben-Israel, I cannot let you in."

As he spoke his hand had been in contact with the inner fold of his garment.   As he withdrew it something jingled.   The keys of the valley were there, then—within the room, at the distance of a few paces.   I saw a strange expression pass over my father's face.   It was not joy; it was not sorrow; it was the shadow of a dark resolve. "My daughter's health," he said, "makes it inexpedient to prolong the interview; but I hope at this late hour you will not think of resuming your long journey. My house is at your disposal; rest here till morning." And while they were assenting, I beheld again upon my father's countenance that shadow which was destined to extinguish a star.

CHAPTER XVIII

MY NEW CORRESPONDENT

WHEN the guests had retired, Phœbe came into my room bearing a letter. Phœbe's spirit of helpfulness had made her a favourite with the guard. Although the originally suspected party, she had perhaps more liberty than any of the household, and even at the decline of day a pass was seldom refused her. On the present occasion she had been out somewhat late, and had been accosted by a messenger, who delivered to her an epistle. It was addressed, "To the Lady Ecclesia, House of Moses ben-Israel." I opened it with some curiosity. It was written from an address bordering on the estate of Hellenicus— which accounts for the fact of Phœbe's being recognised as an inmate of our house. The last letter I had received from this region had been one that had caused me much pain ; it was the offer of marriage from Hellenicus himself. My eye therefore lighted on the superscription with some tremulousness. But any trepidation I felt was soon turned into wonder. This letter was not from Hellenicus, but from one I had never seen— one whose name for the first time I had heard to-night—the man Paul.

He began by introducing himself. He said that, though a stranger to me in the flesh, he was united to me by a bond more close than that of blood— the fellowship in the cause of him who was called the man of the valleys. He had heard of my meeting with him in the valleys, of my zeal, of my devotion. He himself could not claim the same origin for his faith. He had never met King Jesus in the valleys, never seen him in the vicinity of our clan. He did not say it as a matter of pride; he was himself descended from our clan, and felt proud of his origin. But, as a matter of fact, his experience had always been outside. The man that to me had been associated with the valleys had to him been linked with the uplands. His first sight of him had been after death. He had received a revelation all by himself, had entered the service by a private door. There had come to his ears a new and unheard-of message—that the God of Moses ben-Israel had a mission for the Lord of Palatine, nay, that in this very hour

the Lord of Palatine was fulfilling God's mission.
It was a message that at first had taken away his
breath, appalled him, paralysed him. But hour by
hour he had become familiarised to it. Yesterday,
it was his penalty ; to-day, it was his duty ; to-
morrow, it would be his joy.

And then, with equal originality, the letter went
on to deliver a sentiment which, to any member
of our house, would have been the most startling
of paradoxes. It declared that at the present
moment the Lord of Palatine was the greatest
existing barrier to the submergence of the island.
Why, it asked, were we of the house of Israel so
eager to get rid of Palatine Hill? That hill was
a moral breakwater. It restrained forces which
otherwise would sweep with relentless violence
over all that hitherto we had deemed dear. It was
God's hindrance to the anarchy of human passions.
Take it away, and wickedness would be revealed
in open form. It was the only wall which at the
present moment had strength sufficient to stem the
tide of insubordinate desire. Its premature removal would be the greatest calamity which could
befall the men of this island ; let them beware how
they sought to undermine it.

So ran the letter. It made me very uncomfortable. I had an inner persuasion that Paul was

right. But if Paul was right, my father was wrong. I had a disturbing memory of the night's interview. I felt, and I felt with pain, that my father's attitude had compared unfavourably with that of his three associates. I was haunted above all by his last look. It was not what it revealed that troubled me ; it was what it did not reveal. It was the sense of something unspoken, something underground. I ought to have felt happier to-night than I had done for weeks. I was in the immediate vicinity of the three men who had been nearest to him whom I loved. And yet there was a fear at my heart which I had never felt before— a fear which was not the dread of calamity, but the dread of something darker. The shadow of a coming grief is hard to bear, but the shadow of a threatened dishonour is beyond all bearing.

I lay down that night in feverish excitement. Do what I would, there was one sound in my ears, and one image before my eyes ; I heard the jingling of the keys, and I saw my father's face. For a long time sleep refused to come. When it did come, it was of short duration. I awoke in the middle of the night. I felt oppressed, uncomfortable, the prey to a new sensation. Hitherto I had always an impression that the man of the valleys was with me. To-night I felt something

impeding his presence. It seemed as if a screen
were drawn between me and him. I had an unwonted sense of solitude, a feeling that would have
made me cry out but for the fear of disturbing
others. It was as if I were passing through an
impure medium where the air of heaven was
corrupted and the breath of God was stifled. No
moment of my physical weakness had to me been
so prostrating as this.

Hark! Was that a step in the passage? Did
I know that step? Undoubtedly; there was no
dream this time; it was the foot of my father.
He was moving at midnight through his own
house; but not as the master moves. His tread
was stealthy, suppressed, slow. It was not the
darkness made him timorous; I heard the rattle
of a lantern as he passed my bedroom door. The
uncertainty of his advance must have come from
within. He moved along the corridor with a foot-
fall so soft that I believe no other ear than mine
could have detected it. He made his way toward
that wing of the building which we called the
guest-chambers. He paused at the room on the
east side, and my heart paused with him. I knew
who slept there; it was Peter bar-Jona. In the
intensity of the moment my hearing seemed preter-
natural. I heard the lantern laid down on the

outside floor ; I heard the door softly opened ; I heard my father go in. Then followed a silence, broken only by the beating of my own heart. It was but a few minutes ; yet it seemed to me like a century. Then the door re-opened, and I heard the tread returning. Step by step the journey was retraced through the corridor. I heard the feet draw nearer, pass my room, and then fade away toward my father's room. I drew a long breath, but not of relief. Whatever was to happen had happened. My fear had ceased to be a thing of the future ; it had become a thing of the present. One suspense had ended ; another was to begin.

What had happened? As long as it was a future possibility I had feared to translate it into words. But the prosaic nature of the facts around me made me bold. I began to render into common speech. What was that hungry look I had seen on the face of my father? It was the desire to get an entrance into the valleys. What was that lurid gleam that had flitted across his countenance when he learned that the man beside him had a key? Was it not the lust of possession? Why had he asked Peter bar-Jona to remain all night—especially after his deliberate refusal to trust him? Why had he accepted the refusal

without an argument, without a protest, without
even a flash of anger? Why had he been so quick
to end the interview he was so eager to begin?
Why was he treading at midnight and by stealth
in places not his own? What took him to that
room, of all rooms? Was there any escape from
the pitiless logic of the facts? If not, what then?
Anarchy, bloodshed, death, my house left unto
me desolate. I looked into the vista, and I
shuddered.

The excitement of the brain overpowered my
yet feeble strength, and I slept again. When I
awoke it was full daylight, but the impress of the
night was still upon me. Phœbe entered my room.
I inquired if the guests were up. To my surprise
she answered that they were gone, that they had
left at earliest dawn. A gleam of hope flashed
into me. Had I not been premature in my sus-
picions of my father—unfilial, undutiful, unchLarit-
able? Did not the facts admit of an explanation
not less natural and far more innocent? How
knew I that it was midnight when I first awoke?
Might it not equally have been the hour of dawn?
Had I measured the precise intensity of the
shadows? Was there such a contrast between the
last moment of night and the first moment of day?
What more fitting, what more expedient, what

more courteous than that my father should go to
the room of Peter bar-Jona to apprise him of the
dawning of the day? Was not the old chain of
circumstances quite as becoming when attached to
the new theory? Why should not my father have
moved with stealth? Was it not natural he should
wish to avoid disturbing the household, specially
natural that he should wish to avoid disturbing
me? Surely I had been too fast in my conclusion;
I had mistaken the lark for the owl.

As time passed and brought no sequel, as day
after day glided on, and still the catastrophe came
not, events seemed to lend confirmation to the
brighter view. And yet I was not convinced.
The greatest part of our evidence rests not on fact
but impression. Do you know what it is to get
an explanation of a thing you cannot refute and
remain unsatisfied still? That was my position.
The facts might have lent themselves to either
side. But what startled me during these days was
not a positive but a negative element. My father
made no sign of suspicion; but as little did he
make any sign of vindication. Indeed the most
suspicious thing about him was just his persistent
reticence. Towards me his manner became peculiar,
and increasingly so as I grew in strength. He
met me with evident reluctance. When he spoke

to me, he was ill at ease, and always in a hurry. His words on all subjects were vague and general. When I put any question regarding the three visitors, he would answer either by a commonplace or by an evasion, and then would suddenly remember that he had an engagement elsewhere. A girl just returning from the gates of death, and with the weakness incidental to such a condition, might well have been crushed by the sense of unkindness. Will it be believed? I was crushed by the fear that it was not unkindness. Startling as you may think it, and unmaidenly as you may deem it, it would have been a relief to me to know that my father's conduct proceeded from the fact of a coldness towards myself. That could have been explained consistently with honour, for there are states of nervous debility which cloud the heart and leave it no power. But this fear of mine was for my father himself —for his integrity, for his name. Looking back upon that dark past, that tragic past, I feel bound to endorse this sentiment of my girlhood. It is a very ungirlish sentiment; but I have received it from my meeting with a higher life than mine. I felt then, and I feel now, that the noblest manifestation of love is to desire the nobleness of its object. There is a joy in winning a heart; but to make a heart worth winning should be a joy deeper still.

What distressed me most of all at this time was the state of my own mind, to which I have already alluded. I have said that, for the first time since the advent of my new life, I had experienced a sense of interruption in my communion with the man of the valleys. It was the feeling of one not being in the room who used to be there. No doubt the contemplation of a moral shadow had much to do with it; the mind, like the body, may be disturbed by an atmosphere of whose existence it is quite innocent. After a few days the thought struck me that I might consult my latest correspondent. He was evidently a man of large mind and larger heart, full of human sympathy, and free from local prejudice. I wrote to him; I poured out my soul to him. I told him that, although the first outward revelation had come to me in the valleys, the spirit of the new age had impressed me as it had impressed him. I had felt from the very outset that it was not a question for the Lord of Palatine, nor for Hellenicus, nor for Moses ben-Israel, but for the island as a whole. I told him I could stretch a hand to him through the distance, by reason of that common love in him and me which had annulled the difference between

the mountain and the valley. I told him how a
sense of communion with that love had been to
me the joy of all joys, the compensation for all
sorrows. Then I touched on that which disturbed
me—the interrupted sense of communion. I
threw myself upon his pity, upon his counsel,
upon his larger experience ; I asked him to tell
me how it was that I felt the former days to be
better than these.

I sent the letter by the hand of Phœbe ; and on
the second day after I received a reply which on
all my depressed moments has ever since exercised
a healing power. It had all the more force because
it was given in the form of an autobiography.
Paul unburdened himself. He told me his inner
history. He described the rapture of his morning.
It had been to him as if the heavens had opened
to reveal what mortals cannot see. Then there
had come a cloud, or, as he called it, a thorn. The
flower of faith had lost its perfume, he could not
tell how. He struggled against the change, he
prayed against it ; but he struggled and prayed
in vain. It always seemed as if there were interposed a shut gate between him and the heaven
of his morning. At last there had come to him
a strange inner light—a light which had fallen
upon the barred gate itself and gilded it with its

glory. There had broken upon him the thought that the interrupted communion was itself a part of the avenue, that the minor chord was a note of the revealing music. He had come to feel that this cloud over his morning was a special gift of God. He had asked himself if it were well for a mortal to live so near the sky when his fellow-mortals were so far below. Was he not in danger of forgetting what he had most need to remember—the weakness of his brother-man ? Was he not losing sight of the human struggle in the vision of the divine calm ? He had come to the conclusion that the thing which united men was the thorn, and not the flower. Prosperity was often a dividing-line ; but suffering brought together. The touch that joined the world was the contact of a common pain. The flower was the promise of light ; but the thorn was the talisman to love.

And then, on the wings of this latest note, the letter burst forth into one of the most wonderful flights of eloquence I have ever witnessed ; and its burden was this, " Love is better than light." I could not have believed that this man was capable of such passion. You have seen a blaze of sunshine breaking from the bosom of a dusky day. Even so flashed out this message from the calm soul of Paul. In language which no hymn ever rivalled, he implored me to believe that the common love which grows out of the common thorn is more unfading than the radiance that is born of cloudless day. The power of prophecy might fail, the memory of language might cease, the forms of human knowledge might vanish away ; but love was immortal, evergreen, without beginning of years or end of days. It was the greatest even amongst abiding things. It was greater than faith ; it was greater than hope. Faith could see through a glass darkly ; love beheld face to face. Hope could endure as long as the sun ; love could remain after the sun went down—could bear all things, believe all things, endure all things. It was through the bars of the shut gate that man touched the hand of his brother ; the crown of love was a crown of thorns.

CHAPTER XIX

ALONE IN THE STORM

I AM now approaching a day of my life which will remain in my memory as long as life endures, which will remain in the memory of the island as one of the great landmarks of history. As I look back upon it, and on the days which preceded it, I feel now, what I did not know then —that the change which it ushered in was not sudden. These hours of seeming commonplaceness which I was passing in my own room were in reality big with portents both within and without. You have seen the flight of birds before the storm. The birds were flying now—flying round my couch of convalescence, flying through the apparently torpid air. Beneath that torpor there was movement. Wrapt up in the deceptive calm lay the elements of unrest, of revolt, of transition. I see it now clearly, unmistakably. There were signs of the times in my heart

and in my surroundings. Let me try to read
them.

And let me begin with the portent in my own
heart. Do not think that portent was simply the
fear of which I have spoken. No ; it was something deeper than that. The flight of birds that
predicted a change of atmosphere was a radical
change in myself. It was quite true what I had
said in my letter to Paul—that my sympathy with
the valleys had never originated in the fact that
they were adjoining to the house of Israel ; I had
sympathised with them because I believed them
to be the depressed parts of the island. None the
less, my solicitude had been limited to *them*. It
had never occurred to me that the valleys were not
necessarily the most depressed part of the island.
I had ever commiserated the thorn ; but I had
always taken it for granted that the thorn belonged
to the low-lying districts. That it could live in the
uplands, that it could abound in the region of sunlight, that it could be associated, not with corruption, but with nobleness, was a thought which
it had not entered into my heart to conceive.

But this strange man Paul had struck a new
chord in me. Here was a man who himself had
never been a resident in the valleys, who from
birth upwards had dwelt in the region of the

higher air ; yet he spoke of his thorn.   Nay, there
was more than that.   He claimed his thorn itself
as a product of the higher air.   He wore it as
men wear a flower ; he appropriated it as a mark
of his aristocracy in the sight of Heaven.   The
idea was to me unique and overmastering ; it
filled my heart ; I could not let it go.   If suffering
attached itself not only to the vales but to the
heights, if sorrow came not only through the sense
of want but through the sense of repletion, surely
I and my father's house had gone far astray.   I
had tried to stimulate the sympathy of Hellenicus
for the valleys ; I had never thought that Hellenicus himself was a subject for perhaps greater
sympathy.   I had condemned the Lord of Palatine
for the coldness of his charity to the poor ; it had
never occurred to me that the poor might be cold
in their charity to the Lord of Palatine.   A new
light began to dawn, and ere long it was broad
noonday.   I had called my ideal the man of the
valleys : but why ?   What had sent him to the
valleys rather than to the uplands ?   Was it because the former were privileged ?   No ; it was
because the sorrows of the valleys are the sorrows
of man as man.   There are sorrows in the uplands
which may belong to you and not to me ; but the
pains at the foot of the ladder are the pains of all.

It broke upon me like a revelation in these hours
of silence, and the thought made a new world to
me.   I had ceased to be the representative of a class,
the partisan of a section.   I had become a humani-
tarian, an advocate for man all round—as round
as the island.   It was a change purely within, but
it transformed my view of the theatre of life ; old
things had passed away, and all things had become
new.

And while this was happening in my heart, what
was befalling outside ?   I know now ; I write from
the light of memory.   There was within my own
house a movement in the opposite direction, but
still in the direction of change.   If before the eyes
of the daughter there swam the vision of a common
love, before the eyes of the father there glittered
the image of an island dominion.   I have shown
how, since that night of suspicion, there had sprung
up between me and my father a wall of separation.
During my severe illness I had of necessity been
withdrawn from intercourse with him and with
every one.   But the withdrawal had on his part
now become voluntary.   He began, as I have said,
by avoiding long interviews, and by shunning
special subjects of conversation ; he ended by
preventing all interviews, and refusing to converse
at all.   As the days glided on he seemed in-

creasingly to glide apart from me. His momentary
presence in my room was replaced by the inquiring message, and ultimately the message itself
ceased to come. I would hear him pace his own
apartment for hours together, with that slow and
measured pace which denotes anxious thought.
But it was the nights and not the days that mainly
disturbed me. The most disquieting circumstance
was not his presence in his own room when he
ought not to have been there ; it was his absence
from it when he should have been there. In the
old days he had retired to rest early ; he now came
in late. He took his walks in the open air by
night instead of by day. The guard did not fear
him ; they thought him the friend of Caiaphas,
and they knew that Caiaphas was their friend.
They feared *me*, but they deemed me vanquished
and dying. They had no notion that there was
any key of the valley outside the possession of
the Lord of Palatine.

Had my father such a key ? Was he using
such a key ? Where was he spending these nights
of absence ? Was it in the valleys ? If so, for
what and with whom ? Was he seeking to revive
the patriotism of the clan ? Was he fanning the
flame of discontent against the Lord of Palatine ?
I asked the questions with a trembling heart, and

the trembling of my heart seemed to communicate itself to the ground beneath my feet. Everything appeared to be shaking, vanishing. I felt as if my father's house were on fire, as if I, its last member, were being enveloped in destruction. There was something awful in the sense of solitude. If there had been some one to dispute with, to argue with, to strive with, it would have been bearable. But to be alone, so far as companionship was concerned, in a building which I believed to be condemned; to be the solitary representative of a house which I fancied to be even now in flames; to have no one of my own class to speak to, to cry to, to appeal to; above all, to feel that the cause in which I was the victim was not the cause of the ideal I loved,— it was the most forlorn moment I had known since the night of my disappointment in the valleys.

At last one morning I said to myself, "I shall bear it no more." Come what would, I resolved to speak out my dissent, to tell my father that the kingdom which I sought was not the kingdom sought by him. I could not charge him with taking the keys; but I could tell him my view of the question. For once I would have welcomed the presence of Caiaphas; for once our paths would have coincided. But Caiaphas had not returned; doubtless he felt no desire to be immured in a guarded house. My only chance was to deal with my father himself. Clearly he was more to be pitied than blamed. Had he not suffered by the want of my influence? During these hours, days, weeks, in which I had been withdrawn from his side, there had been nothing but his own morbid thoughts to feed on: was it strange if his thoughts should have overcome him? Was it not high time that on my part all this should end? Why was I lingering here in idleness and uselessness? Why was I content to be a drag upon the wheels of the household? Had not this convalescence of mine been too tardy, too protracted, too slow of completion? I would wait for it no more. I would resume my place as mistress of the house. I would take up again the reins of my domestic duties. I would return to that path of guidance and of suasion in which I had always found my father willing to be led. I would dispel this dreaming of my own and this anarchy of my surroundings. I would begin to-day, now, here; this morning would be my second birthday.

As I made this resolve, I looked out upon the morning. I felt a chill on the very threshold. There are some days which beckon us on; there are others which dissuade us, or try to do so. This was one of the latter. It said to my new enthusiasm, " Don't." It was ominous with clouds ; it was restless with winds. There were mutterings of a storm in the east ; the birds, not alone figuratively, but literally, were flying ; and I heard the concentrated lowing of the cattle as they crowded together in the fellowship of the mystery.

Phœbe entered, and I told her my resolve. I bade her say to my father that I would be with him at dinner that day. She expostulated somewhat. She said I might choose a milder day in which to set my house in order ; but I was resolute. I rose. I dressed myself in my warmest morning garments. I was resolved to begin the resuming of my duties by passing through each of the rooms and marking traces of neglect. Meantime the gloom outside was deepening. The air was every instant becoming more chill. The breeze was fast freshening into a gale. The mutterings from the east were growing each moment more pronounced, and the storm was beginning to speak audibly. Every chink and crevice of the house was becoming vocal. Through the doors whistled the wind ; up from the front of the building moaned the sea ; and at the back, where my room was situated, swept the gusts over Palatine Hill.

Phœbe returned. She was deadly pale ; and

a chill went through me keener than that of the atmosphere. My father, she said, was not in his room, not in the house; he had not slept in his bed last night. My first impulse was to utter a cry; but I checked myself. Why should the servants be made to feel that there was anything wrong? I resolved to make light of it. I said my father had probably been called away on sudden business; he would write and explain. Meantime I told Phœbe to summon the servants for the hour of morning prayer. I wished to show the household that there was no loosening of the old ties. In the absence of my father and in the absence of Caiaphas, I had taken the resolution of myself conducting the service. It was a rare thing in our family for a woman to do; but one or two of my female ancestors had done it—notably the distinguished Deborah. I was not anxious for a precedent. I was quite aware that I was on the borders of a new world, and I was not sorry that to my own household I should be privileged to be its pioneer. I took therefore in the common hall the seat which was usually set apart for Caiaphas, and which in his absence my father was wont to fill.

Perhaps for the first time since the days of

Deborah our household now listened to an extemporaneous prayer. I did not read my petitions from a book; I poured them forth from my own heart. I addressed the God of the heights; but I prayed to the man of the valleys. I spoke to him as I had spoken in my wanderings—these blessed wanderings. I spoke without literary form, without even an attempt to be grammatical. It was more a child's cry than a priest's orison. I just entreated him not to leave us alone in the big storms of this island. I told him our ship was rocking in the waves; I asked him to come and take the helm. I implored him to guide amid the tempest. I said that the storm *with* him would be better than the calm without him, that his presence was itself our haven, that no wind could blow too strongly if it drove us into his arms. And the servants stared in astonishment to hear the Object of human worship addressed in such terms of endearment.

After the morning prayers came the morning orders. I surveyed the different rooms one by one; I gave instructions for what needed repair. When I came into the sitting-room, which fronted the sea, the spectacle which met me was sublimely awful. The storm had burst its bounds, and was sweeping all before it. The waters were a sheet of foam, whose whiteness gleamed more apparent over against the ever-blackening sky. The waves came on like a series of successive ridges, towering up, breaking, and levelled on the shore. There was a chorus of unsuppressed voices. The wind shrieked; the ocean moaned; the sea-gulls cried; the billows lashed as they struck the beach. Never had this island home looked to me so terrible, so desolate, so pent within itself. Never did I feel so sympathetic with that ancestor who climbed the peak called Nebo on the chance of seeing land.

It is in these moments of vastness that we notice trifles. I turned my eyes for an instant from the storm—perhaps by an impulse of reaction. They rested on a small table. They rested on something smaller still lying on the table. It was a sealed letter marked " Private," and addressed to me. I tore it open. It was written with a quivering hand, not always very legible, here and there leaving a blot behind, yet full of character withal. It was unsigned; but by me there was needed no signature; it was from my father.

" Ecclesia," it said, " to-night or never. For weal or woe, the prayers of the house of Israel are ended. I have never sought a land beyond the sea. Whether there be such a land I know

not; it is not the heritage I claim. The heritage
I claim is the home of my fathers. I have asked
no immortality but the immortality of my house.
It has been the one article in my creed, the one
faith in my God. My Ecclesia, your name has
been associated with the valleys. It ought not
so to be. You were born for the mountain
ranges. The red blood of the morning sun is
in your veins. You have sprung from a race
whose birth-hour surveyed from the hilltop the
promised land. It was no land of shadows, no
land at the other side of the ocean—if other side
there be. It was this island home in which
we dwell—the food of it, the good of it. Why
pant you for mansions beyond the wave? Your
mansions are waiting for you here. This island
shall be yours—the length of it, the breadth of
it. Something tells me you are destined to reign.
Think you I have been blind to your beauty,
though I have made no sign? Think you my
heart has not swelled with unspoken pride as
I have seen you bloom? You have been my
immortality, Ecclesia. I have seen my race revive in you; I have seen it climb the heights
of Palatine; I have seen it bounded only by
the sea. You have been to me what the man
of the valleys has been to you—the star of a

new empire. I follow the star to-night. This night shall tell whether the house of Israel shall or shall not be free. This night shall say whether your home, the home of your fathers, shall be a prison or a palace. I shall enter its gates in freedom, or I shall enter them no more. I shal return to you victorious, or I shall never return to you. You shall be sharer in my crown; but I will not let you share my cross. If I succeed, I shall meet you at the gates of my liberated dwelling; if I fail to conquer, and at the same time fail to die, I shall not expose my house to the track of the pursuer. Ecclesia, fair weather, or farewell."

CHAPTER XX

THE DAY OF CRISIS

THE letter dropped from my hand. Do you know what it is when a long-expected calamity actually happens? Those who do not know think it must have come without its sting— deadened by the fact of expectation. It is a grand mistake. Let those who have watched beside an invalid, with the sure knowledge that death will be the end, tell you of the pain with which they learned that the end had come. The previous preparation seemed to go for nothing, and the event came like the final shutting of a door. I suppose we never really cease to hope until the future has become the present. So at least had it been with me. Great as had been my fear regarding my father, I knew now that it had been tinged with hope. I learned it from my present despair. Before I received that missive my conviction of the fact had been almost certain; but there is a

world between the almost and the altogether.
The message of my father had annihilated that
world.   I had been holding only a thin thread of
hope ; but that thread had for me bound the stars.
This last stroke snapped the thread asunder, and
the stars fell.

The letter dropped from my hand.   It was all
over now ; doubt was at an end.   The transition
to certainty was a blow, and beneath it I stag-
gered.   Everything else ceased to have any
existence.   I forgot the raging storm ; I forgot the
swelling sea.   I had a sensation somewhat like
that of the night on which Caiaphas brought the
tidings of betrayal.   I had never exactly recovered
from that night.   My nerves had not regained their
wonted vigour, and they had been tried on the very
threshold of the resumed work.   I felt a faintness
coming over me.   I grew very tired.   I lay down
on a couch fronting the casement.   I fixed my
eyes mechanically and unconsciously upon the
cloud over the waters.

Suddenly I became fascinated by the object
before me ; the mechanical gaze was transformed
into a look of interest.   Was there not something
peculiar about this cloud ?   It appeared to be
seeking the island and the window of my room.
It was certainly coming nearer, nearer.   It seemed

to be gathering its folds from off the face of the
sea, that it might throw them over my dwelling. I
trembled at the omen; a cloud had always been
in our house the symbol of an averted heaven.
Closer it drew and closer. And gradually as it
came there broke upon me a revelation. It was
not self-moving; it was only the mantle of some
one. The real mover was underneath; this was
but a garment. Presently it seemed to pass
through the window. For a moment everything
in the room was eclipsed, overshadowed. Then,
all at once, it parted asunder, and from between
the folds there emerged a figure. I looked and
uttered a great cry; it was the man of the
valleys.

I sprang forward; I tried to fall on my knees
before him; but he caught me by the hand. At
the touch of that hand I experienced a thrill of
wonder. In my night wanderings I had felt
wounds on that hand. I had not been surprised;
he told me he had come from death. But I was
surprised to feel them now. Could a wound given
in our island be so indelible that the land beyond
the sea would not heal it? Or, could a wound
given in our island be so valuable that the land
beyond the sea should wish to preserve it? Be
this as it may, I declare that, as my hand rested

in his, I felt again the print of the scars which I had touched on the night of my wanderings.

"Ecclesia." My heart vibrated to the one voice in all the world; and timidly, tremblingly, I raised my eyes to the wonderful beauty of that countenance. "Ecclesia, I have come to you in the cloud to-day. I want you to feel that the clouds are *my* coming—not the coming of an accident. Believe me, I never was nearer to you than now, when the storm is raging round your dwelling. This night shall men tell how the house of Israel is no more. They shall ask where your father dwells. They shall seek him in all the island, and in all the island they shall find him not. They shall say that he is dead. Do not believe it, Ecclesia; he shall be landless, but not dead. He has trusted only in the possession of a soil; his penalty shall be to live without a soil. He has had no faith in the sea; the sea shall be his preserver. He has reposed his confidence in a kingdom; he shall be a king without a kingdom. Men shall look over the waves and say, 'He is drowned.' But your eyes shall see him again. In the light of undawned days he shall stand upon the dust of this island; and lo, the island's crown shall be upon the head of his child. He shall return, and you shall nourish his old age and make him young once more. And his own dream shall be realised, for the island itself shall be no more an island, and there shall be nothing beyond the waves. See!"

As he spoke he pointed to the place of the waters; and I looked, and cried out with surprise at the sight before me. For I saw what John had seen. The waters were not there. They were all dried up, and in their room was a great highway where crowds passed to and fro; and on the other side were hills basking in sun. All the storm had ceased. All the clouds had been withdrawn from the horizon to envelop the one form—the man of the valleys. It was as if the creation which had been groaning and travailing in spirit had caught sight of him passing by and lent him its burden. Everything had burst into bloom. The sky was aflame with glory and the fields with gold. But to me it was all passionless by reason of a deeper passion. My heart was in the cloud— with *him*. He had let go my hand to point me to the splendour; and without his hand the splendour was nothing. I was hungry in the fulness; I was blind amid the glow. I turned back to be with *him*—back into the cloud, back into the shadowy room. I put out my hand to clasp his once more. It grasped the empty air; he was gone. I called on him; I cried out; my eyes swam with tears.

Then the cloud within the room began to expand again. It passed out of the window. It spread over the old place—the place which the light had usurped, the place where the sea had been. And presently I heard the rush of returning waters; and the sea came back, and I was in an island once more. Then came the old sound of the storm, sweeping and roaring to the accompaniment of waves; and I became aware that I was not alone in the room. I was lying on the couch. Some one was bathing my face with water; it was Phœbe.

"Oh, Lady Ecclesia," she said, "you have been ill! I heard you cry, and I felt something was wrong. I knew this exertion would be too much for you."

There is nothing wakes our self-pity like the sympathy of another. I indulged in a momentary weakness, half the result of nerve tension, and half of disappointment at the unreality. And, as at such moments revelation to another becomes a necessity, I poured out to her the cause of my complaint. But this poor girl had something which I had not —at least not in full. Remember, she came from the house of Hellenicus. She had been trained to expect brightness. She caught the silver lining in this cloud of mine. She said I must not believe

that I had simply come back to the old storm. I
had come back with a vision in my heart. Was
not that vision an answer to my own morning
prayer? Had it not been sent to still me amid
the tempest, that in my turn I might make others
still? Dream or no dream, was it not God's
message to me? The man of the valleys had
heard my family service, and had said "Amen."
As she spoke there stole into my heart a great
calm; and I could not but think how she and
I had changed places in the course of the days.
She, the comforted, had become the comforter;
I, the consoler, had stepped down to be consoled.
I had found again the bread which I had cast
upon the waters.

That night came on early; except in my
moment's vision, it had never been day. The
storm raged through the hours unceasingly. At
nightfall there was great rain. Nature's tears
seemed to relieve the tempest at her heart. Her
passion began to subside like that of a child
exhausted by its own excitement. Then it became
intermittent, like certain forms of human sorrow—
an interval of calm succeeded by a burst of feeling.
At last it sank into a sigh, as if it were trying to
restrain itself. A smothered, suppressed wail ran
through air and sea, varied only by the bitter

weeping of the rain. I think it would be more
correct to say that there was less storm *expressed*
than that there was more calm. Every one felt
that the passion and the pathos were there in all
their strength—simply hiding behind the veil; and
I am not sure that the sense of tempest is ever so
strong as when we are made to feel how much
more it could say.

Suddenly there was a new note in the voices.
What was that noise down by the sea? Was it
the roar of the waves? There was something more
in it than either wave or weather. Where, when
did I hear that sound before? It came to me like
a refrain of memory: what song of my past did
it sing? Ah, I remembered—a very sad song.
When last I heard it, it was in the life of my
yesterday. Was not this the very sound that had
broken my girlhood, that had made a woman of
me? Did I not remember the day of that letter
from Hellenicus, when there swam before me the
prospect of a physical crown? Did I not remember
how, in the very middle of my vain imagining,
there had come up that cry from the valleys which
had dispelled it evermore—the cry of the pestilence, the wail of the weary, the clamour of the
stricken crowd? Could I mistake that sound?
Would I not know it among a thousand? Did I

not hear it again to-night? Yes; there was more
than nature in the voices of this night. The soul
of my brother-man was speaking through the sea,
through the wind, through the rain. The plaint of
the valleys was rising once more. Stay, was it
only the plaint that was rising? Were not the
valleys themselves coming up? With all the
likeness to the old sound, there was a difference.
That had been a cry of fear; this was like a voice
of defiance. That had been tragic with despair;
this was tragic with the illusion of coming triumph.
The wail of despondency had been supplanted by
a shout of expectation. I heard and shuddered,
for the shout was more sad than the wail.

Nearer and nearer came the voices from below.
Was it that the subsiding of the storm had
heightened their intensity, as a candle flares
brighter when the flare of the sun goes down?
No; it was more than that. I heard them distinctly approaching; I heard even the direction of
their approach. In the darkness it seemed to me
as if there were a panorama addressed to the ear.
It was a march of voices; but I could mark their
track as easily as I could have traced by day
the footsteps on the sand. On they swept, these
myriad voices, ever growing in volume, ever moving
toward one central point. I could not have per-

ceived more clearly by the eye where was tending
that accumulating crowd.   It was making for the
Sympathy Gate—only it was to get out, not to get
in.   The men of the valleys were trying to scale
the uplands, perhaps the mountains.   Their long
torpor was at last broken—broken by the voice of
the divine man, though not as he meant it to be.
They had seen a distorted picture of his will.
They had caught the rage of dominion, the desire
of empire.   The vision of independence had burst
upon them ; they were coming to vindicate their
freedom.   Freedom ! Were they fit to be free ?
Was there a greater proof of their unfitness than
their very shouts of triumph ?   When the thunder
sends the lightning before it, it bids us prepare for
the crash.   If these men wished to strike fire on
Palatine Hill, why should they have been so eager
to warn the foe of their coming ?   Were they not
placarding their own treason in advance, pro-
claiming to the gaoler that they meant to break
their bonds ?   And my father—the so-called leader
of the band—what of him ?   I saw it all ; he
was not the leader, but the led.   He was holding
reins which he could not control ; the steed had
run off with him ; he was at the mercy of the
crowd which he had gone to command.

And now I heard them climbing the ascent of

the valley—the path which I had striven to *de*scend. They were coming up in the delusion that there was no night here, no care here, no thorn here, dreaming not that humanity is one. As they drew nearer the voices began to be articulate. The breeze was blowing in the direction of the house, and it carried the sound. " Ben-Israel ! ben-Israel ! " " The home of our fathers ! " " The island for the people ! " " The promise of Moses and Mount Nebo ! " " Palatine Hill for the valleys ! "—these were among the cries which came floating through the night up the ascent to the Sympathy Gate.

Then came a sound from another quarter. It was close at hand—within the walls. From the grounds of my father's house there came the blast of a horn—loud, long, and penetrating. The guard had caught the noise and given the alarm. Then the sound was taken up by another horn on a more elevated plane. That again was reverberated by another on a plane still higher, and so on in ascending series, until from the summit of Palatine there rose that great blast which I knew so well— the blast which had sounded the first alarm over my visit to the valleys.

The house was now in confusion. The servants had gathered in the hall, frantic with terror. The signal bore its own message, and it was always a message of danger. Phœbe alone remained calm, and remained with me.   Presently there were footsteps in the passage, and the captain of the guard entered. " Lady Ecclesia," he said, "you can no longer stay here. The men of the valleys have risen ; they are even now on the main road. I cannot answer for the safety of this house. Allow me to conduct you to a place of security."

" I am not your prisoner, sir," I answered, "that you should remove me from my own house."   I spoke with acrimony, for the blood of my race was up.

"This house is under my charge," said the captain ; "I am responsible for it."

" Guard it then," I said ; "but my person at least is free. The charge on which I was imprisoned, though morally true, has legally broken down."

" I have indeed no power to arrest you," he answered ; "if I had, I would use it, in your interest. But I beseech you to consider your position. In half an hour this house may be in the possession of an infuriated mob, to whom your very rank may be your crime. I strongly advise you to seek safety in flight."

" Sir," I answered, " I do not approve of this rising ; none regrets it more bitterly, more poignantly than I do. You have heard me express my sympathy with the man who in the day of pestilence brought succour to the valleys. It is because I profess sympathy with him that I have none with this cause ; I feel that it is a movement contrary to his spirit. None the less, it is a movement of my people. Uninfluenced by me up to this day, concealed from me, this rising is still a rising of those who count themselves my clan. The infuriated mob of which you speak has in its veins the blood of those who, centuries ago, were retainers on this estate. I do not fear them. But if I did, what then ? For what should I fear danger if not for this house—the home of my fathers ? Though it is no longer the old house, though we hold as tenants what once we ruled as masters, though there is mean furniture where there once was gorgeous equipment, yet, poor as it is, worn as it is, dilapidated as it is, its very dust to me is dear. I shall not abandon it in its desolation ; I shall stand amid the ruins of the place which to me is holy. Let the servants go ; let the retainers go—those who grind at the mill and work in the field ; I do not forbid them to leave me. Make them the offer you have made to me. But as long as I have life and liberty I shall abide within these walls."

A voice said at my side, " I at least will never leave you." It was Phœbe ; and I pressed her hand. What course did the others choose ? I cannot express it better than by saying that one was taken and the other left. I never saw such an instance of the inherent difference between individual souls. Grinding the same corn, toiling in the same field, surrounded by the same circumstances, these dependants made an opposite choice ; some went out to seek their safety, and some refused to quit the tottering building. And I learned also in that hour the fallibility of our human judgments, for many who went out were those whom I counted to stay in, and many who stayed in were those whom I expected to go out.

CHAPTER XXI

THE TRAGEDY OF THE INNER SHRINE

THE last of the crowd had now evidently emerged from the Sympathy Gate. The sound no longer came from below, but from a level. It was clear that they were not immediately making for the grounds. They were turning toward the west. Something must have intervened to avert their attention from the possession of the prize which was at once the least guarded and the nearest. Nor was it hard to detect the cause. Counter sounds were audible from the hill; the uplands were coming down to meet the valleys It was as if the sea on one side of the island were roaring to the sea on the other side. I thought of the words of one of our great poets: "Deep calleth unto deep."

As the immediate danger seemed to be postponed, I told the domestics to go and rest awhile, for I felt that rest is an essential part of service.

I had great difficulty in persuading Phœbe, and only succeeded on the plea that I wished to be alone. It was, indeed, strictly true. There are hours in which solitude is our best companionship. This was one of them for me. I felt as if all the day I had been defrauded of solitude. The elements had roared at me; the valleys had clamoured at me. I longed to have an hour of quietness—an hour in which I would be separated from all distractions of the ear. The subsiding of the storm had already removed one of them; those of human passion still remained. Was there any spot where for a brief space I could hide from these?

Yes; I remembered. There was at the back of our house a room called the Oratory. It was a place which for years back had been set apart for private devotion—where any member of the household might retire to pour forth the soul in prayer. Within this apartment there was a door leading into an inner chamber, which was deemed still more sacred, and which for generations past had been regarded as under the jurisdiction of the chaplain alone. In this innermost shrine there were two peculiarities; I mark them carefully in the light of what followed. Resting on the floor there was a large box, to which Caiaphas kept the key. It was filled with gifts—the offerings of those who from time to time had come to Caiaphas to make confession of their sin, and which were supposed to be the possession of the family. Overhanging this box there was another peculiar object, which evidently had its origin in something symbolic. It was an enormous statue, which had been suspended by a cord from the outside roof, and let down through an aperture into the apartment, so as to overshadow the place which held the gifts. I am told it was intended to represent the angel of the clan. This interpretation was borne out by the fact that at the end of every year it had been the custom to encircle this figure with a chain, by which it was designed to indicate that the annual weight of the people's sin had been laid upon the angel. In the process of time the chains had accumulated enormously, constituting a weight upon the statue which I often thought dangerous. Particularly in the storm of the past day had the idea occurred to me, What if the cord by which the figure was suspended should be loosened by the friction of the elements?

But for this last fancy, I would have selected the innermost shrine as the place of my retreat ; there was something in its symbolism which at once calmed and fascinated me. But the thought of the great figure being unable to support its burden was disturbing to me; I felt it would impede my reflection. I resolved, therefore, to take the outer room for my night vigil. How little do we know what we are doing in the most trivial act! My decision determined the destinies of this island.

I lighted a lamp and passed into the Oratory. I carried with me that golden cross which was one of the two possessions I had received from the man of the valleys, and the only one which was left to me. I knelt beside an altar constructed for private devotion; I prayed to him who on this day of storm had come to me in a cloud. A great calm came over me, and I slept—this time a dreamless, visionless sleep. The warm fire, which was kept burning even when the room was unoccupied, conspired with my natural exhaustion to produce a deep repose. My head sank on one of the altar steps, and I became oblivious of all things.

I do not know exactly how long I slept. But when I awoke the lamp had gone out; the fire was also out, but its constant use had made the room habitually warm. There was already in the sky a dim streak of dawn. I had not awakened

naturally; my sleep was broken from without.
I heard again the sound of shouting; but it came
no longer from the valleys, but from the grounds.
I heard the tread of multitudinous feet sweeping
through my father's premises. I heard snatches
of songs expressing the joy of victory, and I knew
where they came from. These were not the voices
of the valley; they were the strains of the men
of Palatine. It all broke upon me in a moment.
The battle was over; the victory was won; and it
was won not by my father's house. The men
of my clan had been crushed—crushed for evermore. I listened to the hoarse voices in the courts
that were wont to be so silent. I heard the jest,
the jeer, the sally of wit and repartee, and the
laughter of response; and for the first time I felt
that my home was in the hands of the stranger.

All at once I became aware of a nearer sound.
Footsteps were coming through the passage, were
approaching the door. They were not like those
in the courtyard—jubilant and bold. They were
covert, stealthy, slow—those of a man who wished
to hide himself. I was breathless with fear. I
have never been greatly afraid of open violence,
but have always dreaded that which comes on
tiptoe. I had not long to wait. The door opened,
and a man entered with a torch in his hand. His

face was deadly pale; but one look at him was enough for recognition. I would have cried out with surprise, if fear had not paralysed me; it was Caiaphas.

He did not see me; he looked at nothing in the room. His eyes were strained on the room beyond—the inner shrine. There was something in that inner shrine which fascinated him, riveted him, made him unconscious of all beside. He began to think aloud.

"The time is come for *me*. Moses ben-Israel is no more. Who remains to represent the family? Ecclesia? No; she has declined to represent it; she has taken up an alien interest. Shall the gifts locked up in the sanctuary fall into the hands of the Lord of Palatine? Not if I can prevent it. Who is better entitled to these gifts than I? Have they not been gifts of the conscience, extorted by my own services? Have they not been wrung out from penitent hearts as a tribute to my power? Are they not all the trophies of my ministry to this house? Has any one such claim to them as I?"

As he spoke he approached the inner room. He entered; he shut the door. I heard a key applied to the lock of the trunk. The vision rose before me of his incredible meanness; it was like one

robbing the dead.   This man had been following
the skirts of the men of Palatine to wait the issue
of events ;   and now, when the house he served
was mutilated, he came to sack it.   My heart gave
a great bound of indignation.   I had encountered
this man before ;   I would do it again.   I would
confront him ;   I would shame him ;   I would teach
him that mine was no alien interest.   I rose from
the steps of the altar ;   in another moment I would
have met him face to face ;   but another was
quicker than I.

For suddenly upon the air there came a deafen-
ing crash and a human shriek.   I rushed to the
aperture.   One look was enough.   I shall never
forget the horror of the sight.   The overburdened
statue, weighted with the chains of the people,
had fallen.   The hold of the cord, already greatly
worn, had been relaxed by the violence of the
storm, and the moment of its final giving way had
been precisely that moment when Caiaphas was
below.   There it lay in fragments on the floor ;
and beneath it there was an awful sight—a
mangled heap that once had been a man.

I could bear no more.   I screamed ; I ran from
the room to shut out the vision.   To get quit of
the dead foe I fled to the living one.   I passed
through the corridor ;   I came into the hall.   I

met face to face with a detachment of the men of Palatine, accompanied by the captain of the guard. It was a relief to meet them; they were alive. The captain evidently thought I was flying in fear.

"Lady Ecclesia," he said, "you are my prisoner *now*; here is my warrant. You and your house have been guilty of conspiracy. By the command of the Lord of Palatine I arrest you for treason against the laws of this island."

"For God's sake," I cried, "take me away from this place!"

"I have also," he said, "in the name of the same Lord of Palatine, to arrest the servants of this house."

"For the sake of Heaven," I repeated wildly, "take us all away!"

Was there in his mind the notion that I wished to prevent a search of the house with the view of concealing some one? I think there was, for he presently resumed: "Are there any guests now within this dwelling? If so, I am bound to arrest them also."

"Sir," I answered, "there is within this dwelling at this moment a guest you do not dream of—an unbidden guest, who comes once to us all. I do not think you will be able to capture *him*."

"What!" he cried, "death here? I thought I had left him where I came from."

"He has fallen," I said, "upon one of your helpers—one who came to spoil the house when he knew the master was away. Go, you will find him in the inner shrine. You know me too well to imagine I shall try to escape."

He returned quicker than he went. His face was ghastly pale—this really brave man, who had just come from a scene of blood. "It is a horrible sight," he said: "do you believe in retribution?"

"To me," I answered, "the horror is not the retribution; it is the fact that I have missed saving him. Do you know, it was the casting of a die that put him there instead of me. I too was in search of treasure to-night; but it was the unsearchable riches. I went to pass an hour of devotion; I decided with difficulty to take the outer rather than the inner room. If I had taken the inner, my hour would have come to-night, and his hour would have been postponed."

I would have said more, but I was startled by the look of his face. If it was ghastly before, there was added to the pallor an expression of the most acute torture. Then all at once it broke upon me, as such things do break. This man, whose associations with me had been so adverse—this man, who

from the night of the betrayal had stood in the
place of my gaoler—this man, whom I had received with sarcasm, invective, obloquy—this man,
whose very name I did not know—loved me. It
was to me a revelation of surprise. That one so
effeminate as Hellenicus should have felt for me
the tender passion was conceivable enough. But
that the rude soldier of the house of Palatine, the
man of stern will and strenuous discipline, should
have shared the same interest with the luxurious
son of pleasure, this was a strange thing. To me
there could be but one explanation. The diverse
power of attraction lay not in me. It lay in my
contact with that mysterious mind which had not
only dominated but transfigured my own—a mind
which seemed to have a hundred doors of egress,
by any one of which it could come out to capti-
vate. It was not I who had taken prisoner two
such opposite types as Phœbe and the captain of
the guard. It was one who had first imprisoned
myself, and who, because his own nature was universal, had brought me into contact with all things.

"What of my father?" I said.

"Lady Ecclesia," he answered, "your father
cannot be found. There has been great carnage
to-night, but he is not among the slain. I know
he was in the heat of the battle, for I saw him by

the light of the torches, and I heard his voice shouting the war-cry, ' The Lord of Hosts is with us ! ' But we have looked in vain for him amid the broken ranks of his house. He is not among the dead ; he is not among the dying ; he is not among the prisoners : he must have escaped. I have sent messengers along the main road, down the valley, up the hill. They will tell us whether they have found any traces or tidings. Meanwhile you have rightly felt that this house is no place for you. Even were it otherwise, I have no choice in this matter. I am commanded to lead you to the tribunal of the Lord of Palatine. See, the dawn is spreading ; in a few hours we must begin our ascent. I withdraw my men to give you time for preparation. As a matter of form I was bound to take hostile possession of this house ; there my hostility ends. Believe me, you have my deepest sympathy."

" And what of the awful guest," I said, " whom we shall leave in the inner shrine ? "

" That shall be my care," he answered ; " dismiss all trouble from your mind on this account. I shall leave a party here to superintend the burial of the priest. I do not know that I shall ask them to bury all his memories. I think I shall get an architect to take a plan of your inner and outer sanctuary for the inspection of the Lord of Palatine. I have a presentiment that some day you will find your own symbols on the top of Palatine Hill."

"You have already one in your possession," I said. "What has become of the little vial which passed into your hands on the night of the betrayal?"

"I have sent it," he replied, "to the Lord of Palatine; this too may yet be heard of again."

CHAPTER XXII

BEFORE THE DEPARTURE

THERE is no feeling more sad than the breaking up of home. I do not think it is felt by all families in an equal degree. There are some who make new friends more easily than others. Our family had always been distinguished for its slowness in making friends. We were said by our neighbours to keep within the house. We were called stiff, unsocial, even unfriendly. The Lord of Palatine and his brother Hellenicus mixed freely with their inferiors ; the house of Israel had a tendency to stand aloof. All the more on this account was there precious to us the idea of home. More than once through the stress of fortune had we been called to break up the old mansion ; and it had always been a moment of unspeakable pain. Such a moment had now come to my own life. I had received the command to quit the house of my fathers. I was about to leave the walls that had sheltered me from infancy. I was to see them dismantled of those retainers that still remained, and to be led forth as a captive on a charge involving life or death.

I knew by presentiment that I would never see these walls again. The few hours left to me of possession were like the hours left to us with our dead before burial—when, unlike Caiaphas, they are our beloved dead. They were a last look, and they had all the bitterness of such. With a bursting heart I went through the old rooms to say farewell. There was not a nook or cranny, there was not a chink or crevice, outside the scene of tragedy, which I did not visit like a shrine. There was not a piece of furniture which I did not water with my tears. A curious temptation came over me to put a mark upon certain articles, that, if I ever met them again, I might recognise them. But then the thought occurred to me that God might have fields for my service in which it was desirable to forget the things which are behind. I said, " Let God be the custodier of our immortalities ; it is not for me to determine what shall be saved from the wreck of time."

There is one thing which to the future reader of these pages may seem strange. He may wonder why, with such a desire to keep memorials of the

past, I had never during all the days of my convalescence made a single inquiry regarding the
burial-place of him who had extinguished for me
all other loves. He may ask why it was that even
at this moment I did not try to procure from the
captain of the guard a relic of the spot, were it
only a twig or a stone. Did I forget? No.
Startling as it may sound, it was not want of
memory, but want of interest. Remember my
peculiar experience. It was not merely that the
man of the valleys to me was not dead: that was
the view held by all his followers. But it was that
to me there never had been a time in which I had
said to myself, " The man of the valleys is dead."
His death had been revealed to me as a past fact,
not a present one. I had to go and pick it up
from the road I had left behind. When I did pick
it up, it had already been more than half swallowed
up in victory. To me the true relic of that grave
was the risen man; I had no wish to have any
other memorial of it. I can understand how others
might think differently. To Peter, James, and John
there had been a moment of actual bereavement—
a moment in which they had exclaimed, " The man
of the valleys is dead." But mine had been more
like the experience of my correspondent Paul : the
news of life revived had anticipated the tidings of

the grave. To me, as to Paul, the thorn had been covered by the flower.

Let me resume my narrative. I conducted the family service again as I had done on the previous morning. I told the domestics everything except the death-tragedy within the house. My reason for keeping that back was not the horror of it. The chaplain Caiaphas stood to our house in the position of a faith. The domestics had always associated every religious act with him; the first exception had been my own service of yesterday, and I doubt if it had full effect. Whatever they felt of Caiaphas personally—and they feared rather than loved him—he was still to them the embodiment of the idea of worship. I felt that to tell them their prop had been removed, before any other foundation had been suggested, would be a cruel thing. To me the death of Caiaphas was no blank in the religious life; I had already caught light from another altar-fire. But to them this was the only fire; to put it out was to leave nothing but cold and darkness. I would not put it out until I had kindled something new. Let them expect the priest's return till another comforter should come. It would be time enough to tell them that the old candlestick had been broken when their eyes had caught one streak of the new and rosy

morn.   And so I kept the big tragedy in my heart
that was lying in the silent room.   Ye who carry in
your breast a pain you can tell to no one, pity me.

After the morning service I did a new thing—a
thing newer than the service : I asked the domestics
to sit down with me at a common meal.   I put it
on the ground that the time at our disposal was
short ; but on any ground it was significant.   Our
house had always been kind to its dependants, had
always claimed the valleys as within its original
boundaries.   But it had never for a moment
forgotten the principle of subordination.   I had
been trained in a school supremely conservative.   I
had been taught to look upon family descent as
the great ground of privilege.   I had always a
tendency to remind myself that I was the Lady
Ecclesia.   I think it was the last part of my old
nature to be conquered.   That night in the valleys
I had seen the vast multitude partake together ;
but I was not one of them, and they were all of
a class.   I think my relations with Phœbe were
the first influences that softened me.   My days of
protracted weakness made me dependent on the
ministrations of another, and that other one whom
I was wont to rule.   Be it as it may, this morning
the Lady Ecclesia was dead and the woman
Ecclesia was alive.   We were sharing one common

peril—my servants and I. Those who shared it with me had elected to do so. Some had turned aside yesternight; perhaps if in the days of the past there had been less of the Lady and more of the woman in me, they would have loved me more. At all events my heart went out to those who remained. They had refused to separate their lot from mine : would I at this moment divide my lot from theirs? The relation of mistress and servant had been shattered by a common blow. We were fellow-creatures, fellow-prisoners, fellow-sufferers ; we would partake this meal together.

And before it was over there came to me another strange experience—a deeper stretch of charity still. The captain of the guard returned. He stood in the hall and sent a message that he desired to speak with me. Quick as lightning the thought came to me, Should not this man be asked to partake the repast with his prisoners ? Had he not last night been far travelled ? Was he not to-day the most burdened man in the service? Would it not be only courteous if I invited him to sit down ? Then rose up pride and said within me : "Lady Ecclesia, you forget yourself. Are you not the daughter of Moses ben-Israel ? Is not this man the enemy of your father—a fighting retainer of the Lord of Palatine ? Is it not to him we are indebted for all this present misery? Is it not to him and to his master we owe the fact that the ordained of Heaven are not the possessors of this island?" Then I seemed to hear another voice— the refrain of words that I had read and which I now remembered. It was that strange message of my strange correspondent, Paul. What if the Lord of Palatine himself was meantime the ordained of heaven? What if he possessed the island because at this hour he was the only man fit to possess it? What if God had consecrated him to the regency until the heir was ripe for his inheritance? In that case, was he not the injured rather than the injuring party? Were not *we* the disturbers of *his* peace, of God's peace? Were not his fighting men the unconscious servants of a Providence that loved order rather than anarchy? Might not my house be the real aggressor?

Then the last voice prevailed. I went out and met the captain in the hall. " Sir," I said, " the time is so short at our command that I have asked the servants to sit down with me before starting and partake of a common meal. If you deem it not degrading to be at the same table with your prisoners, I shall be glad that you join us."

" Where the Lady Ecclesia is concerned," he answered, " *I* am the captive ; the condescension is all hers; the honour all mine. I gratefully accept your offer. But first of all let me give my message. Those whom I sent to seek tidings of your father have returned. He is neither in the valley, nor on the plain, nor among the hills; he has put out to sea."

"Put out to sea!" I cried: "how can you tell that? The space gone over in so short a time must have been very small. Have your messengers tracked the tenth part of the valley or the plain, or the twentieth part of the recesses in the hills?"

"No, Lady Ecclesia, you speak truly. It is not on the ground of a complete search that we know your father to have put to sea; it is on positive grounds. Last night there was a sailing vessel on the beach; this morning it is gone. A band of fishermen, known by sight and name to the men of the valleys, were observed during the week to be busily engaged in stocking it with provisions, and these have also disappeared; they have evidently volunteered to become the crew. Your father, Lady Ecclesia, has made a wild escapade. Does he imagine he can live outside of land? What will he do when the stores have been exhausted?"

Then a great thought flashed over me. I

remembered the vision of yesterday. Had not the
man of the valleys told me that my father would
live without land? Did not that prove that he
was under the protection of the man of the valleys?
Was he indeed beyond the sight of land? No ;
only beyond the sight of our island. Was there
not land on the other side of the sea? Had
not its existence been guaranteed to me by evidence stronger than sight? Had I not the testimony written in my heart that from the farther
shore love's eyes were watching? Were they
not watching now that lonely vessel on the
great deep? Would they not keep that vessel
in its desolate wanderings? Why should men
say, when the ship was cut off from the island,
that it was cut off from supply? Were there
no supplies from the other shore? Were there
not, far out from our island home, meetings of
ships upon the sea—meetings in which the
transport vessels from the invisible land brought
sustenance to the mariner whose island stores
were exhausted? So would it be with my father.
He would not die upon the wave; I felt it, I
knew it. He would be nourished from another
soil till the times of enmity had passed from this.
Homeless, landless, companionless, he would not
die. Without a place left for him on the map

of the traveller, he would still be the leader of a race. With his house in the hands of a stranger, he would keep his family name. He might be despaired of in the island ; he might be forgotten ; he might be deemed dead ; but the salt sea would preserve him alive, and in my heart the words of the night vision would be ever sounding, " He shall return, and you shall nourish his old age, and make him young once more."

" I am grateful to you," I said, " for this information ; it gives me a strange comfort. I am glad my father is hiding on the sea and not on the land. I think we are more in God's hands on the sea ; less in man's. There are always two currents on the land—the human and the divine ; but the current on the sea is all God's. Come, let us join my fellow-prisoners at the morning meal."

And that morning there was exhibited a wondrous spectacle. The day on which our house reached its lowest fortunes was the day in which it attained its widest charity. Whenever I think of that morning, there rises before me the figure of a triangle—narrow at the top and broad at the base. The progress of our house had been a steady progress downwards ; it had begun at the zenith of hope and ended in the present

despair. And yet the present despair had produced what all the years of hope had failed to
win. For the first time in the history of my
home there was displayed within its walls an
act of free hospitality. There, in the last hour
of its possession, the representatives of our diverse
island life sat side by side in social unity. The
servant was at one table with the mistress, the
clansman with the alien, the friend with the foe.
Branches that had never met unitedly on a single
tree were joined this morning. *There* was the
house of Israel, represented by myself—the proud
Ecclesia. There was the household of Hellenicus,
embodied in the presence of the gentle Phœbe.
There were the retainers of the Lord of Palatine,
prefigured in the person of the man who had just
struck a blow in defence of his master's claim. It
was a strange, a heterogeneous, some may say an
unnatural group ; yet I do not think I was ever
more loyal to the honour of my family than when I
made the season of its depression the hour of its
enlargement. There are days which only get
bright as they near the setting sun. Looking back
to that last moment in the house of my father, it
almost seems to me as if amid its storm and stress
the words of one of our poets found their fulfilment : " At evening time there shall be light."

CHAPTER XXIII

OUTSIDE THE GATES

THE morning sun had already climbed far into the heavens as we emerged from the precincts of the old home. By the precincts of the old home I do not mean merely my father's grounds. There was a whole village adjoining these grounds, whose dwellers had always looked on my father as their feudal master. They lined the road as we passed by. They made no concealment of their sorrow: rustic nature rarely does. They wept; they sobbed; they wrung their hands; they uttered exclamations of despair: and if the women were more vociferous, the men were not silent. It was not merely that the old tenant was going; in the afternoon a new tenant would be there, commissioned to hold the house by the Lord of Palatine. I think, when a loved family has departed from a dwelling, there is something sadder than the sight of the house empty; it is the sight of the house in other hands. The first is only a blank ; the second is a revulsion. I do not wonder that they wept.

We left the village behind. We came upon a path which, when last I saw it, was the open country. But now to my startled eye it was a military city. Since the day of my illness I had never been on this road. I had left it a solitary common ; I found it a hive of life. It was covered with soldiers' tents ; it was guarded at every post. But that was the smallest part of the change. It was not the military parade that shocked me ; it was the survivals of a scene of carnage. There were no dead bodies, but there were many dilapidated living ones. In addition to the tents of the soldiers there was a very large tabernacle, which had evidently been improvised for an emergency. In front of the door lay a multitude of wounded men, with eyes eagerly strained upon the edifice. They were clearly under medical inspection. To and fro moved a company of men whom I took to be physicians. They examined the sufferers one by one. At the end of each examination they made a sign, and according to its nature there was a different result. In one case the sufferer was carried into the pavilion ; in the other he was left at the door.

"What is that tenement?" I said, addressing the captain of the guard.

"That," he answered, "is a military hospital."

"But," I said, "large as it is, it seems quite inadequate to this morning's demand."

"As it is merely a stretch of canvas," he replied, "it might be extended indefinitely. But you do not suppose a hospital is meant to meet all the demands for it?"

"Why not?" I cried in extreme wonder.

"You would not," he said, "have those admitted who are not qualified?"

"But what is the qualification?" I exclaimed. "Is not a man qualified in proportion as the amount of his hurt is great?"

"Exactly the reverse," he returned. "The more deadly the wound, the less right has the man to expect care. Look now." (He pointed across the field.) "Do you see those two men whom the doctors are examining? They are hurt in very different degrees. One of them is lying prostrate; the other has broken an arm. Yet, I tell you, that the man with the broken arm will get in, and the man with the broken life will be kept out. There! did I not say it would be so?"

And truly he was right. He who was able to walk was presently conducted into the pavilion, and he who was prostrated was passed by. "Why is this?" I cried in strong indignation. "Are the medical men in the service of your house intended only to cure those who look curable beforehand?"

"Exactly, Lady Ecclesia; you could not have expressed it better if you had studied the subject for years. It is not even a question of curable or incurable. The entire consideration is whether the disease or injury can be removed to such an extent as to render the patient fit for active service. If the doctors think not, they refuse to take care of him. No man among the retainers of our house has his life valued for its own sake."

Where had I heard these sentiments before? Oh yes, I remembered; it was in that last interview with Hellenicus, in which I defended the claims of the valleys. I had shuddered at the theory; but I think there must have been in my mind a faint hope that Hellenicus was somewhat romancing. It is the only way in which I can account for the actual horror with which I saw it in practice. I felt as if some one had struck me. Never since the night in which the woman was stoned in the valley had I experienced such an emotion. "It is shameful," I cried; "it is brutal; it is abominable! If things are bad within *my* gates, they are worse within yours."

The captain laid his hand on my arm, but gently. "I implore you, Lady Ecclesia," he said, "do not say anything that may prejudice your position with the Lord of Palatine. He is already sufficiently incensed. You can no longer even in name speak of *your* gates and his gates. He has threatened to demolish the walls of your old dwelling, and transform it into a military station."

"My house," I answered proudly, "is independent of my dwelling ; it is where my father is, and will return with him when he comes back. Meantime I want to prevent the Lord of Palatine from demolishing his own house. Will you grant me one favour ? Will you allow me to speak a word of kindness to the disappointed man in the scene to which you directed me ? "

"Why to him more than to others? Is he not only one of a disappointed multitude ? "

"Yes," I replied, "but I think we sympathise with units more than masses. Won't you let me go ? You don't fear I shall try to break my bonds —to run away, or to sail away like my father ? "

"Go by all means," he said ; "I trust you implicitly."

I hurried over the field to the point where my eye and my heart had been last centred.

I found the object of my solicitude not only prostrate in body, but completely prostrate in mind. There is a boundary line of physical weakness which tends to obliterate the distinction between the coward and the brave. I have always been told that the retainers of the house of Palatine were conspicuous for courage. That has not been my experience. The opinion is based upon the fact that, when things have come to an extremity, the retainers of this house have preferred to avoid the extremity by meeting death with their own hand. To my humble judgment the fact would seem to point to the opposite conclusion. It appears to me to indicate that the hour of extremity is to these men insupportable, and that they shun the foe which they have not courage to meet.

Be this as it may, the man before me was in mental prostration. I have no doubt he was among the bravest in last night's battle ; but that is not the ultimate test of bravery. It is something to stand fast in the evil day ; but to stand when the night is come—this is divine. He was utterly unmanned by the denial of human sympathy. He had been so accustomed to move in companies that the solitude appalled him. He had not either the material or the strength for taking away his life ; if he had, I have no doubt he would have done it. As it was, he cried like a girl.

I took his hand in mine ; the new life within me had taken away much of my reserve, had made things honourable to me which I once would have deemed improper. "Don't think," I said, "that all the island has deserted you. I am the Lady Ecclesia, daughter of Moses ben-Israel ; and I have come to comfort you." For once it was not pride made me use my designation ; it was the wish to let him feel that he was not neglected.

He looked up quite startled at the sympathy. I greatly missed my little vial at that moment, for I remembered the case of Phœbe. Suddenly it occurred to me that I had still a relic of the night of vision—the little cross of gold which the man of the valleys had given me. I took it from my inner garment and pressed it on the palm of his hand. "Clasp that for a moment," I said ; "I am told it has great power of healing." The effect surprised even myself. In an instant his pale cheek was lit up with a flush not unlike the rose of health ; his languor seemed to vanish, and the light of interest flashed from his eye. "I have the oddest sensation," he said. "I feel as if all the weakness and pain had left my body and passed into the body of that other wounded man opposite. I still have a sense of them ; but I feel as if they were his, not mine. I wonder if you could do anything to relieve him ; I am not speaking quite unselfishly ; for I have a sensation as if he were a bit of myself."

The doctor passed, and I accosted him. "Would you examine this man again," I said ; "it seems to me he shows symptoms of amendment." He answered gruffly that he was not in the habit of reversing his decisions; none the less he proceeded to re-examine. The patient himself protested. He said he had been already pronounced too ill to be succoured. He urged the doctor to go in quest of more hopeful cases and not waste time on him ; he could meet his fate without a shadow of fear.

In a few minutes the doctor looked up from his work. "What is the meaning of this," he said. "This man is certainly fit for the hospital. What has effected the change?"

"Doctor," said the patient, "this lady has a skill beyond you ; she has applied an instrument which has probed deeper, and cured in the probing."

"Let me see it," said the doctor. He took the cross and examined it. He asked me how I had applied it, and he received the information with a cynical smile. "Take your cross," he said, "and try it on that man opposite; he has also been rejected, and is also in despair. I shall wait here till you come back. Let me know the result. A single swallow does not make a summer."

I gladly availed myself of the offer. I crossed the field to the spot indicated—the same where the former patient had felt his pain to be transferred. The doctor followed me with his eye, closely, critically, as if to make sure that the cross and the cross alone were the applied instrument. I did not keep him waiting above five minutes. "Well," he said, with a strongly sceptical air, "what success have you had?" I answered, "Come and see." He accompanied me across the field. We found the man in a high state of mental energy. It took the form of an intense sympathy for those around him. He seemed to have forgotten that he was anything more than a spectator. He had ceased to realise that he was himself one of the company whose case he commiserated. He directed the doctor's attention to cases in the field which seemed to promise recovery. "It is a pity," he said, "that these fine fellows should be lost to the service of the island." He was oblivious of the fact that no one gave greater promise of recovery than himself. At the end of a brief but searching examination the doctor exclaimed with surprise, " This man is also fit for the hospital."

The doctor was now in a strait betwixt two. On the one hand professional pride prompted him to get rid of me as soon as possible. But on the other hand was a more potent agent than pride— self-interest. He knew that every man saved to the Lord of Palatine was a step in his own promotion. The recovery of every patient was a personal gain to him ; it was property saved from the wreck. I possessed an influence he did not understand. But, however unintelligible to him, he felt he could utilise it for his own interest. Pride died hard. He asked me again to let him examine the cross. This time he made an effort at personal experiment. He tried the effect of the instrument on some of the patients with his own hand. He returned crestfallen. " I can make nothing of it," he said.

This was a revelation even to myself. Up to this time I believe I had the notion that the little cross had an efficacy of its own apart from the hand which held it. To me its value was increased rather than diminished by the discovery that it required to be united with a phase of the human spirit. " Doctor," I said, " are there no cases in your profession in which the hand that administers is as important as the thing administered ? " Then the pride died altogether. " You are right," he said ; " take the cross in your own hand and do what you can with it. So far as I am concerned, you have the liberty of the field."

I was not slow to take his permission ; and the result amply justified and rewarded him. I do not think the military hospital had ever been so filled as it was that day. I do not think the Lord of Palatine ever received so many restitutions of seemingly lost property as he did on the morning when I made my inspection of the wounded. The greatest gain of his life came from that very man of the valleys whose interest he deemed at variance with his own. To me the main satisfaction was the opportunity I had of connecting the cross with the name of him who had given it. I did not wish any one to think that the source of the power lay in me. And yet I am bound to confess that I did not wholly succeed in my efforts at self-burial. As I traversed the field, as I was seen ministering in turn to the need of each sufferer, as one by one the cases accumulated in which recovery had come after hope's abandonment, the excitement of the victims hitherto unreached became intense. The vision of a beam of light passing over their comrades, and the frantic fear that the beam might set ere it reached themselves, was almost too much for them. My name had been passed from lip to lip through the sorrowful band. Presently it became came a united watch-cry, or rather a prayer-cry. "Ecclesia! Ecclesia!" rang through the field, in accents half supplicating, half admiring. It was charmingly irreverent. My title was left out; my designation was suppressed. There are pauses in music which are more eloquent than a note would be. So to me at that moment was the leaving out of the word "Lady." I think I never heard so musical a silence.

At last the captain recalled me. "Lady Ecclesia," he said, "my sympathies are with you, and, if it depended on myself, there would be no obstruction to your benevolence. But I fear the interpretation which may be put upon the act by the Lord of Palatine; I dread it for myself, and I dread it for you. Remember you are ascending to his judgment-seat. You and your house are under his ban. What if it should be said that you have attempted to prejudge his sentence by winning the popular ear? In your interest and in my own interest I must ask you to desist. Meantime during this march I have placed my pavilion at your disposal for rest and for refreshment. Retire there for an hour and recruit yourself; I shall allow your own servants to minister to you. We shall resume our journey by-and-by."

I did not refuse his kindness, for I was still easily exhausted. But regarding the danger he apprehended I had no fear. I thought then, and I think still more now, that to one standing before the judgment-seat of the Lord of Palatine, there could be no stronger ground of defence than just the fact that I had caught the ear of his own most faithful retainers, and had been able to minister to the needs of that military force by which he himself had supported his claim to island dominion.

CHAPTER XXIV

THE FIRST WORLDLY TEMPTATION

FROM the moment we left my father's grounds our path had been an upward one, but its rise was at first so gentle that it was practically a plain. After resuming our journey it showed more symptoms of climbing. It was designed on my account that the progress should be effected by slow and intermittent stages. About an hour after noon we reached what might be called a temporary landing in the stair. The estate named Palatine Hill stood on the top of an eminence. There were roads leading up to it from every part of the island, as if it had been designed to be the centre of all things. Nevertheless the communication was by no means easy. The approaches, though many, were long and winding. Palatine Hill, like the summit of every hill, looked nearer than it really was; it tempted by a seeming facility of access which was not there in fact. In none of the roads was the ascent maintained continuously. There were intervals of flat surfaces interposed between the climbings—periods in which the upward progress was suspended and the expectation baffled which predicted an early goal. It was to one of these flats that we attained after the meridian sun; and instinctively I paused to survey the prospect.

For the first time since we began our journey the form of Palatine Hill burst clearly on our view. On the lower ground it had been comparatively hid, but the superior elevation brought it into prominence. In the rays of the midday sun it looked positively gorgeous. I could not help expressing my admiration to the captain. " Yes," he said, " it is very fine, but I think it has passed its full glory. If you were near, you would see signs of decay in the building ; it wants repair. I have seen the House of Palatine exhibit a splendour to which this is as twilight to the day. Besides, it has suffered much of late."

" How so ? "

" Did you not hear of the great fire some time ago, when the house was almost burnt to the ground ? "

" No ; it must have been during the days when I was imprisoned in my room and heard nothing. Was it an accident ? "

" That is just what nobody knows. The Lord of Palatine himself did not scruple to express suspicion of some of your retainers. I do not think he has been the same man since. I remember the time when his solicitude was for the island I think it has become personal. It is on that ground I am anxious about his meeting with you."

I was eager to change the current of the conversation. Affection was having its influence on this man's mind; and I could not bear that even indirectly I should be the means of shaking the loyalty of a subject of the Lord of Palatine. I therefore asked irrelevantly, " At what time do you expect we shall arrive? "

" I think," he said, " the setting sun will be there before us. I do not imagine you will be in time to see it by daylight. Meanwhile I have made every arrangement for your comfort and convenience. I have directed that your tent shall follow as long as the march continues; but I have arranged that the last part of your journey, which is the steepest, shall not be on foot. At the next landing in the ascent we shall dine, after which you and I shall mount horse and ride forward in advance; the others will follow."

I was about to thank him for his kind consideration, when an event occurred which introduced one of the most striking episodes of my life—an episode which had an effect on my mind quite disproportionate to its actual magnitude. A soldier came up from the rear, and, addressing the captain, said, " A singular-looking man has just arrived in the camp who urgently desires to speak to the Lady Ecclesia ; he says he has a message for her of great importance."

" Where is he ? "

" We have left him in the tent set apart for the use of her ladyship."

" Why have not you brought him here ? "

" He says his communication is strictly secret, and must be made to the Lady Ecclesia alone."

" Will you not trust me to go ? " I said, interposing in the dialogue.

" I will trust *you*," he answered, " but not him." Turning to the soldier he said, " Take a company and escort the Lady Ecclesia to the tent ; you can stand outside till the interview is over."

As I crossed the plateau my mind was a prey to fancies. But in all the fancies that floated through my brain I did not hit upon the real one. I conjured up many possibilities. The thought even occurred that perhaps after all my father might have been found on the land. But the thing which really happened was the one thing which I never expected.

I entered the tent with a palpitating heart, and the sight which met my eye at once transfixed me. There stood before me a gigantic figure with breadth to match, colossal in hand and foot, and coarse in feature. His countenance betokened above all other things unrest, and it was centred in his eyes, which flashed wildly, incessantly. He came forward and at once addressed me.

" Lady Ecclesia, daughter of Moses ben-Israel, latest scion of the most royal house in this island, I have come again to visit you. Do you not remember me ? "

" No," I cried, " I never saw you before."

He smiled with great condescension. " I do not wonder," he said, " that you have failed to recognise me, for I have put off all the trappings of weakness and taken a new form. I used to be known as the man of the valleys." (I shuddered.) " Ah ! no wonder you shrink with disgust. That was in the days of my flesh. I have put away childish things. I have come back from heaven with a new body and a new name. I am called no longer the man of the valleys, but ' the son of the star '—the conquering star foretold in one of your poems, The Song of Balaam.' And I am come specially

to you. I am come to raise the fallen fortunes of
your house, to make it not only free but master.
I see you a prisoner in the hands of the Lord of
Palatine ; he shall yet be a prisoner in your hands.
You shall weave the chain for him which he weaves
for you. You shall give back the sneers to him
that he has given to you. You shall deny the
privileges to him that he has denied to you. You
shall put his men down in the valley and put the
men of the valley on Palatine Hill. I am weary
till the work is done, that I may get back to my
glory. Think you it is a light thing to leave my
glory ? Think you I am made of your common
clay ? Nay, Lady Ecclesia, I have descended as
far beneath myself in coming to you as you have
descended beneath yourself in becoming a servant
of the Lord of Palatine. Truly I am called the
son of the star. I am unused to toil ; I am
unpractised in sorrow ; I am a stranger to tears.
And I shall make you, Lady Ecclesia, toilless,
sorrowless, tearless. You shall stand upon the
hill and dictate to valley and plain. You shall
make others do your work ; your enemies shall
bear your burdens. You shall dwell aloft like
my star ; you shall shun the battle and the strife.
You shall look down with calm unconcern upon
the dwarfs beneath you, for the spray of the sea

of trouble shall not touch your feet, and its murmur
shall not reach your ear.   You shall——"

"For the sake of all that is good," I cried, "be
silent and begone; your contrast to the man of
the valleys maddens me!"

The eyes of the giant flashed.   "And does the
Lady Ecclesia deem," he said, "that I am so poor
as to have only one vesture?   Does she think I
am limited to a single form of appearance?   Is
she not aware that I can change my garment con-
tinually, so that none can detect the old covering?
Surely she knows little of the power of God."

"I could detect the man of the valleys," I said,
"in any form—even in your form.   It is not by
the change in your vesture that I feel your contrast to him.   It is by that which lies below your
vesture—your spirit.   Even if you came in his
very image I would know you were not he.   You
are nowhere so unlike him as when you speak.
You talk too grandly to be divine.   *He* never
addressed me as the Lady Ecclesia; he spoke to
me as a woman.   *He* never called me the latest
scion of the most royal house; the most royal
house was to him the servant of all.   *He* never
styled himself 'the son of the star'; they who
have always dwelt among stars are unconscious
of their own splendour.   They know less about it

than those outside. It is their atmosphere, and they feel not that they breathe it. You have never betrayed so small an origin as when you have revelled in your height."

I paused, for the ungainly face before me was lit up by a gleam of lurid fire. Hitherto I had shuddered ; for the first time I trembled. It began to dawn upon me that this was no impostor, but a madman. The glare of insanity glittered in his eye, and his voice grew stern. "And this," he said, "is gratitude ! This is the reward of him who has come to redeem you from slavery, to break the iron fetters and set the prisoner free! You treat me with contempt because I do not proclaim the glories of a quagmire. Then, Lady Ecclesia, I must save you against your will. This island needs you ; this island waits for you. The fugitives of last night's battle require but a stimulus. One word from you will raise the clan of Israel, and that word must be spoken to-day." He drew forth a parchment roll like that used by the man of the valleys, but with gilt edges, and of much finer quality of paper. "There once," he said, "was a roll taken in which the valleys took the lead, and your name was conspicuous by its absence. This roll shall rectify the mistake ; you shall lead and the valleys shall follow. They shall

know that this voice comes not from the vale, but
from the hill.   See, the spaces are as yet all blank ;
in the name of the Lord of Hosts I command you
to write the first signature in the list of those who
elect to follow me."

He put writing materials before me, and bade me
sign.   " I have already," I said, " signed my name
to the roll of the man of the valleys, and it was
signed *after* the valleys.   Every man rises in his
own order, and I dare not alter the order which
was fixed by *him*."

" I unfix it now," he cried ; and his hand was
clenched in anger.   " Has not God power to reverse
His own decrees?   Who are you that you should
raise your will against the Lord's anointed ?   Who
are you that you should gainsay the messenger of
Omnipotence ?   Who are you that you should presume to counsel him whom God has sent to lift
your people from the mire ?   Heaven can wait no
longer on the whims of a mortal. Sign, sign, sign !"

His attitude was so threatening that I began to
congratulate myself on the precautions taken by
the captain.   "Leave me," I said, "or it may be
the worse for you.   I have not come here un-
guarded.   There is a band of the Lord of Palatine's
soldiers outside.   If you molest me I shall call on
them."

The effect was not what I expected. Quick as thought he placed himself between me and the door; and his face became absolutely livid with rage. "And has it come to this?" he cried. "I always knew you were a captive of the Lord of Palatine; I did not know you were an ally. I did not know that the head of a clan ordained by God to smite His enemies could make common cause with these enemies. I did not dream that a daughter of Moses ben-Israel could call out the retainers of another clan to oppress the servants of her own. I pitied you as a slave galled beneath her chain; little did I deem that the chain was dear to you. I thought you a victim; I have found you a traitor. I came to redeem you from another race; I find I must redeem your own race from you. God shall remove the candlestick out of its place and put another in its room. There are others who can take up the cause which the degenerate daughter of the old line has betrayed, and they shall begin by taking vengeance on their betrayer. Say, Lady Ecclesia, will you repent or die?"

He drew from his side a shining dagger. For the fourth time in my life I was very near to death. This was the hardest time. In the valley, in the sick-room, in the oratory, I would at least have had support—that support which comes from the presence of high emotion. Here there was no previous height. I had been in low contact, and I felt lowered. The atmosphere was depressing, degrading, and it affected my courage. I showed miserable want of spirit for one of my clan. I shrank back; I retreated within the curtain of another compartment. He followed me, pointing the glittering blade, and reiterating the words "Sign or die!"

And now, swifter than I can tell, the thought came to me how, in the vision of my night wanderings, he whom I loved had promised to be near me in every hour of danger in which I called. I called now—rather with my mind than with my lips, for I have always felt that the most powerful parts of prayer are the unspoken parts. I fixed my inner eye upon his image—that image which I kept locked up in my heart. I gazed on my fancy's picture with a look so intense that the image was burned into my soul. I do not know whether this inward sight of mine had anything to do with the strange thing which followed.

The fanatic came on, brandishing his weapon. He stood within an inch of me, and his eyes glared. "Do you accept me as your redeemer?" he said. "Sign or die!" I kept my gaze steadfastly fixed on the beautiful face in my heart, and said, " I have signed once ; I cannot revoke that writing." I felt, rather than saw, that his hand was raised ; the inner picture was between me and the dagger ; it was that alone which kept me from swooning. I was conscious of an arm uplifted to strike. Then I heard a great cry. It came not from me, but from my assailant. Suddenly he fell back. The glare of his eyes subsided into an expression of abject terror. He turned his look away from me and fixed it on a corner of the tent ; and in broken, hurried accents he began to speak.

" Who is it ? One of the guardian angels of the house of Palatine ? It must be. That is no island visitor. He never came in at the door. Do you not see him ? He bears in one hand a chalice, and in the other a cross of gold, and on his breast is fastened a parchment roll, very like my roll, but plainer. Even at this distance I can read the names on the roll, they are so legible ; and the first name is Ecclesia. He is coming nearer, nearer—this angel of the Palatines. He is burning me with his splendour ; he is blinding me with his light. If he touches me, I shall be consumed. Keep him back, Lady Ecclesia. Send him away. Speak a word of mercy for one of your old clan. I can fight with men, but not with spirits. He is coming nearer still. Save me, and you shall be free. Help! help! help!" And with a shriek that would have raised the dead the fanatic made wildly for the door, passed out into the open, and vanished from my life for ever. With his after fate I have here no concern. I was glad then, I am glad now, that he did not meet his end through me. In my own heart there was no room for aught but grateful love. I poured it out in that hour to him whose image of beauty, painted in my mind, had in some way to me unknown, and perhaps unknowable, been communicated to the eye of another and made to testify to the presence of a protective power.

CHAPTER XXV

THE SECOND WORLDLY TEMPTATION

YOU may be surprised to hear that I was able to resume my journey so soon after a scene so exciting. The truth is, I felt more refreshed after the scene than I had been before it. I had been refreshed by a presence; I had been saved by him whom I loved. I do not think, if I had been rescued by any other means, I would have been ready for the journey. Mere salvation from death would have left a pain behind. But when the hand that rescued was a hand of love, the weight of affliction was transformed into a more exceeding weight—a weight of glory.

In looking back I think the danger was sent to me for the sake of the presence, not the presence for the sake of the danger. I think what I wanted at that time was another manifestation of some sort. My reason for this belief

is that when we resumed our journey our road
became gradually more inland. Hitherto we had
kept sight of the sea. We now began to strike
into an interior direction, where the view of the
coast was impeded by foliage, and where the
murmur of the waters did not reach our ear.
Now I do not know what the men of Palatine
might feel, but to me the transition from the
sea-view to the land-view has always been spirit-
ually depressing. The tendency to look over
the waves, and dream of lands beyond, was born
with me. I could no more help it than I could
help thirst or hunger. And there was more
than that. The more I looked at the sea, the
better I lived on the land. Nothing to me ever
helped the realities of life like its so-called dreams.
Wherever these dreams were rare, wherever the
sight of the sea was faint and its murmur low,
wherever the odour of the brine had failed to
reach me and the breath of the deep ceased to
penetrate me, I had always felt that my walk
was less lofty and my steps less secure.

To lose sight of the sea, therefore, was to me
no advantage. In the depressed circumstances
in which I stood, I required the aid of every
stimulus which nature could furnish; and the
absence of this would have been a great loss if

it had not been counterbalanced by the imparting
of that other and higher stimulus—the sense of
communion with the object of my love. But I
had more to consider than myself in this matter.
I was afraid of the influence of a prosaic atmosphere on my domestics. I heard in the rear two
of my maid-servants laughing hilariously with
some of the military retainers of the house of
Palatine. Now I see no harm in hilarity either
between the same or different sexes. But it
seemed to me that this was not the time for
it. That the servants of my house should make
merry when that house itself was wrecked, its
master on the sea, and its mistress a captive,
perhaps on her road to death—that they should
be merry, moreover, in the companionship of those
very men who had wrecked the house, banished
the master, and imprisoned the mistress—appeared
to me a thing which indicated a moral decline
and called for grave reflection. Then a thought
of charity came to my aid. I remembered that
I had an equivalent for the sea which my father's
servants, with the exception of Phœbe, as yet
had not. I began to think that I had been too
harsh in my judgment. Was not this power to
be amused with trifles itself a gift of God to
those who had not reached the gate of real

pleasure? Should I not thank Him for it, praise Him for it? And about the sea itself there came another thought. Was it really lost? Would it recede farther the farther I advanced? No. It was not the distance which hid it; it was the foliage of the wood. It was hid only because I was not far enough up the hill. When I reached Palatine and looked down from the light of to-morrow's sun, I would get it all back again. It would burst upon me with all its full glory; it would break upon me with all its breezes. Palatine might take much from me—name, freedom, life itself. But even if it was my fate to die, I would have first the consolation of a sight reminding of home—that mysterious expanse where my Divine Father moved and where my human father sojourned.

We arrived at the second plateau. Here, according to arrangement, we pitched our tents and dined. I had the use of my own tent, and two of my domestics waited on me—the very two whose merriment had caused me such anxiety. In the circumstances I would have asked them to partake at the same table; but I felt they themselves would be happier elsewhere. I therefore dispensed with much serving, and dismissed them early to the rear. I kept Phœbe with me.

During the meal I experienced a renewal of my ascetic feelings. It was caused by a fresh outburst of that roistering mirth which had disturbed me on the march. It was now more pronounced because it was more general. The comforts of the dining hour, the relaxation after fatigue, the influence of companionship, perhaps above all the impulse to forget, tended to make my retainers oblivious of their care, and their voices were amongst the loudest. The men of Palatine had seen too much of life's comfortable side to be easily carried away by it; but to the servants of my house the superfluity was a new thing. This was in a measure their excuse. And yet I confess that to me it was like the clapping of hands over some amusing incident at a trial for life or death. The scenes through which they had passed had not been of a nature to dispel gravity in an hour. They had seen not only the sorrows of their own house but the sorrows of humanity. They had just been in contact with a hospital where the most prominent feature visible was the inhumanity of man to his brother, where the weakest were sent to the wall and only those preserved who had little need of a physician. Was this a state of things to make one smile? Was this a picture to evoke laughter or leave room for mirth? If the end of the old things had failed to sadden, surely there was much to make solemn in the aspect of the new.

After the meal I came out upon the plateau. My eyes rested first upon those of my own house. I was already anxious about them; I found something to strengthen my anxiety. I was startled to see that every member of the household, except Phœbe, had undergone a process of physical adornment. Upon the arm of each, whether male or female, was encircled a band of purple silk, into which, with threads of gold, was woven the form of an eagle. What did it mean? I knew well enough to whom the insignia belonged; they were badges of the house of Palatine. The purple was the symbol of dominion over the island, and the eagle was the family emblem of unretarded upward flight. But why did not the house of Palatine keep its symbols? What had they to do with me or mine? I sent Phœbe to inquire of her fellow-servants; I thought she might get more unreserved information than I. She returned in a few minutes and said: "They say they got them as a present from the captain of the guard, and they are loud in his praises. He gave them in simple kindness, with a view to make them look well and feel happy."

Two things were clear to me : they *did* fancy they looked well, and they did really feel happy. The first was a delusion : nobody looks well in a costume above his sphere, and none knew that better than the captain of the guard. Of course I detected that there was a concealed reason. But I was very glad my servants did not detect it. I was glad it took in their minds so harmless a form as the providing of a means of decoration. It was plaintive, if somewhat pitiful, to see how proud they were of their new toy—how they looked at it, handled it, dandled it, posed in attitudes where it could be prominently seen. There is no sin in men and women admiring beauty—not even their own beauty. The sole question is, What will they do with it? will they exhibit with it or will they minister with it? Remember, no girl ever had a clearer revelation of her own natural attractions than I had in that old mirror ; but to me it came not as a message of self-conceit, but as a command to self-sacrifice. Let me cease preaching, however, and proceed with my narrative.

While I was meditating on the occurrence, a hand was laid on my arm. I looked round, and the captain stood before me. He held out a band of identical nature to that which I had seen the

servants wear. "Lady Ecclesia," he said, "will
you oblige me by putting on this?"

"Why should *I* put it on?" I said. "It is a
badge of the house of Palatine."

"Lady Ecclesia," he replied, "let me speak to
you; let me reason with you. The pressure of
the time justifies my boldness. You are in great
danger. You are hurrying up the hill to an
unknown destiny. This night, or to-morrow at
latest, you will stand before the judgment-seat
of a man of peculiar sternness—a man who claims
to have received from fate the sovereignty of this
island, and who can brook no interference with
his prerogative. He has been much fretted of
late. He is suspicious of his own household;
he is more than suspicious of yours. You cannot
deny that your family has given him reason to
be angry; your clan was yesterday in open revolt.
With that movement you have professed to have
no sympathy. Show that you have none. Put
on this badge of loyalty to the present system of
things. Your servants have already assumed it."

"You forget," I said, "that they are no longer
my servants, or rather the servants of my father;
if they were, they would have had no choice in
this matter. But if I could assume your badge
as the servants do it, I would not scruple for two

minutes. It is to them a simple gew-gaw, a pretty
thing. If I could think it merely pretty, I would
put it on with pleasure; I believe I admire beauty
more than the house of Palatine does. But this
badge is not merely pretty; it is very solemn.
It is the statement of a creed; it is a confession
of faith. It is the declaration that I have taken
a particular life as the ideal of all life. I have
done that once, and I can do it no more. There
can be no two ideals in my universe."

"Lady Ecclesia," said the captain, "you are
wrong; your conscience is leading you mad. It
is no confession of faith you are asked to make;
it is no ideal of life you are pledged to follow.
You are desired merely to attest a present fact.
Let me put but one question. Do you or do
you not acknowledge that the Lord of Palatine
is now the ruler of this island?"

"I not only acknowledge it," I said, "but I
believe that up to this time he has been the ruler
of the island by divine right."

"Then," cried the captain, "all I ask is that you
should state that fact and that belief by wearing
on your arm the signs of his dominion."

"Pardon me," I answered, "to wear these signs
would imply very much more. What is a badge?
Is it not a mark to indicate that what I profess

is the best thing known to me? Do you think
the Lord of Palatine is the best thing known to
me? Do you think he is the hill to which I lift
up my eyes for aid? A starry night is better than
a starless one, and he that has never seen the
day may assume a badge in its honour. But I
have seen the day, and I cannot worship the star.
I believe the Lord of Palatine to be the best man
for the hour; but I do not believe the hour will
last for ever. Will he outlast it? That depends
on himself. He is fit for the old hour: will he
be adequate to the new? Who can tell? Shall
I presume to tell? Shall I take a pledge of
eternal fidelity to that which to-morrow may be
out of harmony with all things? I cannot; I
dare not. Over the servants I have no control,
and what they wear is to them no badge at all.
But in me it would be an act of treason. I have
already a badge. You saw it this morning at
the front of the military hospital. I cured by
it then; I live by it now; I can never replace
it by another."

"Lady Ecclesia," said the captain, and he had
lost his wonted calmness, "think you it is for the
sake of the Lord of Palatine that I plead with
you? Think you it is to preserve *his* ideal that
I ask you to wear this emblem? No, Lady

Ecclesia, it is to preserve your own. It is because I wear a badge for you that I ask you to wear one for the Lord of Palatine. What interest have I in him beyond the fact that he holds your life in his hands? Listen, for at last I shall speak. I am a rough soldier. I have been commissioned from youth to curb refractory spirits. I came to put the bonds on *you*. You were the physically frailest foe I had ever tackled; it was the meeting of extremes. But you conquered me—conquered in the moment of your surrender. You put the bonds on me which I meant for you. What is it, Lady Ecclesia, that has attracted my life to yours? Is it the contrast between man's strength and woman's weakness? No; it is the discovery that the weakness may be strong. It was your *strength* that made me admire you; I have been true to the instincts of my clan. Your beauty might have sufficed for a retainer of Hellenicus, but hardly for a servant of the Lord of Palatine. What I admired in you was the kindred element of power. I saw you stand in your father's house and plead for your own condemnation; and the iron of your courage attracted my soul. I saw you in that house again—in the terror of yester-eve and the tragedy of this morning's dawn. I saw you alone, yet undismayed, deserted, yet fearless, clinging like the ivy to a ruined wall; and I swore a great oath within my heart, and cried, 'This is not a life which I shall suffer to perish.'"

I grasped his hand, for I was touched. "And do you know," I said, "why your words gratify me? It is because I feel that they are not meant for me. That which you admire in me is not mine. It is a reflection. It is what the blue is to the sea, what the red is to the rose. It has been painted into my heart by a great light—the light of love. I have seen one who has transformed me—him whom I followed down to the valleys, him whom I now follow up the hill. Men say that he is dead, but it is not true. He is the light of all my days; he is the flower of all my ways; he is the hymn of all my praise. If I could sing from morn to eve, there would be but one cadence, 'I love him, I love him, I love him.' I am not ashamed of my love. I hide it not; I blush for it not; I veil it not in the face of the Lord of Palatine. I vaunt it; I am proud of it; I rejoice in it. I bear on my breast the badge of my devotion, and no other badge shall ever come near it."

As I finished speaking I drew forth the little cross and kissed it. There were two things I

wanted the captain to feel—that I accepted the
sympathy he expressed, and that I had warded
off the hope he had left unexpressed. I felt that
if to the mind of this man I myself should become
a substitute for my cause, it would be building
for him an impossible aim. I wanted to keep
him for the cause, not for me ; therefore I threw
into the foreground the preoccupation of my
heart. For his part I am bound to state that
I think anxiety covered every other feeling. "Are
you determined then," he said, "to refuse this
conformity ? " "Absolutely," I replied. "Then,"
said he, with a strange identification of interest,
"may the God of your fathers help us ! "

CHAPTER XXVI

PALATINE HOUSE

YOU will remember the arrangement was that after dining on the second plateau I was to abandon the foot march, and, mounting horse, was to ride forward with the captain in advance. This latter part of the journey therefore, though the most difficult, was likely to be that of the quickest movement. It was like the stages of life itself. The later stages are more arduous than the earlier; yet I think we move quicker through them.

As I was now within measurable distance of the House of Palatine, I began to contemplate the nature of that house. Of course I had seen it before. During the days of my friendship with Hellenicus I had been more than once within its courts. I was no stranger to its peculiarities either outside or inside. It was this very fact which gave me food for contemplation. If Palatine had been to me an unknown quantity, anxious thought might have been forgotten in curiosity.

I think, therefore, this will be the best time to indicate the peculiarities of the house into which I was going. I am no advocate for occupying a narrative of life with a description of buildings. I shall not consider this building in detail. I shall confine myself to that which was distinctive about it—to that which is significant of the House of Palatine. There is a correspondence between the dress and the mind. The house of the Lord of Palatine was like its master. It was the miniature of his dominion everywhere. It expressed in small compass the whole character of the man. The plan of such a dwelling deserves a moment's notice.

When one had proceeded for some way through the grounds of Palatine, the avenue leading to the house broke into two paths—one sloping upward, the other running level. These two paths were joined by the house, which had two entrances—one on the low ground, the other on the high. The former faced the south; the latter looked to the north. The first, or ground-floor entrance, was approached from the low road, and was set apart exclusively for the domestics and household retainers. This lower part of the house contained two stories. They were both appropriated to the servants—that on the ground floor for culinary operations, and that immediately above for sleeping accommodation. The entrance on the upper road, which faced the opposite direction, was kept exclusively for the Lord of Palatine and his guests. This part of the building differed from the lower part in having windows both to the north and to the south. Here also there were two stories. The first story consisted of dining-rooms, sitting-rooms, libraries, and the great hall of judgment; the second contained a suite of bedrooms.

Between the lower and higher parts of this building there ran an inside stair, which formed the channel of communication for the domestics. I say "for the domestics." The only communication desired by the Lord of Palatine was on the part of the servants. It was essential that they should come up to *him*; but he did not wish ever to go down to them. In point of fact he never did go down. He went in and out by a different gate. He walked on a higher level. He moved on his own ground. The voices of his domestics, except when they served him, never reached his ear; their laughter and their tears were alike inaudible. He provided for their wants, but he provided at a distance. He was to them what the God of heaven was to us—a majestic power in the air, a presence they were bound to obey, but which in their own sphere they could never meet.

The house was, in fact, an architectural deception. Looked at in the distance, it presented an aspect of unity. It seemed to be a gigantic centre for all classes in the island, a place where could meet the representatives of every order of men. One felt that he was beholding an umbrageous tree, beneath whose ample shade the different ranks of mankind, caught in a common shower, could gather together for a few moments, and forget their differences in the sense of a common protection.

But how unlike all this was the fact. When the traveller came near, the illusion vanished which the distance had yielded. Here was indeed a single building : but was it really a single house ? Its parts were rigidly connected so far as stone and lime could connect them. There was even provided a means of inward communication between the lower and the higher stories. But there was also provided a means by which the inmate of the upper stories could avoid this communication—a means by which he could, if he liked, pass by on the other side. And he did like ; there lay the barrier. No inmates of any two dwellings could be farther apart than the occupants of these two respective stories. Architecture had provided for their union, but the will of man had severed them. As one of our poets would have put it, the fire and the wood were there, but not the burnt-offering. All the materials were present for a sacrifice of human pride ; but human pride itself refused to be sacrificed. So far as the descent of the master was concerned the inside stair was useless. The house was very like an allegory of what this island might have been ; and I have more than once caught myself thinking what a splendid residence it would be if the Lord of Palatine were to become an adherent of the man of the valleys.

The shades of evening had already fallen when, in company with the captain of the guard, I rode into the avenue which led to this remarkable building. He had signalled his arrival by the shrill blast of a special instrument devised for the purpose, whose sound carried far. A messenger met him at the gate. He told the captain it was impossible the Lord of Palatine could see the prisoner to-night. I was to be kept in the state prison till the morning. It was an edifice in the lower grounds. It was set apart exclusively for offenders of the graver sort—that is to say, for those whose crime was supposed to have not merely an individual but a public interest. The charge against me was that of no private wrong. I was impeached with treason. I was accused of conniving against the established order, of inciting to rebellion against the recognised ruler of the island. The imputation was based on the fact that I had advocated the cause of the valleys, declared myself a disciple of him who broke the gates of brass and brought humanity to man. I gloried in the avowal ; but I denied then, and I deny now, that it implied any detriment to the Lord of Palatine.

We came to the cross roads ; we took the lower. On the way to the prison we had to pass the ground floor of Palatine House. The avenue looked very cheerless amid the gathering shadows, and something of its gloom began to steal in upon myself. It was to me the road to prison, which to me meant a state of practical uselessness. Examine your life and you will find that its saddest moments were the moments of its enforced inactivity, the days when it was walled in and compelled to stand still. Such a prospect did this avenue present to me. I felt as if I were stranded, buried, cut off from the development of the island. And yet, would you believe it, this moment in which I trod the lower ground of Palatine was, quite unconsciously to me, the most effective moment my life had ever known.

There was about to happen a circumstance, not only too trivial to be noticed by any history, but too trivial to be put in any diary, which was to produce an effect on this island, compared with which all its pageants were but dust and ashes.

At a short distance from the house we found the way blocked. A crowd of male and female servants stood round a hand-barrow which held a sack of provisions. Two men were quarrelling violently over it, and there was evidently the prospect of a free fight. The cause of the dispute was really the question of the division of labour. One of the men asserted that to wheel the barrow farther was beyond his province, that the portion of ground allotted to him ended at this particular spot, and that the rest of the process devolved upon his neighbour servant. The other with equal vehemence maintained that it was not a question of ground at all, but of special work—that this special work had been assigned to him, and that he was bound to finish it on his own account.

Now do not imagine that in the mind of either of these belligerents the grievance was one of hard work. The barrow was so light that a child could have wheeled it easily. The sack which it carried was long, but of no weight whatever. The distance to which it was to be rolled was very short—only to a neighbouring cellar, which I had to pass on my way to the prison. Neither of the men would have pretended that it was a question of fatigue. It was not even a question of soiled hands, though the hands might get a little soiled. It was a question of dignity. It was assumed by both that to work was an undignified thing. Both had been compelled to work, and therefore both were more or less undignified. But it was better to be less than more. Each felt that the man who did least work was the nearest to the gentleman.

As we came up the wrangling ceased. Many eyes were directed towards me. I saw that by some at least I was recognised, for I heard the words pass from lip to lip, " Lady Ecclesia." They evidently did not think one less a lady because she was going to prison, though they deemed one no gentleman who could drive a wheelbarrow.

When I had ascertained what was the matter, and inquired the destination of the contemned vehicle, I asked the crowd to stand aside, and offered to reconcile parties. " I am going just in that direction," I said, "and shall relieve both of you." So saying, I stepped forward, lifted the handles of the barrow and wheeled it towards the goal.

The domestics followed. The feeling in their

minds was not amusement, not even curiosity ;
it was awestruckness. They felt as those feel
who are beholding a new sign in the heavens.
That the Lady Ecclesia should go to prison was
in the order of things ; but that the Lady Ecclesia
should do common work was something which
took away their breath. I spoke to them as I
rolled my burden on. " Do not think," I said,
" that I am condescending ; I am educating myself.
Have you not heard of the great discovery which
has been made ? After long searching we have
at last received tidings of a land beyond the sea.
We have learned that there is a country where all
the higher people do the work, and all the lower
orders are served. Now I am quite sure there
is a time coming when the sea will be dried up,
and all the people in this island will be transported
by land to the other side. When we get there,
we shall find that the men and women most fit
to do menial work shall be put at the top. And
as I am the Lady Ecclesia, and have been accustomed to be at the top, I would not like to come
down. I am therefore training myself to be a
servant. Servants are all the rage there. The
fashion of this island passes away, and the fashion
of the opposite land is coming. What we here
call ' up ' will there be called ' down.' Should

not you and I be preparing ourselves by hard work ? "

I saw I had produced a profound impression, and it was not long in taking definite form. In a few minutes the two belligerents came up. They were still at variance, but they were no longer at variance on the old ground. Each insisted on resuming his work—not as a matter of chivalry to me, but as a matter of personal privilege. It was like men who had sold a piece of ground suddenly finding that there was a treasure buried beneath it. Each asserted with vehemence his claim to be the carrier ; each urged the argument his rival had used against himself. Words ran high, and the crowd again gathered, in search of that which is dearest to the Palatine mind—a trial of physical strength. I really feared they were coming to blows. I prevented it by running on in the same strain. "Do you think," I said, "that I am going to give up the barrow to either of you ? You would never be so selfish as to take from me my chance. It is the only chance I may have for years. You have a great privilege ; you have so much work to do that, if you are not in the front row, it will be your own fault. But I have had few opportunities. Till the age of eighteen I was a dreamer ; after that I was a gay lady ; then I was a poor invalid. I want to be something more than any of these. How am I to get a high place in the land beyond the wave if I don't get into service? No, no; you must not rob me of my burden till I reach the cellar door; and while I am here you must give me every chance of helping you. If the steward has any difficult accounts to add up, he might send them to me in prison."

Reader, what had I done? "Made yourself immensely popular," you say. "Reconciled two servants," thought I. Both answers are wide of the mark. Little did I know that by the most trivial of all acts I had turned the stream of history. What I had reconciled was not the minds of two servants, but all service to the heart of man. At that moment, quite unconsciously to myself, I was standing in the dawn of a new day; looking back, I can say with an old writer, " Surely the Lord was in this place, and I knew it not." I have heard much in after years of the abolition of compulsory service; but the first step in that abolition had been taken to-day. By a stroke whose potency I did not dream of, I had made service voluntary for evermore. I had made it an object of desire, not of aversion. The real chain is not on the body, but on the mind. I had broken the chain on the mind, and without a change of place I had set the prisoner free. These primitive souls had been captured by a new association. Work, menial work, had in their imagination been dignified, glorified. It was no longer the part of a slave; it was the profession of Lady Ecclesia, daughter of Moses ben-Israel. It was no longer a barrier to promotion; it was the necessary training for promotion. It was no longer a distinction from the men and women of fashion; it was itself to be the fashion of the age which was to come. I think, for the first time at that moment, the words of an ancient poet began to receive fulfilment: "Every valley shall be exalted; the crooked shall be made straight, and the rough places plain."

CHAPTER XXVII

IN THE HALL OF JUDGMENT

IT was morning, and my summons had come A message had been sent by the Lord of Palatine that he would meet the prisoner at noon in the hall of judgment on the upper floor, and that in the first instance he would meet her alone. I was struck with this latter announcement. Surely the Lord of Palatine was becoming more arbitrary, more self-asserting. He never used to act alone—never wished to be thought of as an autocrat. In the conclave where last I had seen him he had laboured to impress the assembly with the belief that he sought their advice and desired their countenance. He had given a representative voice to every part of the building, and had asked the physicians of a past generation to prescribe for the present need. Now he had set every one aside. He was calling no assembly; he was summoning no conclave. He was acting as if he were the island personified. He was breaking the very semblance of a constitutional rule. I could not but look with dismay upon the prospect of being subjected to the scrutiny of a private individual, whose will had been rendered imperious by the troubles of his own house.

Later came another message. The Lord of Palatine desired that the prisoner should be led up from the ground floor by the inner stair. For a moment my old pride blazed out. Who was he that he should treat me as one of his domestics? Then a voice said within me, "Ecclesia, have you forgotten your own saying of last night, that domestics shall be all the rage in the fashion of the future? You ought to be ashamed of yourself, Ecclesia." And so I was; and I breathed a little prayer—shall I not say, rather, a little wish?—to him whom I loved, that he would keep my spirit ever in the thought that the way through the valleys was the way to life.

By-and-by there was a tap at the cell-door. I opened it, and my heart leapt for joy; it was Phœbe. She had followed in the rear with the other domestics. As the journey by foot was long and steep, they had pitched their tents for the night, and had only arrived this morning. She told me the captain of the guard had given her free permission to come and prepare me with my toilet for meeting the Lord of Palatine.

Phœbe was very anxious that I should dress well ; she retained even yet the influence of the house of Hellenicus. She wanted me to make an impression, with a view to my acquittal. She had put in my trunk some of my costliest articles of raiment, and they had been brought by one of the waggons which carried the camp baggage. I was deeply grateful to the poor girl for her devotion, but I firmly refused her advice. "No, dear Phœbe," I said, "I shall keep the dress of yesterday—the plain travelling dress suited to the dusty way. Have not I declined to wear the badge of the Lord of Palatine ? Do you think I shall wear one of myself. I do not wish to defend myself ; I wish to defend him whom I love. It would be no joy to me if he were accepted for my sake ; it would be the worst pain I have ever known. I go to speak for *him*, to clear him, to glorify him. There is no acquittal for me which is not an acquittal for him. If he is condemned, I am condemned with him ; if he is absolved, I am well content to die."

At five minutes before noon I was led forth by the captain of the guard. I passed through the adjoining walk of the lower grounds ; I entered

Palatine House by the servants' door. They were all there, crowded in the hall. Their faces were all sorrowful, some tearful; they bowed to me with deep respect. I ascended the long stair, which was the symbol of domestic obedience. The first room on the summit was the great hall of judgment. My heart palpitated as the latch of the door was lifted. "Now, Lady Ecclesia," said the captain, "I must leave you; you are alone; be discreet as well as brave."

I entered, and the door was shut behind me; it was as if I had parted from my past for evermore. It was an apartment of enormous size, furnished chiefly with benches, chairs, and busts of the Lords of Palatine. In the centre was an elevated platform, with steps leading up to it; but to-day it was unoccupied. My first impression was that the whole room was unoccupied, save by the busts of the dead. Presently my eye lighted on a figure seated at a writing-table. He looked up as I entered, and I recognised him.

Did I? Hardly. Was that indeed the Lord of Palatine? Was that the man I had known in past years as the brother of Hellenicus? Was that the man I had last seen presiding with eagle eye over the conclave of the island? I would almost have imagined that the old family had become extinct, and that the estate had passed into other hands. His face was at once more impetuous and less commanding. There was the old fire, but not the old confidence. He had an air of unrest about him, as that of one who has lost his way.

But if I was surprised at the change in *his* appearance, so evidently was he at that in mine. He started visibly when he looked at me, and for a few moments he gazed in astonishment. Yet he had seen me before. Had anything happened in the interval to alter me? Oh yes; it all flashed upon me in a moment. I remembered that night in which I had first seen the vision that became the ideal of my love and of my life. I remembered the strange increase of beauty that had come to me. I remembered the fascinated gaze of the servants next morning at the hour of prayer. I remembered the expressed admiration of my father. I remembered the sight of my own face in the mirror. I began to understand how, in spite of my plain attire, the Lord of Palatine was attracted.

All this observation and reflection occupied only a few seconds. Suddenly the master of the island seemed to recollect himself. He replaced the look of interest by an expression of haughty disdain. He was evidently determined to treat me as his prisoner.   He did not salute me in any way.   He signed to me to be seated—rather with the air of one who issues a mandate than of one who offers an invitation. I obeyed, and presently he addressed me.

"Lady Ecclesia, it is not without regret that I meet you thus to-day.   You are descended from one of the oldest lines in this island, and with some of your clan I have found friends in council.   But my position in this island makes it imperative on me to be no respecter of persons ; and no height of descent shall induce me to ignore the claims of justice."

"My Lord of Palatine," I said, "my confidence in coming into your presence is not the remembrance of my descent, but of my ascent.   You have done me a very great service in making me climb from the ground floor instead of entering by the upper way.   You have caused me to remember what I am sometimes in danger of forgetting—that I have become a child of the valleys.   It is as such, my Lord of Palatine, that I come to you.   I come to-day not from the height, but from the vale—from the land of those who labour, from the touch of those who toil.   Do not think of my long ancestry ; the ancestry I claim is the length of your stair.

I am proud of having come up to you from the
ranks of your people. I am proud to stand before
you as one whose only claim to recognition is
the possession of the common want and the
sympathy with the common weal."

"Ha!" cried the Lord of Palatine, "here is a
refrain of that new evangel of which we have
heard so much lately. And this reminds me of
the accusation on which you appear before me.
In what you call sympathy with the common weal
you have sought to subvert my personal dominion,
and to alter the constitution of this island as by
law established. You have been the ringleader
of a pestilent superstition rooted in the spirit of
anarchy. You have lent your name to the cause of
a man who has claimed still higher credentials than
yours, and claimed them with the view of stimu-
lating popular revolt. There are charges of the
gravest character labelled on this paper before me;
and, by the house of my fathers, you shall answer
them or die!"

"And let me begin," I said, "with that which
you have just made—that I have been the ringleader of a pestilent superstition. The superstition
you speak of was intended to take away pestilence,
and it fulfilled its design. I was never privileged
to be its ringleader; I was at first a mere spec-

tator; I have at best felt myself to be only a
follower. But I have seen what you have not
seen. I have seen this man of the valleys giving
beauty to ashes, the oil of joy to mourning, the
garment of praise to the spirit of heaviness. I
have seen him take the burdens of the weary
and the pains of the wounded and the crosses of
the careworn. I have seen him transform that
valley which adjoins the house of my father from
a scene of misery into a land of promise. I have
seen——"

"Stop!" cried the Lord of Palatine: "to what
end is this harangue? Shall we judge the day by
its morning when we have seen its afternoon? Do
I not know, do *you* not know, what has been the
outcome of all this? Anarchy, rebellion, the dis-
solution of social ties, the breaking of old bonds,
the trampling underfoot of the established order.
Have you not yourself come red-handed from the
scene of revolution? Have not you and your
father cherished in your hearts a scheme for sub-
verting the government of this island? Have you
not devised by secret counsels a plan by which the
ascendency in this commonwealth shall pass from
my hands to yours? How do you reconcile this
with the ideal of humility which you profess to
follow?"

"I do not reconcile it," I exclaimed; "my defence is that it is irreconcilable. I say it is impossible for any follower of the man of the valleys to approve of that rebellion. *I* do not. I lament it; I deplore it. My father, unknown to me, has been borne down by the stream. He has done wrong, and I shall plead for his pardon. But meantime I plead not for pardon, but for justice—not for justice to myself, but to him whom I love. I ask you to believe that none would shed such bitter tears over this rebellion as he whom they call the man of the valleys."

"What right had the man to be in the valleys?" cried the Lord of Palatine; "what right had *you* to be in the valleys? Did not a conclave of this island forbid it? Did not I myself give the choice between obedience and death?"

"And he *accepted* your alternative, my Lord of Palatine. He did not seek a course between the extremes. He did not slink into the valleys by stealth; he *chose* to die because he loved so fondly. I too have accepted your alternative. I too have gone down into the valley—not to avoid your decree, but to receive the fruit of its violation. I have braved death to follow him."

As I uttered these words the face of the Lord of Palatine again betrayed that appearance of admiration which had so struck me. If I had broken into sobs, I believe he would have suppressed it. What attracted him was the glimpse in a woman of his own ideal of manliness. By-and-by he resumed something of his sternness; but from this point in the interview I had the impression that he was a man battling against himself.

"You say that the movement in which you were interested was unconnected with your father's rebellion. What do you make of this?" He drew something from a private drawer. Great Heaven! It was the roll I had seen in the valley—the roll I had signed in the vision of the night.

"This," he resumed, "was found in the possession of him whom you call the man of the valleys. Whether it has the atmosphere of humility about it I leave you to judge. It purports to be a list of those who have already inscribed their names in a document modestly styled the 'Book of Life.' It is called the 'Book of Life' to indicate that the names therein written shall survive all other names —especially, I presume, the name of Palatine. Is this the offspring of humility?"

"It is, my Lord of Palatine, for there is nothing that can survive but the spirit of self-sacrifice; and if your house shall survive, it must be by that spirit. But think you that this roll is meant to lessen the roll of your retainers? Why then did I labour yestermorn to increase the number of your men preserved from war's destruction? May I ask if the captain of the guard has told you what happened?"

"He has sent me a report this morning, but I have never opened it."

"Could you kindly open it now?"

He obeyed. Strange that in circumstances like these I should speak of the Lord of Palatine obeying. Yet I had a curious sensation of becoming the active instead of the passive party in the interview. He bent for some time over the parchment. The silence was broken by a few involuntary exclamations on his part. Then he looked up and asked, "Is this true?"

"My Lord of Palatine," I said, "you can verify it for yourself. You have the command of the hospital. Seek, inquire, investigate. You will find that the wards are full which used to be almost empty. Is not this a hopeful sign?"

"And how has it been done? The captain speaks of a golden cross which your hand alone could use. Have you the instrument about you? I would fain examine it."

I drew out the little cross and gave it to him.

In the process my hand for a moment touched his hand. It was the first outward contact between the valley and the mountain. I felt a thrill of vibration in the hand of the Lord of Palatine. Had an influence passed from me to him? He looked for a long time fixedly at the little instrument. There are children who are so eager to know the secret of their plaything's charm that they break it in pieces to see what is inside of it. The Lord of Palatine looked as if he would like to do that. "You can't break it," I said. "You can piece it on to other things if you like, but you can't take itself to pieces; it is one and indivisible; it will submit to no analysis."

"May I keep it for a while?"

I started—not at the proposal, but at the request. "Certainly: but why does the Lord of Palatine ask of his prisoner as a favour what he can demand as a right?"

"Do not think me more generous than I am. If the cross were of any use to me without your aid, I would have taken it, not asked it. Stay, this reminds me there is something in this room which we did take unasked. We took from your father's house one of those vials which the man of the valleys filled. It was found on the person of a servant-maid, and declared by yourself to have been given her by you. That vial is suspected of containing matter destructive to life. What say you, Lady Ecclesia?"

" That it contains matter vivifying to life."

" Have you any witnesses?"

" Hundreds among the men of the valleys; only two here—myself and the servant-maid you speak of. I shall taste the liquid in your presence to prove its harmlessness."

" I am afraid, after the experience of the hospital, the testimony would not be deemed altogether conclusive. You seem to have a power over disease; perhaps you may have given it to your maid also."

For an instant I felt as if the way was barred. Then, flashing like an inspiration, there came to me a great thought, a bold thought, one of those thoughts that rise to us only in emergencies. " Be it so, my Lord of Palatine," I said ; " I shall produce a witness from whose testimony there shall be no appeal—a witness whose evidence shall be undisputed and indisputable, and whose authority shall be paramount even with you. Bring forth the vial, and I shall call the witness."

CHAPTER XXVIII

THE JUDGMENT

HE held up the little vial, and the red liquid sparkled in the sun. My heart went back with a great bound. I stood again in the shadows of the night, and saw the one form to me in all the world.

"Now, Lady Ecclesia," said my judge, "fulfil your pledge. I have produced the altar: where is the victim? Have you found a man or woman outside of your interest who is willing to be your witness to the innocuous character of this liquid?"

"I have."

"Name that witness, and I shall summon him at a moment's notice."

"There is no need; he is here."

He cast round the room a quick, suspicious glance. Then compassion overspread his face He evidently thought I was under the influence of insanity, and believed an unseen help to be in the room which would be made visible when the time came. "Ah, Lady Ecclesia," he said, "the aid you seek is not admissible to courts of law. We require a witness of flesh and blood."

"And he is here," I repeated. "I bring no ghostly agency to testify to my truth. My witness shall be in the flesh, not in the spirit."

"And who is this remarkable man who is so near that he needs no summoning, yet of whose presence I see no sign?"

"You, my Lord of Palatine—you yourself."

His face expressed blank amazement. For a moment he seemed to doubt if he had heard aright. I fixed my eyes full upon him; I had observed that whenever I did so the fascination returned. "You, my Lord of Palatine, shall be my witness this day. Yours shall be the testimony which shall go forth to all the island and to all the years that this is not a draught of death. The records of your house tell how your ancestors of old time vindicated the honour of woman. You shall do it again to-day. You shall trust me; you shall taste this liquid; you shall make the plunge of faith. And why shall you trust me? Because I, your prisoner, have trusted you. I have put into your hands the

dearest possession I have ; all the riches of the
island would not make up for its loss. I might
have concealed my possession of the treasure ;
but I trusted you. I knew you to be a man—
a man of Palatine. I felt that, however arbitrary
you may be, however relentless, however inexor-
able, you are just. I recognised a stream of
blood in your veins as free from the taint of
meanness as the red liquid in that vial. I trusted
you. I paid you a more true act of homage
than if I had put on the badge of the house
of Palatine. Think you that chivalry can be
given only from the strong to the weak? It
can come from the weak to the strong. I have
been chivalrous to you, my Lord of Palatine.
I have reposed my faith in you in the hour of
my dependence, in the hour when you have
broken my wing. Give me back the trust I gave
to you—not the thing I entrusted, but the spirit
in which I gave it. Repose in the bird with
broken wing that faith which, even with broken
wing, the bird has reposed in the honour of her
fowler."

I ceased. There was a moment's silence, like
the pause of the traveller at the meeting of two
crossways. Before my eyes floated the image
of him I loved, and with my heart I called on

him. Then a soft light swept over the stern face of the Lord of Palatine—a light which mitigated its sternness without lessening its character. In that moment he left his brother Hellenicus far behind even in the race for beauty. He poised the vial an instant in his hand; then calmly, fearlessly he raised it to his lips and said, " I will be your witness, Lady Ecclesia."

It was done. With almost any other man I would have awaited the result with some anxiety. It is true I knew that the liquid was harmless; but I knew also that the most harmless things may become hurtful if they are drugged by the imagination. This vial had been tabooed throughout the island as a dangerous thing. It was like the traditional water of Marah. Men had called it bitter beforehand; and what we prejudge as bitter is apt to become so in its effects. As it was, I knew the Lord of Palatine was incapable of fear. What would be the influence of this liquid? I had seen how it acted on Phœbe; it had supplied her one need—strength of character. The Lord of Palatine had too much strength of character already; what he wanted was a sense of dependence—shall I not rather say, the confession that he had it? No one shall convince me that he did not already feel the burden to be too heavy for him. If he could only accept a higher power, I knew he must give in.

Presently he sprang from the chair on which he was sitting, with a quick, convulsive movement. Was he ill? Was he angry? Was he ashamed of having played the part of a disciple? I thought he was going to address me. No; he was looking right ahead. He was staring into the corner, like the man I had seen on the first plateau—but with a difference. That had been a look of fear; there was no fear on the face of the Lord of Palatine. There was an expression no one had ever seen there before, the only thing wanted to make him look noble— wonder. For the first time in his life he was awestruck, passive, reverent, conscious of a greater power in the island. One moment he gazed spellbound; then on the floor of his own judgment-hall he dropped upon his knees.

"Man of the valleys," he cried, "you have conquered. Be you whom you may, come you whence you may, you have beaten me in the battle, and I yield. You have burst the bars of my dwelling and surprised me in my judgment-hall; yours is the last judgment, and I bow. I throw my crown at your feet to take it from your hand. Henceforth I shall reign for you—only for you."

I was now seriously alarmed. I had never feared the Lord of Palatine's power; I trembled before his humility. Those who have seen a strong man for the first time weep will know something of my sensation. Never had the Lord of Palatine been to me so awful as in that moment of prostration. I felt as if I had extinguished an oak of the forest. I forgot the gulf between the prisoner and the judge. I forgot the etiquette between the man and the woman. I ran forward. I took him by the hand. I led him back passively to the old place. "Are you ill, my Lord of Palatine?" I said. "Do you not know me? I am Ecclesia, your prisoner."

"No," he said, "I am yours; the last judgment has reversed the first. Let me feel the touch of your hand; there is a light in my eyes which hides the sight of you. Did you not see that presence?"

"I have seen no presence in the room but yours."

"There has never been such a form within the walls of Palatine. I have seen beautiful men like my brother Hellenicus; but their beauty seemed a reproach to them. This man's beauty was power—invincible power, compelling power. My pride went down before him like a leaf before the hurricane. He stood there with the figure of a man and the face of a God; and in his hand was a golden cup which sparkled with the very liquid in this vial; and on his breast was a golden cross—the very image of the cross I hold; and on the cross were written golden letters, and the words were these, 'By this conquer.'"

He rose hurriedly and paced the room, as if to dispel sentiment. Even at this hour the Lord of Palatine was true to himself; he made a strength of his very humility. "And by this I *shall* conquer," he said. "I shall make a new empire in this island, and the sons of Palatine shall bow to the man of the valleys. I shall have his picture hung in every hamlet, that the mothers may know what I want their children to be. Lady Ecclesia, do you know that wondrous art by which men inscribe upon the canvas the likeness of what they love? It is not common either to your clan or mine; but you are above your clan and mine. You have the lineaments of this man's face and form painted in your heart. Could you express them to the eyes of the island? I could get thousands of impressions taken."

"I am an indifferent artist, my Lord of Palatine; and were I great and gifted, this form and face would transcend me. But if my art is poor, my love, I think, is almost perfect. It may be that love may lend wings to soar where the feet cannot climb. As you say, I need no creative genius; the lineaments have been painted within me. Can I express that which is within me? Poorly, dimly. My pencil can only follow afar off. His beauty runs before me and escapes me. All I could hope to catch would be the sight of him in the distance. I tremble, but I shall try."

"Yes, and you shall succeed; and a new morning shall dawn; and this aged island shall grow young again. And I shall plant the impress of this picture at the threshold of every path of youth—in the market-place, in the forum, in the camp, in the chapel, in the festive gathering, in the servants' hall. It shall be to the young men and women of this island what the bush was to your ancestor Moses; it shall set them on fire before they go. The mountain shall be kindled by the rays of the valley, and Palatine shall bask in the light of the evening sun."

"And what of mature years, my Lord of Palatine? You speak of those on the threshold: what of those who have passed the threshold and gone wrong? My ancestor Moses was no youth when he saw the bush. What of my father? You have heard from the captain's report how he is out on the salt sea. Shall no effort be made to rekindle *his* morning?"

"Yes, yes, yes; my ships shall scour the waves in search of him. We shall seek him; if alive, we shall bring him back to you. That sea has for me a new significance. It used to be but so much salt and water; it now beckons me on by its mystery. Never fear, Lady Ecclesia; we shall yet pierce the veil. But have you nothing more to ask than this? I at least have something more to offer." And the Lord of Palatine uttered words which demand a chapter of their own.

CHAPTER XXIX

THE THIRD WORLDLY TEMPTATION

WHAT I am going to relate may be deemed a psychological absurdity. That a judge should pass in a brief interview from a conviction of the prisoner's guilt to a persuasion of the prisoner's innocence is not a strange thing. But that a man in the course of a brief interview with a woman should pass from an attitude of vituperation into the extremest possible opposite may seem contrary to all rule. I would remind the reader, however, whether he be in this island or in regions yet unexplored, that the time passed in this interview was time on the mount. I was conscious all through of an accelerating process by which every moment carried the weight of a day. There are flowers which spring up in a night. Do you think they are specially privileged? Do you think they have been allowed to escape a little bit of the process of natural growth? No, gentle reader, a thousand times no. Their process has only been quickened; not a link has been wanting which is found in the ordinary chain. So was it here. There are moments in our lives which do for us what they do for the flowers—concentrate much work into a very small space. We measure such moments as God measures them—not by their length, but by their largeness. I can only say that in the whole course of this interview there was nothing which came to me with a sense of abruptness—nothing which seemed to break the sequence of the seedtime and the harvest. One day may be as a thousand years; but it will climb the steps of the years.

The Lord of Palatine had something to say. He signed to me to be seated; but he placed me no longer opposite to him, but beside him. Then he uttered one word which startled me—" Ecclesia." He had never used that form of address to the prisoner at the bar; the handle was dropped, and I trembled. " Ecclesia, will you reign with me? Will you help me to train the youth of this island to be followers of the man of the valleys? Are you surprised, Ecclesia, that I am so prosaic? Every bird has its own song, and I have mine. I have never been a man of romance—never looked beyond the needs of the common day. My brother

Hellenicus would have poured forth the notes of the lark ; he would have told you of your beauty and of his desire. I too know your beauty ; it has a touch of the form I saw to-day. But from my youth up I have weighed everything for what it can bring. Hellenicus would say, 'What a source of joy!' I say, 'What a power for good!' I do not think even your beauty would have moved me if I had not seen this power. I have beheld fair women in my day. I have seen them flash through the courts of Hellenicus ; I have beheld them sparkle at the board of Palatine. But never till now have I looked upon her of whom I could say, 'This woman would help me to reign.' Never till now have I seen the possibility of a helpmeet. Never till now have I believed that woman has a place in the history of man. You may deem mine a prosaic wooing ; but no daughter of Palatine has had a tribute like yours. Will you be my bride, Ecclesia?"

As he ceased the room ran round. Never in all my life before or since have I felt so excited. What! says the reader, after such a wooden love-making? Yes. Leaving the daughters of Palatine out of the question, it was the greatest tribute I at least had ever received. It was more than that It was the greatest temptation which had ever

befallen me. You will remember how as a girl
the dream of empire had swam before my eyes—
not for myself, but for my father. Now again it
glittered, and again it was not for myself. I say
calmly, conscientiously, there was not in my soul
one thought of personal ambition. "Will you help
me to train the youth of this island to be followers
of the man of the valleys?" So had run the words
of the Lord of Palatine; so ran the refrain in my
heart. An empire for *him*—him whom I loved:
was it not the crown of all desire? To reach at a
bound what might take years of pain, to compass
at a step what centuries might not see—it was a
thought of maddening joy. It seemed as if God
had rolled His purpose into my hands, and bade
me act for Him; a thousand voices kept singing in
my ear, "Answer 'Yes,' Ecclesia—answer 'Yes.'"

You will see that this temptation at the top of
the hill was different from those on the first and
second plateaus. Those were suggested from without. They had never had a voice within me. They
had been rejected as soon as proposed. But this
was my own desire personified. It sounded like
an echo of the divine will. It said: "Ecclesia,
here is a short and easy method for you. You can
change the worship of this island in a day. You
can command that the life of the valleys shall be

the life of the hill.   Heaven has put a rod into your
hand by which you can force the world into virtue.
Take the rod, Ecclesia.   Grasp the reins of empire
and drive the steeds where you will—nearer to
him, nearer ever to him   Leave not these un-
tutored lives to choose their own way.   Choose it
for them, Ecclesia ; drive them into it ; refuse to
let them ponder ; only reign, reign, reign."

Then it all flashed upon me—the utter wrong of
this seeming right.   The mask fell from my eyes,
and I saw it could not be.   There was only one feeling in my soul, gratitude—gratitude for the gift I
could not take.   I threw myself on my knees before
the Lord of Palatine ; I took his hand ; I bedewed it
with my tears.   "O great, noble man !" I cried—
" never so great, never so noble as now ; I could
wear your badge to-day.   I never was so completely
your captive as at this moment ; your trust has
indeed gone beyond mine.   And yet I cannot, I dare
not take the boon you offer.   To reign with you
would be to follow your mode of reigning.   That is
command.   I dare not command.   The empire I
follow is an empire of love, not of law.   It is an
empire where every one feels he is dead to the
law—living from choice.   I dare not force the
flower into its bloom ; the man of the valleys would
not know his own garden.   He would miss the

freshness of tint and the fragrance of perfume.
You and I might not detect it, but he would. I
think he would rather have the flowers less faultless
than faultless by artificial power. I may seem
deeply ungrateful ; but I know you will understand, I am sure you will forgive." I finished in a
burst of weeping.

He raised me ; he clasped my hands in his ; he
spoke again. "Ecclesia, there is deep truth in
what you say. Be it so. You cannot reign beside
me ; then you will reign after me—reign alone
reign as you will. You may not be my bride
be then my child. Listen, and I shall tell you
a secret—a thing which the island knows not. I
could not have made you my bride in ignorance of
this secret ; I would have told it from honour ; I
tell it now from choice. Ecclesia, my life cannot
be long. I have known it for some time. My
physicians have apprised me that I have a mortal
disease. I have not one pang of fear, but I am
struggling to die in harness. I dread not death,
but I would not have men see my failing powers.
I strive to veil my weakness ; I live to hide my
pain ; I——"

He was interrupted by my emotion. There was
something so grand, so touching, so characteristic,
in this man hiding his burden as other men hide

their treasures, that I quite broke down. The
captain had told me I would not see Palatine in its
former glory. I doubt that. To me the solitary
burden was greater than the solitary power. I had
chafed at the one ; I sank before the other.

"Ecclesia," he resumed, "you have no cause to
weep ; you have robbed me to-day of half my pain.
I looked round the island to adopt a son ; I looked
in vain. There was none strong enough to stand
alone. I saw the towers of Palatine disappearing
in the descending mist, and I was sad. But the
mist has lifted this morning, and the towers re-
appear. I have found among the daughters what
I have lost among the sons. You shall be my
child, my heir, Ecclesia. You shall revive the
glories of Palatine when my day is done. Yours
shall be the broad lands of this island, bounded
only by the sea. Yours shall be the sea itself—the
power to traverse waters once forbidden. Yours
shall be the union of the present and the past ;
to-day shall clasp hands with yesterday. I shall
be your father on the land, and ben-Israel shall
be your father on the sea. I shall build for you
a palace on the hill, and I shall make it like your
old home, and within it I shall put a shrine which
shall remind you of the days gone by."

"Not on the hill," I sobbed—" not on the hill.

Give me a dwelling on the ground below. I am a child of the valleys. Will not you, my second father, be the father of the valleys? Will you not help me to teach men the kingliness of being helpful? I began yesternight to tell your toilers of the dignity of toil: but what is my voice to yours? In vain the daughter of Israel seeks the valley, when the Lord of Palatine stands on the hill. Will you not help your new-found child? Will you not descend with me that stair by which I came to you? Will you not teach the rulers of coming days that to be the greatest is to be the servant of all? Will you not come down and see how in the region beneath they weave and spin and sew? You speak of dying; there is glory for you first—glory which the house of Palatine has never known. I ascended that stair as a criminal; I am expected to descend as a convict. What influence has a convict to make his brethren good? Come and stand beside me, that I may be beautified in your light."

" I have never been down before," he said in deep meditation.

" No," I answered; " it is the one part of the island which the Lord of Palatine has yet to conquer." There was a moment's stillness in the great room; then he put his hand in mine, and we descended the long stair together.

CHAPTER XXX

CONCLUDING REFLECTIONS

READER, here for the present I shall pause. Perhaps at some future time either my hand or the hand of another may continue this history. Every end is a beginning, and the evening of to-day is the morning of to-morrow. Yet I have come to a temporary landing-place, to a stage which, in relation to the past, may be called the evening. Here therefore let us sit down and look back. It is the ordinary plan of writers to put prefatory remarks at the opening of their books. I am quite sure, however, that, though they come at the beginning of the book, they have been conceived at the end of it. We do not really know where we have begun till we have got to the end, for it is by the light of to-day that we read the skies of yesterday. We all write our preface last. I am going to follow the universal example. Here, on the ridge of Palatine, I shall

rest awhile ; and casting back my eyes over the
road I have traversed, I shall try to estimate the
value of the way.

Perhaps there is a preliminary question—For
whom do I design these memoirs ? For the men
and women of the island ? Yes, undoubtedly ; but
not exclusively. I have all along had an imaginary audience. I have never accepted the belief
that this island is permanently isolated. I have
seen something *in* it which never came *from* it,
and which therefore must have come from elsewhere. The gulf has been bridged once to the
outer life of man. If it be so, then the distance,
however great, cannot be infinite. I have felt that
what *has* been done *may* be done. I have always
looked forward to a time when, directly or indirectly, we shall be united to a mainland. How it
may be, when it may be, I know not. Whether
our ships shall penetrate further than those of our
ancestors, whether there shall be new modes of
conveyance compared to which our swiftest shall
be creeping, whether, as in my vision, the sea itself
shall be dried up and this island become literally a
continent, I cannot tell. But I have cherished the
expectation of what I may call a glorious appearing—of an hour when the waste vacancy shall be
broken by the sight of an opposite shore. And

because I cherish this hope, I live for it, I write in the presence of it. I believe our books shall all be opened one day. I believe our records shall be of as great interest to the dwellers beyond the wave as their records would be to us, and I try always to keep before me the solemn conviction that the history I am writing will be read in places and by persons whose very existence is now undreamed of.

What then has been the course of this memoir ? At a first view it might seem to describe an aimless circle in which the end repeats the beginning. Looking back from the place which I have reached in my narrative, there rise before me three successive scenes. In the first and farthest back I am a girl with a dream of empire in my heart. I have waked to the sense of my beauty. I have realised it rather as a gain than as a pride. I am rushing into the pleasures of this island world, not for the sake of the pleasures, but with a view to the promotion of my house. Then the curtain falls, and, when it rises again, I am a girl no more. I am a woman, and a woman in solitude. I have broken with the island world altogether. I have caught sight of something which transcends it, eclipses it. I am living in a region of my own, keeping my own counsel, holding in my heart an incommunicable secret. I am separated from those around me by the wall of a great passion, which hems me in and will not let me go. I am in love with one who was an ideal to me before I knew him to be a reality. I am divided from my kind by an abnormal experience. I am an island within the island.

Then the curtain falls once more; and, when once more it is lifted, everything seems to have come back. I am no longer alone. I have come out of my solitude; I am in the world again. Again there floats before me the vision of empire— no longer as a far-off prospect, but almost at the door. Palatine is at my feet. The island is mine potentially—in a few years will be mine actually. What my fathers have dreamed of, what my poets have sung of, what the prophets of my clan have told of, has become a sober fact, a prose reality; and I stand amid the fulfilment of these ambitions which made my girlhood a life for the world.

But is this progress? Has there been any real advance in my journey? Have I not been treading a labyrinth which, while it seemed to lead me on, has simply brought me back to the place from which I came? Was it worth while to have had a moment of solitude, of separation, of isolation? Entrancing as it was, elevating as it was, soul-

inspiring as it was, was it not a waste of time, if
the world were after all my goal? What need to
be made a child of the valleys, if only to be transformed at last into the Queen of Palatine?

Nay but, most inquiring reader, there has been
no transformation. It is the child of the valleys who
has become the Queen of Palatine. Do you think
the vision I met in solitude has ever faded from
my eyes, ever lessened its brightness by a single
ray? Do you think I left *him* to come to Palatine?
Nay; it was he who brought me to Palatine.
Together we climbed the great hill—together we
faced the three temptings—together we ascended
the long stair. Do you know the difference
between treading the same road *before* and *after*
love? To the common eye it is a monotonous
repetition; to the eye kindled by love it is a new
scene. It is not merely that something is added;
it is that everything has changed its meaning;
the twilight has become the dawn. So has it
been with me. I have passed *from* the world
to the world; but in the passage I have met
one who has illumined my days. To outward
appearance I have simply come through the
labyrinth to the spot where I used to dwell.
But the labyrinth itself has been the progress.
I went in alone; I have come out accompanied,

and that makes all the difference between the flesh and the spirit.

When the Lord of Palatine saw in the glare of busy day the cross with that inscription, " By this conquer," he saw the new world into which I had come.   It was revealed to me through him that my empire itself was to be my altar.   It was proclaimed in letters of gold that the head of the stair was to be the foot, now, henceforth, and for evermore.   It was written upon the air of heaven that the ruler was to be the servant, the king the priest, the master the menial.   I was not disobedient to the heavenly vision.   I took the crown as a cross, the sceptre as a sacrifice.   When the Lord of Palatine closed his eyes in death, I was called to be a queen.   It came to me as a call to service —service more lowly than I had ever known. Instead of standing at the top of the stair looking down, I felt myself to be at the foot of the stair looking up.   I had the sensation of being the property of another—bought with a price.   It seemed to me that henceforth I was bound to take my orders from every one.   Even the lowliest appeared one step above me, and a voice kept ever ringing in my ears, " Ecclesia, they are all your masters now."

In the years that have come this has always

been my attitude. I do not say it has always been the attitude of the band of workers whom I have gathered round me. Often have they forgotten themselves. Often have they returned to the pride of the old house of Palatine. Often have they made others weep with the vaunting of their power—but none so bitterly as me. I have never varied. From morn to midday I have been the child of the valleys. When my followers have lorded it, I have hid my face and blushed. I have never varied, and Phœbe has never varied. At the time when others have been showing pride on the upper ground, she and I have generally been down on the lower, helping the needs of man. I do not think we have ever paused in this part of our work. Other things may have been interrupted, but not charity. There is one work Phœbe and I are prouder of than all other improvements. We have planned and superintended the erection of a new and additional hospital. We have written on it the inscription, " For the benefit of those who are not likely to live." It is to be in all time for the men, women, and children who are unfit to run, who give no hope of ever being fit to run. It is just the opposite of the old building. We have let them in on the very spot where the ancient hospital put them out—the steps of despair. It is a home for the stranded, for the island's rejected. Phœbe and I have each lent them something. I have brought them the golden cross, and the little vial, and the picture of him with the marred visage ; Phœbe, with the true instinct of her clan, has carried flowers to make them glad. We are striving to undo the ravages of the olden time.

And yet I would not have you think that I am no longer anchored to the past. I am—although my anchor is not on the shore, but in the sea. The father of my adoption sleeps amid the woods of Palatine ; but the father of my life is still alive. I know not where he dwells ; I have failed to find him. We have pierced farther into the mystic depth of waters than ever mariner sailed before ; but we have found no trace of the land which preserves without a possession the name of Moses ben-Israel. Years have passed, and he must now be an old man ; but the promise of the storm-cloud keeps sounding in my soul, " He shall return, and you shall nourish his old age and make him young once more." The future holds my past ; therefore it cannot die. It is preserved by the salt sea ; it is wafted back by the breeze of ocean. That is why I have not returned to the old home. If my father had been to me only a memory, I would have made my dwelling in the scene of his sojourn.

But my father is not a memory; he is a hope. He is not behind; he is before. Therefore I feel that I am nearest to him looking out upon the blue waves, watching the breakers' foam, listening to the hum of waters. As I gaze on that scene— the first joy of my childhood—it is not my childhood that chiefly comes back to me. It is the thought of the day when, as a woman, I shall meet him on the shore, and, pointing to the broad fields of Palatine, shall say, " Your prophecy was true after all."

Printed by Hazell, Watson, & Viney, Ld., London and Aylesbury.